KAVANAGH *QC II*

Tom McGregor is a journalist and author of five novels.
He lives in London.

Also by Tom McGregor

BETWEEN THE LINES

The Chill Factor
Close Protection

Peak Practice

Kavanagh QC

KAVANAGH
Q.C. II

Tom McGregor

PAN BOOKS

First published 1996 by Pan Books
an imprint of Macmillan General Books
25 Eccleston Place
London SW1W 9NF
and Basingstoke

Associated companies throughout the world

ISBN 0 330 34624 5

1 3 5 7 9 8 6 4 2

A CIP catalogue record for this book is available from
the British Library.

Phototypeset by Intype London Ltd
Printed and bound in Great Britain

PROLOGUE

Strasbourg. Lizzie Kavanagh looked out of her office window and reflected that while her new job still left much to be desired its location couldn't be bettered. The city was beautiful: the canals, the half-timbered buildings, the cobbled squares and the magnificent cathedral were just some of its many delights. And the cosmopolitan atmosphere was something that appealed to Lizzie. With the Plenary Sessions of the European Parliament taking place for a week each month, the city was positively buzzing with a chatter of different languages and disparate nationalities. There were, thought Lizzie as she forced her mind back to the mountain of paperwork on her desk, only two disadvantages. One was her uphill struggle to get the grants she needed for her charity work. She could live with that: the situation would improve with time and as she made her mark. She wasn't so sure that there was room for improvement in the other: the fact that her husband and children were in London.

She and Jim tried their utmost to maintain a proper family life, and it was a far from easy task. Weekends were supposed to be sacrosanct; a time to leap on planes and resume that life. In an ideal world, it should have been possible. But then, whoever said the world was an ideal place?

1

Not me, thought Lizzie as she looked up from her desk and, with a half-smile, acknowledged the man walking into her office. Philippe Kaplan, she had long ago decided, proved that the concept of the 'archetypal Frenchman' wasn't, after all, a cliché. Suave, dapper and good-looking, he managed – as did few of his British counterparts – to be ruthless and sensitive, charming and sincere, and beautifully dressed without appearing effete. He was also an unabashed 'caviar socialist', something that was regarded as perfectly acceptable in France yet distinctly dodgy in Britain.

Philippe returned Lizzie's smile with a broad grin and eased himself into the seat opposite her. He even manages, thought Lizzie, to make sitting down seductive.

'Wonderful news, no, Elizabeth?'

'Well . . .'

'You've been granted the funds you need to start your project.' Philippe frowned. 'You should be pleased.'

Lizzie sighed. 'Yes, but I've been granted barely a tenth of what I asked for.' Then she crossed her arms and looked him in the eye. 'I've been fobbed off and you know it.'

'Nonsense.' Philippe flicked a non-existent speck of dust off his perfectly creased trousers. 'The feasibility study unlocks funds for research. From research it's a short step to Planning, and once you're in Planning . . . well . . .'

Sure, thought Lizzie. Once you're in Planning you're practically in heaven. She had been in Strasbourg long enough to appreciate – and mistrust – the interminable and rickety bureaucratic steps you needed to tread before you could even say boo to a goose. Trying to

2

control her increasing irritation, she said to her boss, 'And how long will that take, Philippe?'

Philippe waved his hand in a peculiarly Gallic gesture. 'Longer, of course, than is strictly desirable, but the system here is a delicate machine, Elizabeth. If you treat it too roughly, it breaks down.'

Before Lizzie could reply, they were interrupted by a discreet knock, which was followed by Lizzie's assistant, Fabien, popping his head round the door. 'Your husband has just phoned from the restaurant, Mrs Kavanagh. He's, er—'

'Oh, God! Waiting for me!' Uncharacteristically flustered, Lizzie looked in mounting panic first at Philippe and then at her desk. What was it she had been thinking about her disrupted family life only a few minutes ago? So disrupted was it that she had even forgotten today was Friday; that Jim was coming out to Strasbourg for the weekend. Wearily, she asked Fabien to phone Jim at the restaurant.

'Tell him I'll be . . . an hour. At the most.'

Sensing that Lizzie was in no mood to respond to charm, Philippe stood up. 'Be patient, Elizabeth,' he said, with an appreciative smile. 'Everyone is most impressed with your work. I know you're going to be an outstanding success here.'

Without much warmth or conviction, Lizzie returned his smile. At that moment she couldn't care less about being successful. All she wanted to be was absent.

Three-quarters of an hour later, a waiter poured the last of a bottle of wine into Jim Kavanagh's glass and asked if monsieur would care for another bottle. Looking up from the book he had been reading, monsieur smiled and nodded in a faintly sheepish manner. The waiter knew he was expecting to be joined by a companion for dinner, but judging by the look on the man's face as he departed with the empty bottle he reckoned that he should have given up long ago. Then he shrugged. What was it to him if the middle-aged grey-haired man had been stood up? He was still spending money, wasn't he?

Back at the table, Kavanagh was well aware of how the situation might look, but he didn't care. He was also well aware that he had already drunk more than was good for him – but again he didn't care. And he knew what the sniggering waiters and pitying customers didn't know: that his dinner companion would, without doubt, arrive. He looked at his watch. With any luck, she might even arrive soon. He hoped that, for her own sake, she would arrive before he had done much damage to the second bottle of claret.

Laying his book aside, he played with the stem of his wine glass and thought about the weekend ahead. It was going to be one of those extremely rare ones when he and Lizzie would be together without work commitments, without children and without, hopefully, any worries. When Lizzie had first taken the post in Strasbourg, the worries and the children had been synonymous. Kavanagh, holding the fort in London during the week, could never guarantee that his work as a high-ranking barrister would enable him to get home in time to look after the children. It had been the 'children' themselves who had pointed out that they didn't need any looking after. Kate, at eighteen, was hardly at home. She was at pains to inform both her parents that she was now an adult and that she would soon be leaving home to begin her degree in English literature. As for Matt, he didn't appear to notice that his mother was absent for much of the time. Nor, mused Kavanagh ruefully, did he seem to notice when his father was present. Matt's concerns, like those of every other self-respecting sixteen-year-old, were himself, his computer, his social life, his awakening libido and – when he was too tired to concentrate on any of those – the television. On the rare occasions when Matt talked about the fragmented family life his parents had fretted so much about, he pronounced it 'cool'. To have one of Britain's leading QCs for a father and a glamorous international fund-raiser for a mother was fine by Matt – and a source of envy to his friends.

At that point the glamorous international fund-raiser, not looking especially glamorous, burst into the restaurant and approached her husband's table. Her finely chiselled features wore a look of contrition, relief – and pleasure.

'I'm sorry, Jim,' Lizzie began as she pecked him on the cheek and then threw herself into the chair opposite him, 'it's just that . . .'

Kavanagh put an affectionate hand over hers as the waiter appeared with the second bottle. 'It's okay, Lizzie. I guess it's just another two-bottle night in Strasbourg.'

The waiter poured a glass for Lizzie and shot her a covert look. Yes, he said to himself. Definitely worth waiting for. Not, perhaps, as young as she might have been – but, then, women of a certain age did carry with them a definite *allure*, a sophistication that wasn't present in . . . Realizing that his discreet look had become an overt stare which Lizzie was now returning

5

with more than a little disapproval, the waiter coughed and moved away.

Lizzie and her husband caught each other's eye and laughed. The waiter had broken the ice for them. Suddenly they were both feeling relaxed, mellow and looking forward to a weekend of idle togetherness.

It was Kavanagh who unconsciously spoiled the mood when, over his *foie gras*, he asked Lizzie how the job was going. Equally unconsciously, Lizzie suddenly became businesslike and leaned over towards him, eyes blazing with passionate enthusiasm. 'You know, I really think I'm beginning to get the hang of it. The way to get what you want here is to come at things from the right angle. You can't,' she continued as she stabbed the last *escargot* on her plate, 'just go charging in head on. But then again the great point to remember is that everybody has the same ultimate goal, that we're all on the same side. Strasbourg,' she finished, 'really is an amazing place once you get used to it.' Then she noticed Jim's expression. 'Um . . . sorry, Jim. I'm banging on, aren't I?'

'No, no. Go on, I'm interested.'

Lizzie gave him a rueful smile. She knew perfectly well he was bored to tears. Leaning over the table, she patted his arm. 'Thanks, Jim. Putting up with late planes and late wives every week.' Then she looked him straight in the eye. 'It hasn't been easy, has it?'

Kavanagh raised an eyebrow. 'I'm not complaining.'

Suddenly, Lizzie looked forlorn. 'I miss the kids.'

This time it was her husband who smiled. 'You're not the only one. Kate's never in, and anyway she'll be off to Cambridge soon, and Matt's gone AWOL somewhere on the information superhighway. You're not missing much, believe me.'

Lizzie grinned. 'Funny, isn't it, about Kate?'

'Eh?'

'Well, of all the tutors in Cambridge, she ends up with the husband of one of my oldest friends.'

'Oh, God, yes, I'd forgotten.' Kavanagh cast his mind back to Lizzie's surprise when Kate had informed them that her tutor would be a man called Jeffrey Manners, who was married to one of Lizzie's old schoolfriends. 'How long is it since you've seen Angela?' he asked Lizzie.

'Oh, ages. Too long.' Lizzie sipped her wine. 'It'll be nice to have an excuse to catch up with her.'

'What's the husband like?' Kavanagh's tone suggested that he'd already made up his mind: he would be dangerous, predatory and unsafe around young students.

Reading his mind, Lizzie guffawed. 'Oh, for goodness' sake, Jim, stop being so suspicious! Anyway, "the husband" has got a name – and it's Jeffrey, not Svengali.'

'Hmm.'

'I've only met him a couple of times. He seemed very nice. Quite a star academically, apparently.'

'So Kate'll be in good hands, then.'

'Yes, she will.' Again Lizzie leaned towards him. 'Enough about the kids. If they're not pining for us, why should we be pining for them? This weekend is supposed to be about us, remember? Alone, in Strasbourg.'

'True. Any ideas about what we should do?'

'Oh . . . I can think of a few. Relaxing ones, mainly.'

But Kavanagh, looking down at his plate, missed the wicked expression on Lizzie's face. 'Good,' he said. 'I've almost forgotten how to relax.'

Lizzie frowned. 'Hey! You haven't brought any work with you, have you? This is supposed to be—'

'No.' Kavanagh held up his hands in a 'not guilty' gesture. 'No work, Lizzie. I haven't got any work to do. At all. Things are very quiet in chambers.'

'Oh, it'll soon pick up. It always does. I'll bet you lunch at Bibendum that you'll be up to your eyeballs in some juicy case in no time at all.'

Later, Lizzie rejoiced in her flippant remark. Lunch at Bibendum didn't come cheap and, a few months later, Kavanagh took her at her word. The 'juicy case' he became embroiled in was brewing, in London, on the very night that Lizzie had made her bet. It concerned two people from very different backgrounds with very different stories to tell – about the same event.

Miriam Jacobs surprised her mother on two counts as she flew into the house and tore up the stairs. First, Marcia Jacobs was taken aback by her daughter's appearance and the state of her clothes. Second, she was shocked by Miriam's words as she ran up the elegant stairway. 'Get Daddy for me!' she yelled down to her mother.

Accustomed to obeying orders after nearly thirty years of marriage to her rich, powerful and autocratic husband, Marcia headed down the hall towards his study. Alarmed as she was by her daughter's appearance and panic-stricken look, she was nevertheless pleased that Miriam had asked for her father. It was the first time in nearly six months that she had, let alone asked *about* him.

Father and daughter – so alike in both their good looks and volatile temperaments – had fallen out in a big way. It was all because of 'that boy' and, thought Marcia as she knocked on the door of her husband's study, that dreadful cause. The Workers' Action Party or some such rubbish. Marcia had been as appalled as her husband about what Miriam firmly declared to be her 'role in life'. Helping other people was all well and good – Marcia herself was involved in countless charities – but there was no need to take up with unwashed, unemployed people and become, of all things, an ardent socialist. Still, if Miriam now wanted to talk to her father, it boded well for the future. She obviously needed his help and advice. And Marcia knew that, whatever trouble Miriam may be in, Alan would help her – and advise her to keep well clear of the rabble with whom she had been consorting.

Half an hour later, Marcia was proved right. Father and daughter were standing in the garden, watching the flames of the bonfire that was now destroying the clothes Miriam had been wearing when she entered the house. The expression on Alan Jacobs's face was grim; that on his daughter's was more difficult to read. She was at once tired, tearful, relieved – and worried.

Alan's face softened when he turned to her, and he squeezed her arm. Dressed in a fresh cream linen shirt and dark jeans and with her hair wet, she now looked like the daughter he knew and loved. She also seemed younger than her twenty-two years. Younger – and more vulnerable. Alan knew that, even in her present distress, Miriam was too proud to admit that, yes, she had got in with the wrong crowd and that she now deeply regretted her involvement. Her terror at what she had witnessed that evening was enough to convey that message. Alan turned back to the bonfire and watched as it devoured the vestiges of Miriam's leather jacket.

'I'm not taking a chance on what this boy might say to the police,' he said. 'The minute my solicitor gets here you must tell him everything.' Alan fixed his daughter with a steely glare. 'Exactly as you told me. Then we will all go to the police together.'

'It was terrible, Daddy,' said Miriam, in a small voice.

'I know. But it's all over. You're home now. You're safe.'

In a police cell in another, far less salubrious part of London, Mark Holland did not reply to the policeman's question.

'Did you hear me? Do you want a solicitor?' Detective Chief Inspector Knowland was fast losing his patience with the youth sitting opposite him in the interview room. The Workers' Action Party probably didn't believe in solicitors. More fool they, thought Knowland. Mark Holland was going to need the best solicitor in the land to stand any chance of avoiding life imprisonment for murder.

Then Mark raised his head and met the policeman's eye. 'No. I don't need a solicitor. I'll tell you what happened.'

CHAPTER ONE

Mark Holland went on trial for murder eight months later. By that time he had acquired a solicitor – and a barrister to represent him in court. The barrister was James Kavanagh.

'Let me get this straight,' said Kavanagh to his junior colleague Julia Piper, as they looked through the case notes. 'On the night of the murder, Holland said he didn't want a solicitor, that he killed this boy and the girl had nothing to do with it, right?'

'Right.'

'And then the girl goes to the police confirming that story – at which point Holland accuses her of doing the murder, yes?'

'Yes, but it's a little more complicated than that.'

Julia looked up from her notes. As usual when they were working together on a case, they were sitting in Kavanagh's room in River Court Chambers, the 'set' where they both worked. It was a room that Julia coveted, although she acknowledged that, while Kavanagh was nearly thirty years her senior, he showed little sign of slowing down, far less of retiring. And even when he did retire, there was no guarantee that Julia would get his room. Several of Julia's colleagues – and Jeremy Aldermarten in particular – had their eye on Kavanagh's room.

'What are you grinning about?' Kavanagh's half-amused, half-indignant tones roused her from her reverie.

'Oh . . . I was, er . . . thinking about Jeremy.' Well, that was partly true. And it certainly explained the grin. Julia wasn't alone in finding Jeremy comical – when he wasn't being irritating.

'What about Jeremy?'

'He's in court defending a butter-wouldn't-melt-in-my-mouth Sloaney piece with Knightsbridge legs who's just been accused of half-inching a diamond ring from a Bond Street jeweller.'

'Oh.' Kavanagh couldn't see why that should be amusing. 'D'you think he'll get her off?'

'Doubt it.' Julia grinned even more broadly. 'But I reckon he's got his sights set on getting off *with* her.'

'Ah. I see.' That, thought Kavanagh, sounded very Jeremy. 'Anyway, back to this Mark Holland business.'

Although Julia would be Kavanagh's junior in court, she already had all the facts of the case at her fingertips. 'Yes.' She sighed. 'Mark Holland. He is – or was – one of the organizers of some sort of National Front march that turned out, unsurprisingly, to be more of a pitched battle. You know, the usual sort of thing, far-left-wingers – the Workers' Action Party – against a bunch of flag-waving skinhead fascists.'

Kavanagh knew the sort of thing.

'A lot of action,' continued Julia, 'was recorded on video by a news cameraman covering the event. And the police can confirm much of what happened.'

'Except the murder.'

'Except the murder. That took place after the right-wingers realized they were heavily outnumbered and fled. According to the police, Mark Holland and a couple of his pals, including the girl, chased after them and cornered their victim nearby in a garden of a deserted house.'

'That's where they found the body?'

'Yep. And Mark Holland was bent over it holding a knife. His clothes were covered in blood.'

Kavanagh groaned. 'Great. And this is the man I'm going to be defending.'

'Mmm.'

Kavanagh made a pyramid with his hands. 'So. Initially he says he's guilty and then, when the girl – what's her name?'

'Miriam Jacobs.'

'When Miriam Jacobs corroborates his story, he then changes it. Why?'

'Well, from listening to the police tapes of the interview with Holland, he originally said that the skinhead came at him wielding a knife, that there was a scuffle, that lots of people were pushing against them and that the next thing he knew there was blood on his hands and a body lying in front of him. He said that it was an accident. That he was only defending himself.'

'And then . . .'

'Hold on, Jim.' Julia held up a hand. There weren't many QCs she would dare interrupt. There was, in fact, only one, and her working relationship with him was so good perhaps because neither of them stood on ceremony. 'The girl then appeared with Daddy – some sort of big-wig in the city – and Daddy's solicitor.' Julia paused for effect. 'Michael Hopcraft.'

'Ah. So Daddy's a very rich big-wig.'

'So it would appear.' Now pacing the room, Julia cast her mind back to the tape of Miriam Jacobs's version of events. 'Miriam Jacobs,' she said quietly, 'told

13

the police that Holland had been the one with the knife. Here,' she continued as she walked towards the tape recorder in the corner of the room, 'is Mark Holland's reaction to that news.'

Kavanagh listened as the machine crackled into life and the voice of Mark Holland filled the room. A voice, thought Kavanagh, that was surprisingly well educated. Then he checked himself. His own wife used to be active in the Socialist Workers' Party. A militant pest, her father was fond of saying. And Lizzie was about as highly educated as they came. And as well bred.

'It was an accident,' came the pleading, increasingly desperate tones of Mark Holland over the cassette. 'It's the Nazis who use violence. I was only defending myself.'

The next voice, Julia explained, was that of Detective Chief Inspector Knowland. Kavanagh could picture the scene in the police interview room. The hapless Holland and the obviously exasperated Knowland – about to play his trump card. 'Stop messing us about, Mark,' said the policeman. 'We know it was you who had the knife. We know you chased the boy, held him down and then stabbed him. We know,' he went on, with a note of triumph in his voice, 'because Miriam's been talking to us. She's here now, Mark. She saw the whole thing and she's prepared to swear to it.'

The intake of breath from Mark Holland was sudden, sharp – and shocked. 'I don't believe you!'

'She was ten yards away in the road. She watched you do it.'

'She couldn't. She wouldn't say that!'

'But she did, Mark. To her solicitor – and to us. Your girlfriend,' continued Knowland, with barely disguised contempt, 'was right there. She watched you murder him. She's stuffed you, son, so why not start telling the truth?'

And that was when Mark Holland, who had previously refused a solicitor, suddenly demanded to see one.

'What?' Knowland was obviously taken aback.

'Get me a solicitor!'

In the room at River Court, Julia pressed the pause button. 'Patricia Graves was assigned to him. She's in the room during the next bit of the tape.'

As Julia wound the tape further on and then pressed play again, Mark's voice, quieter and calmer this time, again filled the room. '. . . Miriam came through the line with me. She was right there. She took the knife out of her pocket. I couldn't believe it. I thought it was a joke. Then she stabbed him.'

Either Holland is telling the truth or he's a damn good actor, thought Kavanagh. The boy sounded genuinely shocked. 'She stabbed him in the chest – right up close. He just crumpled down. Miriam stood there staring. She'd . . . she'd got blood all over her clothes. Then she dropped the knife and I picked it up for some reason. I shouted at her to get the hell out and she ran away.' From the tone of Holland's voice, it was evident that he knew his last words did nothing to further his case.

'Why did you say it was you?' interjected Knowland.

'I made it all up to keep her out of it.' On the tape, Holland gave a hollow laugh. 'What's the word for it? Oh, yeah . . . chivalry. What a bloody joke. I did that for her,' he continued in subdued tones, 'and she's betrayed me. But,' he added, with a forcefulness that surprised the listening barristers, 'I'm now telling you exactly what happened. It wasn't me. It was her.'

15

Julia switched off the tape recorder and sat down opposite Kavanagh. 'According to Patricia Graves, Holland's still very angry and resentful towards the girl. Hardly surprising, I suppose.'

'Hmm. What's his background?'

'Lower middle-class. Not much money. Worked hard enough at the local comprehensive to get himself to university, then chucked it all in after a year when he got involved with far-left politics.'

Kavanagh groaned inwardly. Kate had now been at Cambridge for the best part of a year: he didn't care to be informed about high-minded strong-willed students who abandoned their education for their ideals.

'The parents were devastated,' continued Julia as if on cue. 'They've never forgiven him. Their attitude seems to be that he made his choice four years ago and now they won't have anything more to do with him. His political chums are about the only family he's got now.'

'Oh. And he lives with them?'

'Yes. In a squat in Hackney.'

After Julia had departed to her own room, Kavanagh found himself unable to shrug off the gloom that had descended as a result of their conversation about Mark Holland. He knew that defending Holland and trying to prove his innocence was going to be an uphill and probably thankless task. But also he had – unusually – let his imagination run riot by drawing parallels between Mark Holland and his daughter. Apart from the odd contretemps over boyfriends, Kate had been an exemplary child and was now, a young adult, both charming and well adjusted. Yet she was also extremely volatile and hot-headed: ripe, mused her father, for rebellion. Unable to concentrate on any work, he wandered into Peter Foxcott's room, ostensibly to discuss the case.

Peter, as usual, was amiable, and amenable to being distracted from his own work. As head of River Court Chambers, Peter had administrative and financial duties connected with the running of the chambers, duties that he often found boring, as well as his work at the Bar. Kavanagh knew that he himself would have found them tedious too and, while others had been surprised that Peter, not he, had been elected Head of Chambers, he had been relieved. He now enjoyed, although he would never voice it, the position of being the barrister to whom all his other colleagues deferred, while not having to deal with any onerous administrative responsibilities.

'Most students,' said Peter, after Kavanagh had outlined the Mark Holland case to him, 'go through a rebellious stage. My David, for instance, was an absolute fire-breathing revolutionary at college. Now look at him, commodities broker at a merchant bank.' Then the proud-father expression vanished. 'Mind you, he's probably doing more damage to the system these days. Charming boy, but rather dense in some respects, actually . . .' Realizing he was on the verge of being indiscreet, he quickly changed the subject. 'Er, how long's your Kate been up at Cambridge now?'

'Getting on for a year.'

Peter grinned. 'You wait. It won't be long before she drags home some embryo Lenin.'

Oh, God, thought Kavanagh, why on earth did I initiate this conversation? 'Well,' he said, anxious not to pursue the subject of Kate, 'it's more than just a phase with Holland. He's been a WAP for five years now.'

'WAP?'

'A member of the Workers' Action Party.'

Peter grimaced. 'Any history of violence?'

'Not to speak of. Rent-a-mob appearances at strikes and demos, nothing like this before.'

'What about the girl?'

This time it was Kavanagh who grimaced. The jury, he knew, would love Miriam Jacobs. 'Wealthy, tolerant parents. Liberal background. Bit of a high-flier, by all accounts. And nothing in common with Holland at first glance.' He looked morosely at Peter. 'She says she was naïve, under his influence.'

'Plausible?'

'On the face of it, very.'

'So,' said Peter, cheerfully, 'what have you got? She says he did it. He says she did it. He admits it, then promptly contradicts himself. His prints are on the knife. The victim's blood is on his shirt. She's a nice, impressionable girl from the top drawer and he's a bolshie oik with a chip on his shoulder.' His grin widened. 'Very promising for you, James, I must say.'

Kavanagh laughed. 'Thanks for the kind words of encouragement. Remind me to come back to you next time I want my ego boosted.'

'Funny,' said Peter, with a faraway look on his face. 'That's exactly what Jeremy said to me earlier.'

'Oh? Has he got a dog of a case on his hands as well?'

'We-ell, I wouldn't exactly call her a dog . . .'

In court at that very moment, Jeremy Aldermarten was, in his own opinion, giving one of the best performances

18

of his career. As he paused in the questioning of the defendant – his client – he reflected on Peter Foxcott's unkind words about his chances of winning the case. 'A snowflake's chance in hell, Jeremy,' was how Peter had rated his chances of ensuring an acquittal for Lucy Cartwright. Jeremy thought differently. As he stood facing his client, imperious and authoritative in his black cloak and wig, he could sense that she was beginning to win the sympathies of the jury. How, anyway, could they possibly think that this fragile, upper-class beauty could have deliberately stolen an expensive diamond ring?

Jeremy cleared his throat and smiled at Lucy. It wasn't difficult. She was incredibly attractive, he thought. And, poor thing, so vulnerable. Jeremy reckoned that all she needed was the love of a good man. 'So, Mrs Cartwright, you were saying . . .'

Immaculate in an understated but hugely expensive Armani suit, Lucy coughed nervously and began to speak. Both her bearing and her cut-glass accent screamed the message: 'I don't belong here. This is all a horrid mistake.'

'I took off my own ring,' she began, 'while I was trying on some others. I suppose I must have left it on the counter and walked out wearing the wrong one.' Lucy smiled apologetically at the jury. The male jurors smiled back. The women of their number didn't: some of them detected a coquettishness beneath Lucy's innocent protestations; others were just plain jealous of her insouciance about being in a Bond Street jeweller's in the first place. For most of them, Bond Street might as well have been Mars.

'So,' said Jeremy Aldermarten, 'you took the ring by accident?'

Wide-eyed, Lucy gazed at him. 'Oh yes. Absolutely. You see, I've been so awfully absent-minded recently.'

'Why recently, Mrs Cartwright?'

Lucy bit her lip. 'Since . . . since my husband left me.'

At that, the expressions of several of the women members of the jury softened.

Jeremy changed the subject. Best, he reckoned, to leave the jury with the image of a bereft, lonely Lucy. 'How much money did you have on you when you were arrested, Mrs Cartwright?' he asked.

'Nearly a thousand pounds.'

Jeremy smiled and sat down. Perfect, he thought. Absolutely perfect.

His opponent didn't think so. Charles Griffiths, representing the Crown, was on his feet in a flash. 'Mrs Cartwright,' he began, in a voice that carried none of Jeremy Aldermarten's unctuous sympathy, 'the value of the ring on your finger when you left the store was much greater than the one you left behind, wasn't it?'

Lucy clutched her handbag tightly. 'In monetary terms, perhaps. Not in sentimental value.'

'You deliberately substituted the valuable ring for the worthless one, didn't you?'

'That's not true! I would never do anything like that.' Lucy paused and then looked straight at Griffiths. 'I am an honest person.'

Half an hour later, the two barristers had addressed the jury, summing-up for the defence on one hand and the prosecution on the other. Then the jury retired to make their verdict.

Jeremy, relaxing in the robing room, was quietly confident. In his summing-up, he had emphasized that Lucy Cartwright, distressed and overwrought by the break-up of her marriage, had simply made a mistake in walking out of the jeweller's with the wrong ring. Anyway, he had stressed, why on earth would Mrs Cartwright steal something she could easily afford to buy?

Griffiths, interrupting his reverie, came up to him and jabbed him, in a not unfriendly manner, on the shoulder. 'Hot stuff there, Jeremy,' he said. 'You almost had me cheering you on.'

Jeremy gave his opponent a withering look. 'I find I'm always articulate in a worthy cause.'

Griffiths sniggered. 'Still, I don't suppose the words "incredibly guilty" mean much, do they?'

'Your cynicism,' said Jeremy, with another pitying look, 'does you no credit whatsoever, Griffiths.'

Fifteen minutes after that it was all over. The court had reconvened for the verdict of the jury – and that verdict was not guilty. The snowflake had battled through hell and won. Jeremy was ecstatic. So was Lucy. Griffiths was disbelieving.

'Well done,' said Jeremy to his client as they emerged from the court.

Lucy looked up at him with something akin to hero worship. 'I didn't do anything,' she purred. 'You were marvellous.'

CHAPTER TWO

The following day Lucy Cartwright arrived at River Court Chambers to demonstrate just how marvellous she considered Jeremy Aldermarten to be.

For once in his life, Jeremy was at a loss for words. After a silent and embarrassed yet delighted contemplation of the gold Rolex watch she proffered him, he finally found his voice. Almost blushing, he looked his client in the eye. 'I can't possibly accept this, Mrs Cartwright.'

'Lucy, please.'

Jeremy shuffled from one foot to another as, with obvious reluctance, she took the watch back. 'You know,' he said, 'some people might think it unwise of me to see you.'

'Why? Am I doing something wrong?'

'Of course not. Absolutely not. Only . . . well, there is a view that it's better to keep the professional life rigorously separate from the personal.' Seeing her evident disappointment, Jeremy leaned closer. 'But I think that's rather a stuffy view, don't you?'

Lucy beamed. 'You saved my life, Jeremy. You simply must let me do something for you.'

It didn't take him long to agree to let her take him out to dinner that evening. As he escorted her through the hallway, having agreed to meet later at the Café

Royal, Jeremy was more than a little discomfited to bump into Tom Buckley, the senior clerk, at the front door. He looked at Lucy with keen interest – and not a little disapproval.

As the door swung shut behind her, Buckley remarked, 'Taking your work home again, Mr Aldermarten?'

Jeremy looked down his nose at the clerk. 'She is an ex-client.'

But Buckley wasn't going to let it go. 'You've done your bit, Mr Aldermarten. I'd leave it at that if I were you.'

Jeremy snorted. 'Really, Tom, you sound positively Victorian at times.' Then he stalked off back to his room. Bloody little man, he thought. Always poking his nose into other people's business.

One of Jeremy's many complaints about life at River Court was what he considered the bolshiness of the senior clerk. While in most professions the term 'clerk' suggested a menial position, barristers' clerks were anything but. A clerk – and especially a senior one like Tom – wielded enough power to make or break the barristers. They were the people who, after receiving instructions from solicitors, assigned the cases. A barrister of James Kavanagh's calibre was sought after on his own merit, but for juniors – those who were not yet or would never be QCs – it paid to keep on the right side of the clerks. It was a lesson that Jeremy Aldermarten seemed incapable of learning. Furthermore, even after fifteen years at the Bar, Jeremy had failed to grasp the notion that most clerks prided themselves on their bolshiness.

'Pretty girl.'

'What?' Annoyed, Jeremy whirled round to find Julia Piper standing in the doorway of her room. From her sardonic expression, it was clear that she, too, had witnessed Lucy's invitation to dinner.

'I said, "pretty girl".'

Jeremy affected disinterest. 'Was she?' Then, seeing the grin spread across Julia's face, he glared at her. 'It's a perfectly innocent situation, Julia. I see nothing wrong with allowing oneself a pat on the back from time to time.'

'Oh, for Heaven's sake! You're so completely transparent, Jeremy. If she hadn't been so good-looking she'd never even have got her foot through the door.'

'Rubbish. Anyway, it's just a meal. Refusal would have been churlish.'

Again Julia grinned. 'Churlishness has never been a problem for you before.' Leaving Jeremy looking wounded, she closed her door and made her way down the hall. Well, she thought to herself, Jeremy *is* churlish. And childish. She cast her mind back to the time, almost two years ago now, when Jeremy had made a play for her. At first he had been uncomprehending in the face of her repeated refusals to be seduced. Then he had become plain annoyed. Finally, he had decided that she was a lesbian: how else could she be impervious to his advances? Julia recalled hearing the rumours Jeremy had spread. Unfortunately, he had spread them at exactly the same time as she had begun a torrid affair with a handsome – and very male – six-foot-two cricketer. Jeremy had been livid. Still grinning as she walked up the Strand, Julia hailed a taxi and began mentally to prepare herself for the meeting ahead: the meeting in the prison interview room with Kavanagh, the solicitor Patricia Graves and the alleged murderer, Mark Holland.

*

Initially, Mark was hostile. Julia correctly attributed this to nerves. Unused to dealing with older, wiser professionals, Mark was intimidated by them. Even Patricia Graves, herself deeply sympathetic to left-wing and anti-racist causes like those Mark espoused, intimidated him with her severity and apparent inability to smile. Oddly, it was James Kavanagh, the eldest of the trio questioning him, to whom he finally warmed.

'So,' said Kavanagh as he looked up from the notes he had been making, 'the knife you say that Miriam took out of her pocket. Had you seen it before?'

'Oh, yes.' Mark thought bitterly back to the time when he had first seen it. 'It used to be on the sideboard at her dad's place. She said it was a holiday souvenir. Indonesia or some such place.'

Kavanagh stared. 'Alan Jacobs says you stole it.'

Mark laughed hollowly. 'Alan Jacobs is a lying git.'

'He says it disappeared after you visited the house with his daughter sometime in March last year.'

'No.'

'Did you go to his house at that time?'

'March? Yeah, I went there. Miriam wanted to see her mum. We waited until Jacobs was away on a business trip.'

'Why didn't you go when he was there?' interrupted Julia.

'He hated my guts for a start. And, anyway, Miriam and him had had a row. They weren't speaking.'

'What was the row about?'

'Politics.'

Kavanagh tried to look encouraging rather than irritated. 'A little more detail would help us with our defence, Mr Holland. Anything you can remember. Anything at all.'

Mark sighed. He wasn't, he silently conceded, being too helpful, and these people, rich Conservatives or not, couldn't help him if he didn't give them a chance. It was a shame he didn't know that James Kavanagh would rather be hanged, drawn and quartered than vote Conservative.

'Okay. Her dad reckoned it was me that got Miriam into direct action. He said I was a bad influence on her. That was a real joke. It was his influence he was worried about, not mine. He couldn't stand her having a mind of her own.' A faraway – and distinctly unpleasant – look came into Mark's eyes as he talked about Miriam's father. 'The only time I met him,' he continued, with distaste, 'all he did was have a go like it was all my fault. I don't need that bollocks. I walked out and Miriam came with me. He hated that.' Then he laughed a venomous little laugh. 'Still, he got her back in the end, didn't he?'

Kavanagh looked down at his notes again. 'How long was that before the rally?'

'About six months,' Mark replied. 'For all I know Miriam didn't speak to her dad for all that time.'

'Were you ever on your own in the room where the knife was kept?' asked Julia.

'No chance. I wasn't exactly her mum's pin-up boy either. She watched me like a hawk the whole time. Probably thought I was going to gob on the Axminster.'

You probably did, thought Kavanagh. But, instead of voicing that thought, he asked Mark if he remembered what Miriam was wearing the day of the rally.

'Um . . . yeah. Black leather jacket. Khaki chinos. Some kind of light shirt. Yellow, I think it was.'

'And are you absolutely sure that her outfit was bloodstained when she ran away?'

Mark met Kavanagh's gaze. 'Yeah. I'm absolutely sure.' Then, suddenly inspired, he leaned forward and told Kavanagh that Kathy Tyler, one of the fellow WAPs who shared the squat in Hackney, would back him up about Miriam's clothes. 'Kathy was there,' he said. 'She'll confirm that.'

But Kavanagh and Patricia Graves exchanged a glance that said otherwise. 'Kathy Tyler,' said the latter, 'is refusing to make any kind of statement.'

Mark leaned back in his chair. 'Oh, yeah, that's Kathy. Stubborn little cow. Miriam was always winding her up.' He paused. 'They hated each other's guts.' Turning to the solicitor, he asked her to talk to Kathy again. 'If you say I asked, surely she'll talk? Kathy'll come through for me.' But even as he said the words Mark doubted them. Kathy and their other housemate Nick Stevens had hated Miriam with a vengeance. They loathed the fact that she lived most of the time with them, polluting the atmosphere with her expensive clothes and upper-class voice, seducing Mark with her high-minded talk – and her little sports car. From the outset of his relationship with her, they had felt that she was on some sort of ego-trip; an anti-parental rebellious jaunt that would end as suddenly as it had begun. They doubted her commitment to the cause and, to make matters worse, Kathy was highly suspicious of Miriam's commitment to Mark. Kathy knew that he would be better off with her: knowledge not shared by Mark.

Kavanagh was astute enough to guess most of that – and experienced enough to know that there was no point in pressuring Kathy Tyler to come forward in support of Mark. Not yet, anyway. Instead, he changed the subject back to the crux of what he knew would be the prosecution's strongest card: Mark's initial admission of guilt. 'Why, Mr Holland, did you tell the police that you stabbed Ian Taylor?'

Mark took a deep breath and then leaned forward again. 'Miriam was a sister. She was one of us. You don't let each other down, do you?' Then, realizing that, judging by the evidence thus far, his 'sister' had let him down very badly indeed, he covered his face with his hands. 'No. It's not just that. Have you seen her? She's just . . . well, I mean, I would have done anything for her. Anything. I was stupid about her, like a kid.' His misery was apparent to Kavanagh and Julia. 'I was in love. Really in love. All I could think when the coppers got hold of me was that I had to keep Miriam out of it. That,' he finished in a small voice, 'is how messed up I was about her.'

Kavanagh glanced at Patricia Graves and Julia. They both nodded in implicit understanding. They weren't going to get much more out of Mark Holland that day.

As they stood up, Mark, now with tears in his eyes, added, 'I thought she was really into it. I mean, I thought she hated the fascists and loved me. Ha! Wrong on both counts. She was just off on some selfish trip of her own.' Almost pleading, he said to Kavanagh, 'I don't want to go to prison for what she did. The guy's dead and she's just going to walk away.'

Several hours after Kavanagh and Julia concluded their interview with Mark Holland, another lady who had, according to barrister Charles Griffiths, succeeded in 'walking away', was raising her glass to the man who had enabled her to do so. 'To British justice.'

Jeremy Aldermarten clinked his glass against Lucy Cartwright's. 'And to you, Lucy, for such a wonderful evening.' It had been, he reckoned, a much better evening than even he had anticipated. Lucy Cartwright was not just beautiful and well dressed: she was also intelligent, amusing and good company. And the pair of them, throughout the duration of dinner at the Café Royal, had discovered many interests in common, many similar likes and dislikes.

'It has been a wonderful evening, hasn't it, Jeremy?' said Lucy. 'You . . . er . . . you probably think I'm shockingly forward. I mean . . . well, I barely know you but . . . one senses a sort of spark.' Then, giggling prettily, she leaned back in her chair. 'God,' she added as she put a hand to her mouth, 'I must be squiffy.'

'Not at all. I feel the same thing. Not squiffy, I mean, but . . .' Seizing the moment and, in a gesture that he hoped spoke volumes, he reached for Lucy's dainty hand.

At that moment, the waiter, looking contrite, appeared with the bill and the credit card Lucy had handed him moments before. 'Er, I'm sorry, madam, the expiry date . . .'

Lucy's hand flew to her mouth. 'Oh, my God! How utterly stupid.' Then she reached for her handbag. I'll give you a cheque, shall I?' But after a few moments of frantic and fruitless searching, she found herself looking at Jeremy in panic. 'Oh, Jeremy, I must have . . .'

Jeremy, however, had already stepped into the breach. He reached into his breast pocket while silencing Lucy with his other hand. 'Please. Allow me.' As discreetly as he could, he beckoned to the waiter and handed him a card.

When he turned his attention back to Lucy, he found that she was crying. 'It's too much.' She sniffed. 'I've made such a hash of everything. I can't even buy a meal successfully.'

Horrified by her tears, Jeremy handed her his handkerchief. 'It's all right. Really, Lucy. It's all right. Please don't cry.' Much to his relief, the waiter returned almost immediately with the credit-card slip and, before all eyes in the restaurant were on them, he managed to usher Lucy out of the room and to the main entrance of the building. 'I'll, em, find you a cab, shall I?'

Lucy, now dry-eyed, looked at him in great sadness. 'Oh dear. And there was me hoping we were going to spend the night together.'

Jeremy barely stopped himself recoiling in utter surprise. For the second time in the space of twenty-four hours, he was rendered speechless.

'Unless,' continued Lucy, 'there is some tremendously fierce ethical objection, of course.'

His wits recovered, Jeremy smiled. 'Not in the least. You are a *former* client, Lucy.' With that, he leaned towards her and brushed his lips against hers.

She giggled.

'What is it?'

'It's just that when this week started I thought I might end up in prison.' She took his hand. 'Instead of which I'll be in bed with my barrister.'

CHAPTER THREE

Lucy Cartwright wasn't the only one planning to spend that night in bed with a barrister. Yet, did she but know it, her prospects were looking infinitely more promising than Lizzie Kavanagh's. Back from Strasbourg for the weekend, Lizzie had rather hoped to find a loving husband waiting for her when she returned to the house in Wimbledon. Those hopes were dashed – and her expectations were still unfulfilled three hours later. Great, she said to herself as she lay on the sofa, idly flicking through what passed for Friday evening entertainment with the TV remote control; no husband, no son and, of course, no daughter.

At least she knew she would see her daughter over the weekend. She and Jim – if he ever returned – were going up to Cambridge to take Kate out for the day, then meet Angela and Jeffrey Manners. Since she had gone to Cambridge, Kate's news, both verbal and written, had been approving and enthusiastic – although she had remained rather quiet on the subject of her tutor. Lizzie hoped that taking the three of them out to dinner wasn't going to be a disaster. Just because she was friendly with Angela Manners didn't mean that Kate and Jeffrey would necessarily get on. Anyway, thought Lizzie as she gave up on the TV, it probably didn't matter if they weren't particularly friendly. Much better to keep their relationship as it should be: a pupil–tutor one. Snuggling down on the sofa, she closed her eyes and wondered what she should wear the next day. A tricky one, she mused. On the one hand she wanted Angela – whom she hadn't seen in years – to notice how little she had aged; on the other, though, she didn't want to embarrass Kate by appearing as mutton dressed as lamb. Lost in these very un-Lizzie-like thoughts, she drifted off to sleep.

Half an hour later her husband woke her up. He looked delighted to see her. She, initially equally pleased, wrinkled her nose in displeasure as she kissed him.

'You smell of Indian takeaways.'

'Do I? It must have been the onion bhaji,' Kavanagh replied. 'Julia's a real fan. Can't say I'm too fond.'

'Ah! I see,' replied Lizzie in mock outrage. 'While I'm lying here pining for my husband, he's whispering sweet nothings into another woman's ear over onion bhajis. Very romantic, I must say.'

Kavanagh grinned. 'Hugely. We even had a video to watch.'

'Oh?'

'Mmm. A newsreel of that march that ended in murder.' He walked over to the drinks tray and poured a large whisky for both of them. 'I'm sorry. If I'd known you were getting back so early I'd have—'

'Brought the video home to watch?'

Again Kavanagh grinned. 'Yes . . . well, I've done that anyway.' Handing one of the tumblers to Lizzie, he continued, half apologetically, 'It's just that I'm not convinced by this girl Miriam Jacobs.'

'The one who was led astray by the boyfriend with the chip?'

'Yes. From the look on her face in the video, I'd say she was having the time of her life. And when the fighting began, she looked positively ecstatic.'

'Well, surely there's someone who can verify that for you. You said there were masses of people around.'

Kavanagh stuck out his lower lip. 'There were – but none of them are willing to talk. Julia's been through the disclosure material with a fine-tooth comb and there's nothing to help us.' Then, seemingly struck by a new idea, he looked at Lizzie in a penetrating, barristerial way.

'I'm not in the witness box, Jim,' she reminded him.

'No, I know, but I was thinking. Remember the anti-Vietnam war demonstrations?'

'Mmm.'

'Did you enjoy them?'

'What – getting baton charged, crushed and trampled?' Lizzie laughed. 'Loved every second.' Then she, too, looked pensive. 'Actually, I suppose I did a bit. I was terrified, of course, but . . .'

'Excited?'

'Very. I'd never done anything remotely anti-establishment in my life before. It felt morally right, and gloriously rebellious into the bargain.' Then, frowning at the memory, Lizzie looked at her husband. 'But I never felt like killing anyone, if that's what you're driving at. Is that what you think this Jacobs girl was after? The ultimate thrill?'

Kavanagh peered over the rim of his glass into the mid-distance. 'It crossed my mind. I'm not sure but I suspect she knows a hell of a lot more than she's letting on.'

But Lizzie's mind was still on the anti-Vietnam demonstrations. 'Do you know what I remember most about that time when I was a bolshie radical?'

'No.'

'The stuffy barrister who was assigned to defend me for disturbing the peace.'

A slow smile spread across Kavanagh's face. 'Ah. Stuffy, was he?'

'Frightfully. I thought, being a left-wing Northern lad made good and all that, he'd be a bit more sympathetic.'

'Oh dear. You poor little thing. He wasn't nasty to you, was he?'

'Well, he wasn't very nice. But,' said Lizzie as she went up to her husband and put her arms round his shoulders, 'I soon brought him into line.'

'And how did you do that?'

'Well, marrying him helped . . .'

Lizzie decided on a print dress that was neither too young nor too old but that flattered her figure. It seemed to do the trick: when they arrived in Cambridge, Kate complimented her on her appearance and Matt, whom they had managed to persuade to accompany them, didn't greet her at breakfast with an anguished, 'Oh, *Mum* . . .'

Cambridge, even Matt conceded, was beautiful, and the Kavanaghs enjoyed a hearty lunch followed by a long walk on the banks of the Cam. From her breezy chatter, it was clear that Kate was enjoying herself immensely at university. Both Lizzie and Kavanagh basked in silent, parental pride at their clever, beautiful and talented daughter. Not, they told themselves, that they were biased in any way.

Yet as they walked along the riverbank to their rendezvous with Angela and Jeffrey Manners, Kate suddenly seemed uncomfortable. 'Wouldn't it be better,' she said, to her father, 'if you met them on your own? You don't want me there.'

Kavanagh looked down at her. 'Why? Is he going to tell us what a useless student you are?'

'No, it's just . . . well, I'd rather not be around if you're going to talk about me.'

'Don't worry, we won't embarrass you.'

Matt, however, had other plans. 'I will,' he said brightly.

Kate poked him in the ribs.

'We're not checking up on you, Kate,' said Lizzie, as she took her daughter's arm. 'He may be your tutor, but Angela and I have known each other for ever. We were at school together.'

Matt chimed in, 'Oh, great. An evening of ripping yarns about high-jinks in the dorm and crushes on the headmistress. Can't wait.'

'Anyway,' said Kavanagh, ignoring him, 'we don't get many chances to sit down together as a family these days, Kate. You know how much your mother's away.'

Lizzie rolled her eyes heavenwards. 'Thanks, Jim.'

'I didn't mean it like that.'

'But it's not family, is it?' interrupted Kate. 'It's family plus my tutor and his wife. It's embarrassing.'

'Don't you like him, Kate?' Lizzie sounded concerned.

'No . . . I mean, he's all right, but—' Realizing her bad grace was in danger of ruining the evening, she stopped. 'Sorry. No, he's fine. It's just . . . well, it's an unusual situation, isn't it?'

*

Unusual or not, the evening proved pleasant enough. Matt, initially bored, was cheered up by being allowed to drink more than the one glass of wine his parents normally allowed him. Lizzie – while she would never have admitted it – was bucked up when she saw that Angela looked older than she did, and as for Kavanagh, he was just happy to have his family around him. His family: but not Jeffrey Manners. Angela, he thought, was pleasant enough, but he didn't take to her husband. He found himself unable to pinpoint exactly what it was about the man that he didn't like. As with so many university lecturers, he dressed exactly like his students. Yet Kavanagh grudgingly conceded that, although he had to be in his mid-forties, he looked youthful enough to get away with it. As the evening progressed, though, Kavanagh decided he felt sorry for Jeffrey. Kate, it seemed, shared her father's opinion of her tutor and had studiedly ignored him throughout the meal. No wonder Jeffrey, in between spells of polite conversation, was taking solace in too much wine.

Yet any *froideur* was offset by Lizzie and Angela's constant chatter. Kavanagh noted with interest that the latter, while not exactly jealous of her old friend, appeared somewhat envious of her working life.

'But I didn't have a career when the children were young,' said Lizzie as they waited for pudding. 'It's something I always wanted to see if I could do.'

Angela nodded in approval. 'Good for you. Maybe I should get myself a top job somewhere.' Then she jerked her head towards her husband. 'See how long it would take Jeff to notice I'd gone. You'd miss me, wouldn't you, darling?'

Jeffrey, who had been staring at Kate, paused before answering. 'Course I would.'

Angela either missed or chose to overlook the lack of passion in his statement. 'What he means,' she said to Lizzie, 'is that he'd miss me when the laundry basket reached critical mass.'

Lizzie smiled. 'Hmm. The trouble is, you don't want work to take you over completely, do you? I hate the fact that career and family has to be so either/or. I want my other life as well.'

Across the table, Jim watched her in appreciation. Lizzie wasn't making those remarks for his benefit; she wasn't even aware that he was listening. That made her words doubly gratifying.

Matt, on his father's left, and now banned from drinking any more wine, had finally descended into boredom. Fed up of listening to his mother wittering on about her job, he turned to his sister and asked her if she had any boyfriends. The question – innocuous enough if a little blunt – had the most startling effect on Kate: she blushed a deep red and told Matt to get lost. In the brief moment of silence that followed her angry, vehement command, Lizzie noticed that, perhaps for the first time that evening, her daughter and Jeffrey Manners made eye contact. And there was something profoundly unsettling about the look that passed between them. Suddenly unsure of what to do next, Lizzie told Matt to behave himself.

'Mum!'

'How is our Kate getting on then, Jeffrey?' interrupted Kavanagh in a manner that itself brooked no interruption. Having noticed the sudden awkwardness, yet not understanding it, Kavanagh asked the forbidden question.

'Dad!' wailed Kate. 'You promised.'

'Perhaps,' said Lizzie, 'we shouldn't talk about academic things . . .'

'No.' Setting down a wine glass which, yet again, was empty, Jeffrey assumed a tone almost as commanding as Kavanagh's. 'It's fine. Kate is doing wonderfully well.' He turned to Kavanagh and, in a sudden demonstration of enthusiasm, extolled his daughter's virtues. 'She's bright, committed and keen. I can't remember when I was last so impressed by a student.'

Again silence fell. Angela and Lizzie looked at Jeffrey. Matt looked at the ceiling. Kate looked down at her plate. Kavanagh, pleased and proud, was the only one who greeted Jeffrey's odd outburst with approval. He took the statement at face value, as praise of an exceptional student.

Lizzie never managed to regain her earlier buoyant mood. Doubt had set in; a doubt that increased when, as the party left the table and drifted towards the door, she noticed Kate and Jeffrey's hands brush. Given that they were edging past another table, the contact could have been accidental. But there was nothing accidental about the firm, reassuring squeeze that Jeffrey gave Kate once her hand was in his.

'I think I can manage without the gory details, Jeremy. A vivid mental picture of your sex life could ruin my entire day.'

Impervious, as usual, to sarcasm, Jeremy Aldermarten leaned over the table towards Julia Piper. It was Monday morning, and he was anxious to share his weekend experiences with his colleague. Those experiences had not been varied.

'But, Julia, this is the real thing! She's beautiful,

smart, funny and absolutely *loaded*. You should see her place.'

Julia took a sip of her coffee and frowned at him. 'You sound horribly mercenary.'

He dismissed that with an impatient wave. 'Oh, it's not money. It's the whole package. This woman oozes class. You know, I've always tried to avoid using the word, but I seriously wonder if this might not be love.'

Julia nearly dropped her coffee mug. 'My God, Jeremy! You've only known her for a few days and for most of those she was in the dock.'

He dismissed that one as well. 'Found innocent. And anyway, how are busy barristers supposed to meet new people?'

By accident, thought Julia. She had met her boyfriend at a cricket match. Yet she had to concede that even that had not been unconnected to her life as a barrister. She had been playing in a chambers team. Jeremy hadn't thought that women could play cricket and had tried to banish her to the boundary. He had had to eat his words when she had proved herself an ace bowler. Her very first words with David had been exchanged after she had bowled him out. It had been much later that the tall, blond and, she reckoned, beautiful man had bowled her over. Jeremy, however, didn't know she was still seeing David – and she wanted to keep it that way. Jeremy was unbearably nosey.

'But, Jeremy,' she said, with a note of real concern in her voice, 'don't you think you should be a bit more cautious to begin with? You know almost nothing about her.'

'Nonsense. You can tell she's blue chip at a glance.'

God, what a snob, thought Julia. Yet irritating though Jeremy could be, she was, in her way, fond of him. And it wasn't his fault if he was a prat. 'I just think,' she said carefully, 'that you're rushing your fences. I'd hate to see you get hurt.'

He looked as if he had been hit. 'Julia, you're beginning to sound as though you actually care about my welfare.'

Julia grinned. 'You're right. Forget I said anything.'

Jeremy and Julia's discussion about love wasn't the only one of its kind that morning. In a quiet, leafy country lane in Bedfordshire, a car had pulled up on the grass verge and two lovers were wrapped in a warm embrace in the front seat. After a moment, the girl pulled away. There was an uneasiness, a certain tension in her manner that unsettled her lover.

'What is it?'

'We have to talk. I . . . well, I've been thinking a lot about things and I'm not sure . . . I just think it's all getting a bit too serious.'

'Kate,' said Jeffrey Manners, after an agonized pause, 'I've left my wife.'

CHAPTER FOUR

Mark Holland pleaded not guilty to the murder of Ian Taylor. Kavanagh and Julia Piper knew they were going to have an uphill job persuading the jury that he was, indeed, innocent of the crime. It wasn't just that Mark, on the night of the murder, had first admitted culpability and then changed his story: added to that was that none of his fellow WAPs had agreed to come forward to support him and the evidence against him was pretty solid. Furthermore, Dominick Blake QC, counsel for the prosecution, had an almost unparalleled record for winning cases and was a formidable opponent for Kavanagh. The icing on the cake, from Blake's point of view, was that His Honour Judge Tremain was presiding over the case, a circuit judge renowned for maintaining a political stance somewhat to the right of Attila the Hun. His distaste as he looked at Mark Holland was almost palpable.

Kavanagh, however, scored a minor victory on the first day by manipulating DCI Knowland into admitting that, yes, Mark Holland had lied to protect his girlfriend Miriam Jacobs. An increasingly irritated Knowland allowed that Mark had initially claimed that Miriam was nowhere near the scene of the crime and that, as the news video clearly showed, he had been lying. Although the murder itself had not been captured on video, it was abundantly clear from the footage that Miriam had been close by. The first seeds of doubt were sown in the minds of the jurors.

But the rest of the day's evidence and testimonies did little to further Kavanagh's cause. The forensic evidence confirmed that exhibit 'A', a long-handled knife, was indeed the murder weapon and that it had been found in the suspect's pocket. Three sets of fingerprints had been identified on the handle: those of the suspect, of Miriam Jacobs and of her father Alan. DNA testing had established that the blood found on the blade was that of the deceased. It was clear from their expressions that the jurors were confused – and highly suspicious. It seemed to most of them that Mark Holland had changed his story not because he wasn't guilty of murder but because he was so enraged about Miriam Jacobs's confirmation of his initial admission of guilt. It was a sort of *crime passionnel* in reverse: Mark, after the event, was trying to get at Miriam.

Kavanagh and Julia, aware of the direction in which the jury were leaning after the first day, were stoical rather than depressed about it. There was still a long way to go, and they still had plenty of cards up their sleeves.

Yet it was Mark's solicitor Patricia Graves who unexpectedly gave them their trump. As the two barristers stood in the lobby of the crown court waiting for their taxi, Patricia appeared looking breathless, excited – and triumphant. 'Kathy Tyler,' she panted, as they looked on in surprise, 'has agreed to give evidence. She was right there, witnessed the whole thing.' Eyes shining, she paused and looked from Kavanagh to Julia. 'It happened just the way Mark said. She saw

Miriam Jacobs do it. We've got her, Mr Kavanagh. We've got her!'

Back at River Court Chambers, Kavanagh and Julia perused the typewritten statement that an ecstatic Patricia had thrust into their hands. It was from Kathy Tyler herself, claiming that she had witnessed Miriam Jacobs murdering Ian Taylor.

Kavanagh, however, didn't share Patricia's enthusiasm about the statement. Noting his scepticism as he picked it up and scanned it for the umpteenth time, Julia took it out of his hands. 'It fits with everything Mark said, Jim. And we know Kathy Tyler was there.'

'Mmm. So why didn't she say this before?'

'We know why. She didn't want any truck with the corrupt bourgeois legal system.'

Kavanagh looked up at his colleague. 'And now all of a sudden she's been overwhelmed by an attack of conscience?'

'Well, why not?'

Kavanagh frowned. 'She says she saw a woman she hated commit a murder – a murder for which a close friend is being blamed. Yet she only comes forward at the eleventh hour. Doesn't that strike you as odd?'

'Not especially.' But from the way Julia refused to meet her colleague's eye, it was clear that she, too, had doubts. 'Jim,' she said, 'she's the best we've got. Don't say you're not going to call her?'

Kavanagh was silent for a moment and then let out a deep, dissatisfied sigh. 'I've never liked gift horses, Julia. They have a habit of ending up in the knacker's yard. But, yes, you're right. She's the best we've got.'

*

Kathy Tyler didn't make for a very impressive 'best'. Summoned by Patricia Graves to court for the next day of the hearing, she made both Kavanagh and Julia stop in their tracks as they walked through the lobby towards the robing room. Making no concessions whatsoever to convention, she was wearing heavy black boots, camouflage trousers and a white sleeveless singlet. Her hair, gathered into a lopsided pony-tail, was braided with a multicoloured assortment of beads.

Julia found herself staring in reluctant admiration. 'I see Ms Tyler is going out of her way to make a good impression on the judge.'

But Kavanagh was looking intently at the girl's right arm. With a torn leather jacket slung over her shoulder, the muscular biceps of that arm was emphasized – as were the leather thongs on her wrist and the Celtic tattoo just above the elbow. Kathy was talking to Patricia Graves and didn't notice Kavanagh taking a few steps towards her before he turned back to Julia. 'You mean that's Kathy Tyler?'

'Well . . . yes. Jim, what's the matter? What is—'

'Get Graves,' he replied, with uncustomary rudeness. 'Meet me in court in five minutes.'

Too surprised to question him further, Julia did as she was told.

Five minutes later she, Patricia Graves and Kavanagh, alone in the court, stood huddled round a TV monitor as Kavanagh, his mouth set in a grim line, inserted a video and switched on the remote control. 'What on earth are we looking for?' asked a now-irritated Julia.

But Kavanagh didn't reply. He fast-forwarded the footage until he reached the scene in the alley just before the murder took place. 'Okay, this is where the camera misses what took place and cuts away to the scenes further up the road. Now look.'

Julia and Patricia Graves watched as the camera zoomed in on a policeman struggling with a demonstrator about fifty yards from the scene of the murder. Both had their backs to the camera as they struggled. The policeman finally managed to grip the demonstrator round the neck, but the demonstrator continued to struggle. In an attempt to release the choke hold, an arm came into view, battering and clawing frantically at the policeman's hand and face. That arm was muscular, covered to the elbow in leather thongs, and sported a highly distinctive Celtic tattoo.

Kavanagh froze the frame and turned to the two women, whose mouths hung open. 'Where,' he asked, 'have you seen that tattoo before?'

Julia groaned. 'Oh, God. I'm getting that distinct sinking feeling.'

'Kathy Tyler,' Patricia said, in a small voice, 'was arrested but released with a caution, but I didn't know—'

'No. Nobody knew.' Kavanagh extracted the video. 'The point is, there's no way she could have seen anything from the position she was in. She was a long way away and involved in a vicious struggle of her own at the time. Kathy Tyler is not telling the truth.'

'Mark will be devastated,' said Patricia. 'She was his big hope. I suppose,' she added without enthusiasm, 'we'll have to go down to the cell and tell him.'

Mark Holland wasn't just devastated: he was completely distraught. Yet after his initial outburst he agreed that it would only serve to damage his case if they called Kathy as a witness.

Kathy, however, thought otherwise. She had to be

45

dragged screaming out of the court lobby. As she reached the doorway, she turned to Kavanagh, her face a taut mask of pure hatred. 'You bastard!' she yelled. 'You're all in this together. It's a sodding conspiracy. Fascist bastard! Mark Holland is innocent!'

It was more than a little unfortunate that both Judge Tremain and Dominick Blake witnessed her tirade. Unaware of who she was, Tremain did his best to ignore her. Blake, however, smiled to himself and looked at Kavanagh. 'That, I take it, was your star witness. I gather we won't be seeing anything more of her.' With that, he walked into the robing room. He knew he had every reason to gloat: his first witness of the day was someone altogether more credible – and commanding – than Kathy Tyler. He was Alan Jacobs; the sort of person guaranteed to impress juries.

Fifteen minutes later, with the court in full session, Jacobs was standing in the witness box, radiating calmness, control and authority. It was abundantly clear that he was the sort of man who made others leap into the air when he said, 'Jump,' and who made people believe him if he said, 'Innocent.'

'Mr Jacobs,' said Dominick Blake, 'do you recognize this knife?'

Alan Jacobs nodded as the court clerk showed him exhibit 'A'. 'Yes. It's mine. I bought it as a souvenir many years ago on holiday in Indonesia.'

'Where did you keep it?'

'It was kept on the sideboard in the drawing room of my house in London.'

Blake nodded. 'Did the accused, Mark Holland, ever come to your house?'

Alan Jacobs winced. 'Yes, he did.'

'And did he know where the knife was kept?'

'Yes. I pointed it out to him once when we were talking about the Far East.'

Mark Holland, flanked by policemen in the dock at the back of the court, shook his head. Nobody noticed. All eyes were on Blake who, with a slight bow to the judge, sat down. He had made his point.

Kavanagh was on his feet in a flash to cross-examine Jacobs. 'When did you realize this knife was missing, Mr Jacobs?'

'Sometime in March. I forget the exact day.' His dismissive manner indicated that the date was irrelevant. It had gone missing – and Mark Holland had taken it.

Kavanagh pretended to read his notes and then looked up again. 'It wasn't you who realized it had gone, was it?'

'No, it was my wife.'

'She told you it had been stolen?'

'Yes.'

'So you went straight to the police and reported the theft?'

'No.'

'No? Why not?'

'It didn't seem an important enough issue to involve the police.'

Kavanagh paused and once more consulted his notes. Jacobs, for the first time, looked unsettled. He knew that Kavanagh was going to change the subject – but he didn't know to what.

'How would you describe your relationship with your daughter, Mr Jacobs?'

If Jacobs was surprised by the question, he didn't show it. 'We are extremely close.'

'But there was a long spell when you didn't get on very well, wasn't there?'

'We had our ups and downs, just like any family.'

Kavanagh raised his eyebrows – and his voice. 'Ups and downs? You didn't speak to her for six months until all this happened.'

Jacobs hesitated before replying. 'It was nothing more than a silly row.'

'It started, Mr Jacobs, as long ago as March last year.'

This time Jacobs didn't reply at all.

'It was March, wasn't it?' prompted Kavanagh.

'Yes.'

'And it was in March that the knife went missing.'

'That had nothing to do with my daughter.'

'How do you know that?'

'It had nothing,' repeated Jacobs, 'to do with Miriam.'

Kavanagh smiled at the witness: a smile that was condescending rather than warm. 'You weren't even there, Mr Jacobs. You were away on business.' Letting that piece of information sink into the minds of everyone in court, he changed course again. 'You don't like Mark Holland, do you?'

But Jacobs had been prepared for that one. 'I have nothing against him personally.'

'Hmm.' Again Kavanagh looked down at his notes. 'So, you hadn't spoken to your daughter for six months, and on the twenty-third of September she's suddenly desperate to see you. That's right, isn't it?'

'Yes.'

'Where were you when she arrived at your house that night?'

'I was working in my study.'

'So she rushed in to see you?'

'No. My wife came in and I went up to Miriam.'

'Up?' For the benefit of the jury Kavanagh looked politely puzzled.

'Yes. Upstairs. She was in her room.'

'What was she doing there?'

'I have no idea.'

'No idea? You just said you went up to see her.'

'I didn't go up immediately. I was busy. It was a few minutes before I saw her.'

'How many minutes?' Kavanagh's tone had suddenly become commanding.

'I don't know . . . ten or fifteen.'

Kavanagh took a deep breath. 'So, to get it straight. Your wife told you that the daughter you had not seen or spoken to for six months needed to see you urgently, yet you kept her waiting for a quarter of an hour?' Out of the corner of his eye, Kavanagh noticed several jurors leaning forward in their seats. And behind him, in the public gallery, an air of tension had gathered. Things were hotting up.

Jacobs refused to be intimidated. 'I had no idea that the situation was so grave.'

'But didn't Mrs Jacobs tell you what state Miriam was in?'

'She told me she was very upset.'

'Very upset – yet your work was so vital you couldn't see her immediately?'

'No,' said Jacobs, through pursed lips. 'Not immediately.'

Kavanagh looked at the witness with something approaching disdain. 'You couldn't have a more urgent crisis, could you? She rushed home to see you, her father, even before going to the police—'

'She did go to the police!' Jacobs glowered at Kavanagh. 'When she got home she had just witnessed a fatal stabbing and she was very upset. She spoke to the police the moment she gathered her wits.'

'Yes.' Kavanagh nodded. 'But she only gathered her wits after she talked to you, didn't she?'

At home that evening, Kavanagh reflected grimly on the events of the day. He wondered if he had succeeded in sowing any seeds of doubt in the jurors' minds regarding the behaviour of Miriam and Alan Jacobs. On balance, he thought, he had probably failed. Reconciliations invariably made people feel happy, and the jurors were probably thinking how nice it was that Miriam and her father were back on speaking terms, even if it had taken a fatal incident to provoke the reunion. And if Miriam had run to her father instead of to the police – well, that was understandable, wasn't it? She had been in need of comfort and security.

No, thought Kavanagh, he had not succeeded in his task of making the jury wonder what Miriam had been doing in the fifteen minutes before her father went up to her. Kavanagh himself was pretty sure what she had been up to: he believed that she had been changing out of the clothes that had been covered with Ian Taylor's blood. The only problem was, he couldn't prove it. He couldn't even prove that the clothes she had been wearing to the rally were different from those she had worn during her interview with the police later that evening. The video of the rally was no use in that department: the only shots of Miriam were mug-shots, showing nothing of her clothing.

Kavanagh's increasingly negative thoughts were disturbed by the sound of a car in the driveway. He looked at his watch. Kate. With a party to go to in London on Saturday night, she had declared she would be coming home for the weekend; a weekend that, by happy coincidence, would be another family one as Lizzie had spent the entire week working from the London office and would be at home until Sunday night.

She was also in the hall when Kate opened the front door. 'Darling! How nice. Good journey?'

Kate came forward to kiss her mother, thereby avoiding her eye as she replied that she had managed to get a lift.

'That's nice. Everything okay?'

'Fine.' Kate, unusually, seemed to have nothing more to say. 'I'll . . . I'll be up in my room.'

Lizzie sensed that perhaps everything wasn't okay. She said, 'Aren't you going to say hello to Dad? He's in the study.'

'Oh. Right.'

She frowned as she watched Kate head towards the study: something was definitely up – it was most unlike Kate to be so furtive. And then she cast her mind back to last weekend's dinner in Cambridge. She hadn't asked any questions – but she had a horrible feeling she already knew the answers.

The bell rang. Still distracted, Lizzie stepped forward to open the door and, before she had registered who was on the threshold, forced a polite smile.

That smile faded abruptly as she found herself staring into the face of Jeffrey Manners. If she was disconcerted to see him, he was even more so. He had clearly been expecting Kate to answer the door. 'Ah. Hello. Elizabeth.' Uncomfortable with eye contact, he indicated the book in his left hand. 'Kate forgot this.'

'Oh.' Lizzie's voice was wooden. 'You were Kate's lift.'

'Er . . . yes. Could you get her for me?'

But instead Lizzie reached out for the book. 'I'll give it to her.'

Jeffrey withheld the book. 'It'll only take a second.'

Lizzie sighed. 'Tell me this isn't what it looks like, Jeffrey.'

Jeffrey's momentary silence and the look on his face confirmed everything Lizzie suspected. Then, as she heard footsteps in the hall behind her, he uttered the words Lizzie hadn't wanted to hear. 'I'm sorry,' he said, 'but you ought to know that Kate and I have been seeing each other.'

As he spoke, both Kavanagh and his daughter appeared beside Lizzie. Kavanagh couldn't believe that he'd heard correctly. 'What do you mean, seeing each other?'

Lizzie held out a restraining arm. The last thing she wanted was for him to go off the rails before she knew exactly what was going on. 'It's nothing, Jim.'

'I should go,' said Jeffrey, taking a step backwards.

But Kavanagh had noticed the look that had passed between Jeffrey and Kate. 'Would one of you,' he said in a voice that suggested calm before a storm, 'please tell me what's going on?'

Jeffrey hesitated and then approached Kavanagh. Realizing what he was about to do Kate tried, too late, to stop him. 'Kate and I,' he blurted out, 'are having a relationship.'

Kavanagh's disbelief outweighed his anger – but only just. 'What are you talking about, man? You're her bloody tutor.'

Jeffrey bowed his head. 'I'm sorry you had to find out like this—'

Kavanagh erupted. 'You're thirty years older than her!' he bellowed.

'Well, twenty-four, but that's hardly the point.'

'Don't talk to me about the bloody point! You come to my house, chasing after a student you're supposed to be responsible for—'

Knowing full well that her father was quite capable of thumping Jeffrey, Kate put her hand on his shoulder. 'Dad—'

Kavanagh shook it off. Stepping towards Jeffrey, he could barely contain his urge to throttle the man as he looked at him with pure disgust. 'This is blatant harassment. I'll have you out of that university quicker than you can blink. I'll make damn sure you're never in a position to exploit young people again—'

'I can assure you, Kate is not being exploited.' Jeffrey squared his shoulders. 'Far from it, in fact.'

'How dare you!'

Suddenly, Kate had had enough. 'Will all of you please be quiet!' she yelled. So surprised were the others that they immediately lapsed into silence. 'I'll handle this on my own,' she continued, more quietly, and to Jeffrey, she added, 'I can't talk to you now. I'll call you when I'm ready.' Then she turned inside and walked towards the stairs.

'I'm sorry,' said Jeffrey to her still numb parents. 'I didn't mean to embarrass you—'

'Embarrass!' Kavanagh was livid. 'You bloody disgust me! You needn't think you can get away with this. I'm contacting the college in the morning.'

Before Jeffrey could protest, Lizzie stepped forward.

'What about Angela?' she said. 'Doesn't she have a say in this?'

'That,' replied Jeffrey, 'is between her and me.'

'Not any more.' Lizzie's measured tones were far more threatening than her husband's ranting. 'You involved us when you took advantage of Kate.'

'Aren't you ashamed of yourself?' spat Kavanagh.

Jeffrey looked him in the eye. 'I'm past the point where shame has much to do with anything.' Then he turned to his car and left the Kavanagh family to face a weekend of anything but togetherness.

CHAPTER FIVE

'I don't think I've ever seen you like this before, Jeremy.'

'Like what?'

'Well . . . good-natured.'

'Contentment does things to a man, Julia.'

Julia nearly exploded. Good old Jeremy, she thought. Only in him could contentment and pomposity grow in equal measures. 'It doesn't sit well, somehow,' she said. 'It's like having a Rottweiler fetch your slippers.' Jeremy, as ever, failed to rise.

'What does Lucy do anyway?' continued Julia.

'Well, she doesn't *do* anything at the moment. She's resting after the abuses of a hideous marriage and considerable emotional turmoil.'

Alarm bells began to ring in Julia's mind. It wasn't the first time. Shortly after Jeremy had bombarded her with tales of Lucy's beauty, intelligence and inordinate wealth, Lucy had been evicted from the elegant house that had so impressed Jeremy. Subsequently, she had tearfully admitted that the house had belonged to a friend who had lent it to her until she sorted out her financial affairs. 'I didn't ever tell you it was mine,' she told Jeremy. 'And how could I have admitted to you that I was temporarily financially embarrassed? I would have lost you.'

Touched by her words, Jeremy had sternly instructed her to tell him the truth from then on – and had asked her to move in with him. Temporarily, of course. He had related all this to Julia, and Julia had been deeply unimpressed.

Now, with this latest revelation, she was deeply suspicious. 'You mean,' she said, 'that Lucy is living off you.'

'That's a vulgar way of putting it. And anyway it's a purely temporary arrangement until she can sort out her financial affairs.'

Julia moaned, 'Oh, my God, you're giving her money.' Then without even a glimmer of her previous jocular tone, she asked him how much.

'Hardly anything.' Jeremy looked away. 'Well, a couple of thousand.'

'Jeremy, do you really think this is wise? You hardly know her.'

'So you keep saying.' Irritated now, Jeremy glared at her. 'I happen to disagree.' Then he gathered up the files in front of him and prepared to leave the room. 'Much as I hate to ruin your recently improved opinion of me, would you kindly keep your opinions about my romantic disposition to yourself?'

Julia flinched as Jeremy banged the door behind him with more force than was strictly necessary. He was right, she supposed: it wasn't any of her business. Yet the old, hackneyed phrase of love being blind sprang to her mind. There was definitely a lot more to Lucy Cartwright than met the eye. Then Julia, too, gathered her papers and stood up. She, like Jeremy, had better things to do – like sit behind Jim Kavanagh and listen to the next witness in the Mark Holland trial.

'Off to court, then?' The question took her by surprise as, a minute later, she walked into the hallway. Turning round, she found herself facing Alex Wilson, the newest recruit to River Court. Julia grimaced in response to the question. 'Yes, the Mark Holland trial.'

'Not going well?'

'Not going anywhere, really.'

Alex grinned. 'Unlike Jeremy, then. Whatever he's off to do, he's obviously confident of winning.'

Julia shook her head. 'He's already won – or so he thinks. That damsel in distress he got acquitted has wound him round her little finger. I don't like it, Alex,' she added, worriedly. 'I think she's dodgy – and I gather it was a miracle Jeremy got her off in the first place.'

'Julia, there's only one rule when it comes to other people's sex lives. Don't interfere.'

Julia gave that suggestion due consideration. 'Normally, yes . . . but what if she *is* taking him for a ride?'

But Alex, more than most, had good reason to believe that Jeremy could do with a nasty shock. He had given her two when she had joined as a pupil a year ago. Initially, he had tried to get her ousted because she was black. Then, in an alarmingly rapid *volte face*, he had tried to make amends by pouncing on her in a manner that was both unsubtle and unsavoury. 'Look, Julia, even if Jeremy is in trouble, and I appreciate you've known him longer than me, this is *Jeremy* we're talking about.'

Remembering Alex's experiences – and her own – Julia replied ruefully, 'I know. Moral dilemma of the day: should one throw a lifebelt to a drowning rat?'

Alex chortled and, with a quick, 'Good luck,' left Julia alone in the hall. For the second time in almost as many minutes, she had to remind herself that Jeremy's problems were his alone. She had enough of her own.

Forcing her mind back to the trial, she allowed herself a small smile. This morning's witness, she felt sure, would prove more fruitful than the last. Alan Jacobs, unsurprisingly, hadn't given anything away. His wife, Julia suspected, would be a different story. You would have to be either extremely strong – or extremely weak – to stand being married to a man like that for nearly thirty years.

From the moment Marcia Jacobs walked into the witness box it was abundantly clear to Julia that she was nervous, ill-at-ease – and unhappy about being the centre of attention. Dominick Blake was also aware of this, and Julia grudgingly admired the way he coaxed her gently through his questions. Yet once he got her on the subject of the knife, he was on firmer ground. Marcia Jacobs was adamant that Mark Holland had stolen it from the sideboard on the day he had visited last March.

'So what did you do,' asked Blake, 'when you realized it had gone?'

'I decided to see if anything else was missing. Then I thought about calling the police. Finally,' said Marcia, with the air of one who knows she has done the right thing, 'I decided to wait until my husband came home from his business trip. I told him Mark had taken it.'

Blake smiled at her and sat down.

Kavanagh, however, wasn't in the mood for smiling. Immediately he got to his feet, he looked at Marcia Jacobs without a trace of sympathy. 'When your daughter visited you in March,' he said, 'she left with the defendant, didn't she?'

'Yes.'

'Mark Holland didn't take the knife. She did, didn't she?'

Marcia looked horrified. 'That's ridiculous. Miriam wouldn't steal from us.'

Kavanagh thought otherwise. 'She took it as a gesture of defiance against her father, didn't she?'

'No.'

Ignoring her denial, Kavanagh continued as if the woman didn't exist. 'He didn't want to report the theft because he feared she had taken it. When your daughter first cáme in on the evening of the twenty-third of September, she was desperate to see her father.'

Perplexed by the sudden change in questioning, Marcia opened her mouth too late to reply. 'And then,' continued Kavanagh, 'she ran up the stairs and went into her room?'

'Yes.'

'And you went to your husband's study and told him what had happened?'

'That's right.'

'And were you surprised that he made her wait for a quarter of an hour before going up to see her?'

Marcia was completely floored by the question. Kavanagh had to prompt her to answer.

'I . . . well, I don't remember precisely . . .'

'Your husband has testified that he worked in his study for a further ten or fifteen minutes before going to see Miriam. Is that not the case?'

A slight sheen appeared on Marcia's upper lip. 'I really can't – well, it was such a terrible evening . . . Yes,' she finished, without much conviction. 'It must have happened like that.'

'Well, what did you do during that time?'

'I went up to see if she was all right.'

'Ah.' Kavanagh waited a minute. 'So you went into her room and spoke to her?'

Again, Marcia looked uncomfortable. 'I . . . I was on the landing.'

'The landing? Why didn't you go in?'

In mounting desperation, she looked around the court. All she saw was a sea of faces, eager for her reply, none displaying much sympathy. Turning back to Kavanagh, she almost pleaded that as it was her daughter's private room one couldn't just barge in . . .

'Oh, come on, Mrs Jacobs. You must have been worried about her. Why didn't you go in to see her?'

Everyone in the jury and the public gallery, sharing Kavanagh's scepticism, leaned forward for Marcia's answer. 'I couldn't,' she said in a small voice.

'Oh, why was that?'

'She'd locked the door.' As soon as she had said the words, Marcia knew she was now on unfamiliar and shaky ground.

'Locked it?' Kavanagh queried. 'Why?'

But Marcia wasn't keen to explain why.

'Mrs Jacobs,' repeated Kavanagh, 'why did your daughter lock the door?'

Marcia hung her head. 'Because . . . because she was in the shower.'

Kavanagh allowed time for her words to sink in before repeating them with theatrical emphasis. 'I see. Because she was in the shower.' He threw a significant glance towards the jury, then sat down with a flourish – in stark contrast to the miserable Marcia Jacobs, who crept away from the witness box like a guilty schoolgirl.

Kavanagh watched grimly as she left the courtroom. Things might be picking up for him in court, he reflected, but home life in the Kavanagh household was far from up-beat. As usual, he had tried not to bring personal problems to work, but this time he was finding it more than a little difficult to dismiss the unhappy events of the weekend from his mind.

Although both he and Lizzie had tried to discuss Kate's affair with detachment and reason, the situation had quickly degenerated into something resembling a bunfight. Kavanagh had blamed Jeffrey Manners for taking advantage of Kate. Lizzie had blamed Kate for knowingly entering into an affair with a married man. And Kate had shocked them both by saying that she was no longer in love with Jeffrey; that the affair had been just a 'bit of fun'. Ultimately – and perhaps inevitably – Kate had become so angry that she had brought up the affair Lizzie had had two years previously, accusing her mother of being an expert on the subject of infidelity. At that, Lizzie had lapsed into shocked silence while Kavanagh, for the first time in his life, had felt like hitting his daughter. Lizzie's affair with barrister Miles Petersham had nearly destroyed the Kavanaghs' marriage and indeed their family life; that both had survived had been due to much hard work, soul-searching and compromising. Lizzie had admitted to her husband that the affair had been due more to frustration at coming second to his work than to passion for Miles. She supposed she had been trying to prove a point. Now, by reopening the old wound, Kate was trying to prove another.

Even Kate had seen she had gone too far. As Kavanagh sat in the courtroom idly flicking through his notes as they waited for the next witness to be called, he remembered the look of contrition on her face after her outburst. If nothing else, it had served to end the family argument – but not before Lizzie had announced that Angela had asked to meet her for lunch on Monday. Today was Monday, and although Lizzie was supposed to be back in Strasbourg, she had declared that work would have to do without her for a day or two.

Kavanagh looked at his watch: twelve o'clock. Lizzie would be meeting Angela in half an hour. He wished he could have accompanied her. Then, he dismissed that thought from his mind. The meeting between the two women was likely to be painful: what was about to happen in court was liable to be important and, he hoped, beneficial to his defence of Mark Holland.

The lights were being lowered to show the court the video that had been taken by the news reporter on the day of the rally. Silence reigned while everyone looked at the monitors and at the figure of Mark Holland breaking through the line of policemen. The video followed him as he rushed down the street. Behind him, and clearly visible on screen, was the person who had replaced Marcia Jacobs in the witness box.

As the video flickered and then stopped, the lights went up and all eyes turned towards Miriam Jacobs, beautifully yet soberly dressed, and now standing staring out at the court. Every inch her father's daughter, she looked magnificent – yet behind her composure it was evident that great strain was being tightly controlled. Dominick Blake, adopting almost reverential tones, asked her to describe to the court the events they had just watched on screen.

Her voice tremulous yet her manner determined, Miriam spoke in a clear, cut-glass accent that reminded

Julia Piper, sitting quietly behind Kavanagh, of Jeremy Aldermarten's paramour.

'I was forced against the police line by the sheer weight of people behind me,' she explained. 'Mark and I were up at the front. Then the line broke. The only safe way to go,' she added with a hint of apology, 'was forward.'

Blake nodded in sympathy. 'It must have been terrifying. Can you remember what happened in the next few moments?'

'Well, I lost sight of Mark for a moment. Then I saw him chasing someone onto the pavement. The man was wearing a Union Jack T-shirt. He fell over a garden wall.' As she spoke, Miriam both looked and sounded like an awed schoolgirl trapped in a situation she didn't understand.

'And where were you by the time this took place?'

'In the road a few yards away.'

'What did you do when you saw what was happening?'

'I moved nearer and shouted to Mark.' Miriam raised her hands in a curious, yet convincing gesture of helplessness. 'I was scared. I just wanted us to get out.'

'Did you succeed in attracting his attention?'

'No. Either he didn't hear me or he ignored me. I . . . I saw him reach into his jacket pocket and then hit the boy who was lying on the ground.' Wide-eyed, Miriam looked at Blake. 'A few seconds later I realized he had a knife in his hand. He leaned down again and when he looked up there was blood all over his shirt.' As she gave her evidence, she avoided looking at Mark. He, however, had been staring at her in mounting disbelief. Suddenly, no longer able to contain himself,

63

he leaned forward and, in a half-whisper clearly audible to those at the back of the court, called her a 'lying bitch'.

Julia Piper turned round to admonish him but, aware that his protest was useless as well as out of order, he had slumped back in the dock and closed his eyes. Dominick Blake looked at Judge Tremain. The judge looked at Kavanagh. Kavanagh looked straight back. The uncomfortable moment passed, but not before half of the jurors had noted the look of distaste on the judge's face.

'Miss Jacobs,' continued Blake, 'why did it take you over four hours to go to the police with what you knew?'

Miriam shrugged helplessly. 'I don't know. I panicked. I just wanted to get away, to stay out of it.' Then she bowed her head. When she raised it again her eyes were moist. 'And . . . and I really cared for Mark. I just didn't know what to do.'

'What made you change your mind?' Blake spoke sympathetically.

'My father asked me if I could live with myself if I didn't own up to what I knew. In the end, no matter how much I felt for Mark, I knew I couldn't.'

Dominick Blake wasn't the only person in court to be moved by Miriam's tearful, heartfelt reply. It was quite clear that, as he sat down and Kavanagh rose to begin his cross-examination, the majority of the court was on Miriam Jacobs's side.

'Can you remember,' began Kavanagh, politely, 'what clothes you were wearing when you went to the rally on the twenty-third of September, Miss Jacobs?'

'Yes. A black leather jacket, white shirt and black jeans.'

Kavanagh nodded. 'And you changed out of those

clothes when you got home before going to the police?'

'No . . . I didn't change. I was in shock.' Miriam tried a tentative smile. 'I wore the same clothes all day.'

For the umpteenth time since he had taken on the case, Kavanagh bitterly regretted that Miriam's fleeting appearance on the video captured only her face. Yet he kept his feelings to himself as he replied, 'I see. Thank you.' Then, after a second's pause, he asked Miriam why she had gone to the rally.

Miriam looked him in the eye. 'I wanted to show I was against racism and violence.'

Kavanagh's face, as he listened to her response, carried not the slightest trace of warmth. 'You went,' he replied, 'because you found the prospect of confrontation exciting, didn't you?'

'No.'

'What did you feel,' he continued, 'when the police line was breached and the violence started?'

'I felt very scared. I didn't want to get hurt.'

'Actually,' countered Kavanagh, 'you enjoyed it, didn't you?'

'That's absurd. It was terrifying.'

But Kavanagh wouldn't let go. 'You got a kick out of being so close to real danger, didn't you?'

'That's rubbish.'

By the increasingly impatient looks Judge Tremain was directing at Kavanagh, it was clear that he agreed with Miriam. Just as he was about to ask Kavanagh to desist from that line of questioning, Kavanagh did so without being told. 'Where exactly were you,' he asked, 'when Ian Taylor was attacked?'

'In the road about ten yards away. I can't remember the exact location.'

'But you were definitely standing on your own in the road?'

'Yes.'

Kavanagh looked up at Judge Tremain. 'With your honour's leave, I would like to take this witness through the video-tape evidence again.'

Tremain indicated his assent. Despite being irritated by Kavanagh's persistence, he knew that the barrister was far from a fool. Something on the tape, he suspected, was about to contradict Miriam's evidence.

The whole court watched, this time with greater interest, as the tape was replayed. They watched as the camera moved from the distant mob surrounding Ian Taylor to the road where Miriam claimed she had been standing. The camera panned up the street, encompassing its entirety and everyone standing there. Then Kavanagh replayed the scene once more, this time in slow motion. He stopped the tape and looked at Miriam. 'You're not there, are you?'

'The camera must have missed me.'

Kavanagh shook his head. 'The camera shows the whole street at that moment. You're not there.'

'I *was* there.'

'No. You're not there because you were in the mob surrounding Ian Taylor, weren't you?'

'No!'

Seemingly unperturbed, Kavanagh suggested they look further back through the tape. Again the court watched, this time in suspense, as the tape showed Miriam breaking through the police line with Mark Holland. Kavanagh froze the tape at that frame, getting a perfect shot of Miriam's face. It bore an expression of wild excitement.

'That's not the face of a terrified woman, is it?' said Kavanagh.

Clearly rattled, Miriam glared at him. 'Appearances,' she said smartly, 'can be deceptive.'

'You're loving every second of it, aren't you?'

'No.'

'You were on a high of excitement, weren't you?'

'No! I was scared.' Aware that she was beginning to lose the sympathy of the court, Miriam also began to lose her self-control. 'I'm not on trial here!' she shouted. 'You're trying to make things look bad when they aren't. Mark did it. I saw him. I had nothing to do with it.'

Taking advantage both of the scepticism that greeted her remarks and of Miriam's own uncertainty, Kavanagh switched off the tape and, equally quickly, began a new line of questioning. 'If Mark Holland was intent on murder, he could have used any knife, couldn't he?'

'Er . . . yes.'

'So why on earth would he go to the trouble of stealing one from your father?'

'I have no idea.'

'You were there when this knife went missing, weren't you?'

Miriam faltered, 'I don't know – I don't know when it went missing.'

'Your mother told you it had been stolen though, didn't she?'

'No.'

'You knew where it was all the time, didn't you?'

'No.'

'You took it with you when you left the house that evening in March, didn't you?'

'No.'

Kavanagh drew breath. 'So you are saying, Miss Jacobs, that Mark Holland went to all the trouble of stealing an easily identifiable knife, didn't tell you about it and then kept it concealed from you until the moment he used it at this rally?'

Now feeling more in control of the situation, Miriam stared straight back. 'That,' she said, in her old haughty manner, 'is exactly what must have happened.'

If Miriam Jacobs thought she had turned the corner, she was in for a rude awakening. 'Miss Jacobs,' said Kavanagh, after a dramatic silence, 'why did you have a shower when you got home on the twenty-third of September?'

The question took the wind right out of Miriam's sails. She hadn't told her solicitor about the shower. Only her parents had known about the shower, and surely they would never . . .

Shock and confusion were written all over Miriam's face as she stared dumbly at Kavanagh. 'I . . . er,' she stammered eventually, 'I can't remember having a shower.'

'Your mother says you did.' Kavanagh deftly put the knife in – and twisted it. 'That's why you locked the door for nearly fifteen minutes after you got in.'

Desperately trying to gather her wits, Miriam gave the barrister an apologetic half-smile. 'Then I suppose I must have done . . . but I don't know. I was very confused.'

Noting that the jurors were looking at Miriam with a mixture of curiosity tempered with dislike, Kavanagh continued relentlessly. 'It wasn't your father who made you wait fifteen minutes. It was the other way round, wasn't it?'

'I don't think it was that long—'

'I'm still having some trouble with the sequence of events, Miss Jacobs.' Julia Piper, sitting behind Kavanagh, knew he was having no trouble at all with the sequence of events. She also knew that his primary concern was to convince the jury that Miriam was lying. 'To be clear,' he continued, 'you ran into the house demanding to see your father, is that right?'

'Yes.'

'You wanted to see him urgently but instead of walking the few yards to his study you locked the door of your room for a quarter of an hour and had a shower, didn't you?'

Miriam lowered her eyes. 'Yes.'

'Very understandable. The events of the day had left you feeling exhausted and dirty, hadn't they?'

'Yes. I needed to get myself together.'

'And having had a shower you then put on fresh clothes, didn't you?'

Only then did Miriam see the trap Kavanagh had laid for her. But it was too late. Through gritted teeth, she ground out her answer, hearing as she did so how absurd it sounded. 'No. I did not put on new clothes.'

Kavanagh looked at her. Then he looked at the jury. 'Are you seriously expecting this court to believe that you went to all the trouble of having a shower only to put on your soiled outfit again?'

'Yes! Because it's the truth—'

'The reason you rushed into that shower,' interrupted Kavanagh, 'was because Ian Taylor's blood was on your face and hands, wasn't it?'

Miriam didn't reply.

'And you did change your clothes, didn't you? You changed them for the same reason you had a shower.

It was because they were heavily bloodstained, wasn't it?'

'I—'

'Miss Jacobs, what happened to those clothes?'

The image of the dying embers of the bonfire she had lit with her father sprang into Miriam's mind. But no words came to her mouth. Leaving her staring helplessly in front of her, the picture of a woman with a great deal to hide, Kavanagh sat down. He allowed himself the faintest trace of a smile as he did so.

While the events of Monday reaped dividends for Kavanagh, they failed to do so for three other people in his life. One was Lizzie. Her lunch with Angela Manners started wearily and ended acrimoniously. Relating her husband's version of events, Angela claimed that Kate had thrown herself at Jeffrey and had taken what she wanted without a thought for anyone else. Lizzie pointed out that Jeffrey wasn't exactly innocent himself: he had abused a position of power. She and Jim, she went on to say, could easily make an official complaint, thereby ruining Jeffrey's career. The already distraught Angela accused Lizzie of making threats – and then the meeting went rapidly downhill. After ten minutes, Angela had got to her feet, claiming that she and Lizzie had 'nothing more to say to each other'.

Left alone at the table, Lizzie put her head in her hands and, for once in her life, didn't know what to do. She didn't want to make a complaint. Deliberately ruining other people's careers was not her style; and such a move wouldn't solve the problem.

Had Lizzie but known it, the problem, back in Cambridge, was about to solve itself. Over the weekend,

Kate had been doing a lot of thinking. Her first thought was that she didn't want to fall out with her parents. Her second was that she had loved the thrill of the affair with Jeffrey more than she loved Jeffrey. And her final and deciding consideration was whether she, an eighteen-year-old with her whole life ahead of her, really wanted to throw it all away for a married man in his forties with three children and – as her mother had hinted rather heavily – a reputation as a serial adulterer. The answer had been a resounding no. Therefore, summoning all the courage she possessed, she asked Jeffrey to meet her in a quiet Cambridge pub.

She broached the subject almost immediately – and was more than a little stunned by Jeffrey's reaction. For an instant he looked shocked; then he looked her in the eye and smiled. 'Well,' he said, 'no point in brooding, I suppose. It's not really so important, is it?'

Kate was horrified. 'But I thought you—'

'Thought what?' Jeffrey's lip curled. 'That I was taking it all deathly seriously? You weren't the only one having fun, you know.'

'But you told Angela . . .'

This time Jeffrey actually laughed. 'You don't seriously imagine I'd have left her for *you*, do you? Our marriage has been through worse things than this. I expect it'll survive.'

Completely nonplussed and not a little upset, Kate stared down into her lap. Was this what it was always going to be like, she wondered. Just a game? Why, then, had Jeffrey risked so much by coming to her parents' house and declaring all? 'Then I don't understand why you got so upset,' she said, after regaining her composure.

Jeffrey smirked. 'Oh, probably a case of my vanity

being bruised. I overreacted, that's all. Don't worry about it, Kate. It was probably reaching its natural conclusion anyway, wasn't it?'

Kate could hardly bear to look at him. 'I suppose so,' she said, quietly.

'All's well that ends well, eh?'

But Kate couldn't take any more of Jeffrey's nonchalance. She stood up to leave. She could only think of one thing to say: 'Goodbye, Jeffrey.'

Only when Kate had left the pub did Jeffrey let his mask slip. Sitting alone at the table, he looked like a man for whom the bottom had fallen out of his world.

The third person that day to receive an unwelcome surprise was Jeremy Aldermarten. Working at home that day, he spent half the time in a daze of happiness, gloating over his good fortune at meeting Lucy. They had made passionate love that morning, and then Lucy, aware of the importance of his work, had said that she would spend the rest of the day seeing her lawyer, lunching with a friend and doing various chores that would enable her lover to be left in peace. Jeremy was touched by her solicitude and, in a surge of happiness, decided to book a table at her favourite restaurant for dinner. He picked up the phone and dialled and, as he waited for an answer, began to doodle on the paper in front of him. Only when he had booked the table and replaced the receiver with a satisfied smile did he see what he had been writing on the paper. Again and again, he had written the words 'Lucy Aldermarten'. He looked at the name for a moment. Well, he thought to himself, it wasn't an impossibility, was it? Then, shaking his head and marvelling at his new capacity for sentimentality, he scrunched up the paper and leaned over towards the wastepaper basket. As he did so, something in it caught his eye. He had been sure the basket was empty. His cleaning lady was most punctilious about such things – and so was Lucy. He picked up the torn scraps of paper and read what was written on them. It was his own signature, written again and again – but not in his own hand. For a moment he sat still, rigid with shock. Then, after a full minute, he reached once more for the phone and dialled a different number.

Barclays Bank answered almost immediately.

'This is Jeremy Aldermarten,' he said without preamble. 'I'd like the balance of my account please.' After a few moments of giving security details, Jeremy was told his balance. He had to ask his banker to repeat the figure not once, but three times.

CHAPTER SIX

In the witness box the following day, Mark Holland stood with the air of a man who carried the entire weight of the world on his shoulders. It was unfortunate, Kavanagh reflected as he questioned him, that he also managed to convey the impression of a man with a chip on his shoulder.

Taking him gently through the events of the day of the murder, Kavanagh had already established that Mark had been beside Ian Taylor when Miriam, to his horror, had extracted her father's knife from her pocket and had stabbed him. She had been incredibly excited about the march, he said, and had kept saying that everyone would soon see the best way of dealing with the Nazis. But no, he had had no idea that Miriam had intended to stab one of them. Nor had he had any idea that she had been carrying a knife. In answer to the question of why he had picked up the knife after Miriam had dropped it, Mark claimed he didn't know; that he had been confused, appalled and bewildered by the scene before him. Then he told Kavanagh that he had shouted at Miriam to get as far away as possible.

Hoping that the jury was beginning to get the impression of a gallant young man willing to sacrifice anything for his girlfriend, Kavanagh then asked him why, in his first interview with the police, he had taken the blame for the stabbing.

With a faraway, yet bitter look on his face, Mark replied that it had been because at that point he had been besotted by Miriam. 'I'd have said anything to keep her out of it,' he continued, seemingly surprised at his own words. 'It probably seems dumb, but I'd never met someone like her before. She had a lot of style, she talked like she really hated injustice and she talked like she really loved me.' He gave a weary, resigned shrug and let out a deep sigh. 'I fell for it all. I was flattered she'd chosen me. I felt like I should protect her.'

'So why did you change your mind?'

'I had a chance to think. Then,' he continued, with a twisted smile, 'I heard all that crap she'd come up with about me doing it. I knew she was going to walk away and dump me right in it. She betrayed me without a second thought. I was on my own.'

Kavanagh waited. If only, he thought for the umpteenth time, Mark hadn't made that first statement. 'Whatever the reason, Mr Holland, you did lie in that first statement. Is what you are now telling the court an honest account of what happened that day?'

Mark nodded and looked fixedly ahead. 'I know people reckon that because she's a woman she couldn't have done it. She's got all the money on her side. The expensive lawyer, the posh family, all the privileges that come with the territory. I don't have any of that,' he added with feeling. 'All I've got is the truth.'

But Dominick Blake believed otherwise. As soon as Kavanagh sat down, he leaped to his feet and bombarded Mark with a barrage of questions.

'Mr Holland,' he began, 'it was Ian Taylor's blood on your shirt, wasn't it?'

'Yes.'

'Your fingerprints on the murder weapon?'

'Yes.'

'And you did make a statement admitting that you killed him, didn't you?'

'Yes, I did, but—'

'Nobody saw Miriam Jacobs with the knife, did they?'

'No.'

'Nobody, apart from you, has placed her positively at your side while Ian Taylor lay dying, have they?'

'No.'

Blake paused and smiled a predatory smile at the witness. 'She wasn't there, was she?'

Fighting to control his temper, Mark Holland clenched his teeth. 'Yes. She was there.'

'This attempt to pin the blame on her,' went on Blake, 'is nothing more than a desperate ploy to get yourself out of trouble, isn't it?'

'I'm telling the truth.'

'And it's just your word against hers, isn't it?'

'Yes. But my word's good for something.'

Blake turned to the subject that he knew would finally make Mark lose his temper. 'Neither she nor her family can be trusted, can they?'

'No.'

'You can't trust any of their class, can you?'

'Too right.'

'They're all liars, aren't they, these class enemies of yours?'

'Yes.' Mark played straight into Blake's hands. 'The whole corrupt, stinking lot of them.'

'You hate them like you hated Ian Taylor, don't you?'

'They're as bad as him and his kind, yes.'

'They deserve to die too, don't they?'

Red with anger, understanding too late that he had been doing himself no favours, Mark fought to regain his composure. 'I didn't kill him.'

'I put it to you, Mr Holland, that the only person lying here today is you, isn't it?'

Mark looked up in exasperation. 'How many times do you want me to say it?'

But Blake was implacable. 'Ian Taylor stood for everything you hated and that's why you killed him, isn't it?'

Mark ignored him. Instead, he looked towards the public gallery and then fixed his gaze on the girl sitting between Alan and Marcia Jacobs. Miriam found herself unable to meet his eyes. As she looked down into her lap, Mark, with all the contempt he could muster, continued to stare in her direction. 'If it wasn't for Miriam, Ian Taylor would be alive today.'

As he said the words, several people in the courtroom looked at Miriam. Among them was DCI Knowland. His expression was easy to read. He believed, beyond the shadow of a doubt, that Miriam Jacobs, not Mark Holland, was a murderer. Kavanagh watched the policeman with interest. He, too, believed his client was innocent. He also believed that, throughout the course of the trial, and especially after Miriam Jacobs's unreliable testimony, there had emerged reasonable doubt as to Mark's guilt. And if the jury found reasonable doubt, they were obliged to find him innocent of murder.

After Kavanagh's and Blake's summing-up to the jurors, the judge, as was customary, had the last word. Addressing the jurors, he emphasized the inconsistencies in Miriam's evidence, pointing out that she had proved herself a 'thoroughly unreliable witness'. Yet he also said that, even if they disbelieved all or part of Miriam's evidence, it did not automatically follow that Mark Holland was innocent. Direct evidence linked Mark to the crime – and also the matter of his confession. All those factors, said Judge Tremain, should be taken into account as they considered their verdict.

As they left to do so, the court adjourned. Kavanagh, Julia Piper and Mark's solicitor Patricia Graves wandered out into the lobby and found themselves face to face with the Jacobs family. They looked, thought Kavanagh, as if they were the ones on trial. All three were pale and silent – and looked highly embarrassed to find themselves facing 'the opposition'. For a fleeting moment, Kavanagh caught Miriam's eye. Her expression told him all he needed to know. Yet it was the jury who were about to reach a verdict. And it mattered not that it was he – not they – who had spent half a lifetime with criminals, whose expressions he had learned to read like an open book.

Sighing, he turned to Julia and Patricia Graves. 'Coffee? I reckon they'll be out for ages.' The two women followed him across the lobby. Neither trusted themselves to speak.

'Members of the jury, have you reached a verdict on which you all agree?'

The foreman stood up and looked at the court clerk. 'We have.'

'On the charge of murder, how do you find the defendant Mark Holland, guilty or not guilty?'

'Guilty.'

The uproar in the public gallery lasted a full five minutes. Some of the shouts were of triumph and relief. More were of outrage. Yet the verdict was final – and unanimous. Mark Holland would go to prison and Miriam Jacobs could forget the whole thing. Kavanagh looked out of the corner of his eye at the Jacobs family. Miriam had flung herself, at once crying and laughing with relief, into her father's arms. Marcia Jacobs found herself looking at Kavanagh and, like her daughter before her, quickly looked away.

Judge Tremain, however, was impassive. As soon as silence had fallen, he turned to the pale, shaking figure in the dock. 'Mark Thomas Holland,' he pronounced, 'you have been found guilty of a vicious and cowardly murder. There is only one sentence allowed by the law in these circumstances. You will go to prison,' he ended in a cold, clear voice, 'for life.'

'But there will be an appeal?'

'No.' Kavanagh inspected the contents of his whisky glass. 'There won't be any appeal.'

'But surely—'

'Mark doesn't want an appeal. He confessed in front of me – and Patricia Graves.' Kavanagh looked around his room at River Court Chambers where, half an hour after they'd left the court, he and Julia were consoling themselves. After the verdict, he and Patricia Graves had accompanied Mark to the court cell before he was escorted to prison. He could still hardly believe what Mark, in a daze, had told them.

'I wish you'd seen her that morning,' he had said with a misty look in his eyes. 'She was magic. So clear. So determined. I was frightened I wouldn't be able to go through with it. I was frightened I'd let her down. I just wanted to be as strong as she was.' Then he had looked at Kavanagh. 'Miriam put the knife in my hand. After that it was easy.'

CHAPTER SEVEN

In the aftermath of Kate's affair with Jeffrey Manners, Lizzie Kavanagh quit her job in Strasbourg.

Her husband was aghast. 'You can't do that!'

'I just have.'

'But Kate's a survivor. I mean, she's practically over it already and anyway—'

'And anyway,' interrupted Lizzie, 'it's not just about Kate. It's about us. The family. And it's also about me.'

'You?'

Lizzie couldn't help but grin. It wasn't often she could describe her husband's expression as 'vacant'. 'Well, it was my job, Jim. But I'm beginning to realize that it wasn't the job for me.'

Kavanagh sat down and cradled his coffee cup in his hands. After his initial shock at Lizzie's announcement, he was experiencing a new sensation: relief. Only now was he beginning to comprehend the strain that the Strasbourg situation had imposed on their marriage. Yet he was also puzzled. 'When did you come to this conclusion?' he asked Lizzie. 'Isn't it all a bit sudden?'

Lizzie reached over the kitchen table and put her hand over his. She could tell from his expression that he was surprised, relieved – and rather miffed at being, until now, left out of the equation. 'I'm sorry to spring this on you, Jim,' she said, 'but I didn't want it to become a family debate. It's a decision I had to reach on my own and, no, it's not sudden. I've been feeling increasingly sidelined in Strasbourg, and not getting the funding I needed was the last straw.'

'Mmm.' He knew all about that. Lizzie's boss Philippe Kaplan, whom Kavanagh had long ago decided was smarmy, had dropped that one on her only last week. 'Next time,' he had told Lizzie, 'I'm sure they'll agree to your request.' Lizzie forbore to point out that as 'they' included Kaplan himself, he wasn't exactly rooting for her. And it was then that she had decided there wouldn't be a next time. 'I haven't been putting pressure on you to do this, have I?' said Kavanagh.

'No, Jim.' Lizzie smiled broadly at him. 'You've been brilliant about the whole thing. It's just . . . everything. Maybe I'm just too old for this commuting lark.'

Kavanagh, too, smiled. 'You mean you're now going to stay at home and devote your life to cooking my meals?' He said the words with an exaggeration of his normally mild Northern accent.

Lizzie giggled. 'Oh, I think I'll play the role of Her Indoors for a while – until I get another job.'

'You'll still have to commute.'

'I'd rather do it from Wimbledon than from Strasbourg.'

After a month Lizzie was beginning to tire of playing the role of housewife, yet Kavanagh was starting to relish having her at home. While she had been working in Strasbourg, he had tried his best not to let standards slip. It had been a difficult task. With Matt spending most of his time in mysterious teenage pursuits and

Kavanagh working long hours, delicious home-cooked meals had become a thing of the past and the two of them had survived for much of the time on Indian takeaways.

It was just such a meal about which Kavanagh was thinking as he prepared to leave chambers on a rainy autumn day. Lizzie, he remembered, was off to some bash this evening and wouldn't be at home for dinner. Perhaps, he mused, he could sneak in a takeaway. Lizzie's cooking was all very well – all very brilliant, in fact – but sometimes he did have a yearning for old habits . . . Lost in contemplation of chicken tikkas and the debate over plain versus spicy popadoms, he was barely aware of Tom Buckley, the senior clerk, coming into his room. When he did acknowledge Tom's presence, it was with a rather desperate, 'I'm staying at home tomorrow. Mountain of paperwork to catch up on.' Why, he thought as he said the words, does Tom always make me feel guilty? I'm a QC, for God's sake. I shouldn't feel intimidated by my clerk.

But Tom saw intimidation as part of his job description. Normally, he was good-humoured about it, but he had of late been increasingly brusque with the barristers at River Court. Today he didn't bother to attempt a smile. 'Working at home might be difficult, sir.'

Kavanagh rolled his eyes. He didn't have to ask why. Tom wasn't prone to making courtesy calls: he was much more likely to attack his barristers with last-minute cases. 'Customs,' continued the clerk, 'are sending down a brief for next week.'

Kavanagh was surprised. 'Prosecuting? I thought you were lining me up for a GBH?'

Tom, at last, managed a grin. 'Mr Foxcott got to it first.'

Then, seeing Kavanagh's thunderous look, he opted for a more placatory approach. 'There can't be much to the Customs matter. It's a return from Ted Fellows in King's Bench Walk.'

Kavanagh was even more surprised. He wasn't accustomed to accepting cases that had been rejected by barristers in other chambers. And especially from barristers more junior to himself. Ted Fellows wasn't a QC, or 'silk' in barristers' parlance. 'Ted Fellows,' he replied icily, 'isn't even—'

'I know, sir, but he had a coronary this morning.' Taking advantage of Kavanagh's momentary loss for words, Tom quickly changed the subject. 'I didn't think you'd say no to a healthy fee.'

'I don't have much choice, do I?'

At that, Tom made his retreat. He knew to quit when the going was good. Irritated, albeit with a twinge of guilt, Kavanagh picked up his briefcase and decided that, Customs and coronaries apart, he was now in need of a pint before making the journey home. Closing the door of his room, he made his way down the hall to Peter Foxcott's. He knocked and went straight in, looked at Peter's bald head bent over his desk, and said, 'Fancy a quick pint?'

Foxcott glanced up and shook his head. 'All right for some, Jim.'

Kavanagh grunted and closed the door. Another person trying to make him feel guilty. Well, let them try, he thought. I'm still having that pint.

His next port of call was Jeremy Aldermarten's room. Jeremy, he reckoned, needed cheering up. Yet as he entered his room, he noted that Jeremy was already being cheered up, by an efficient, spinsterly looking woman. They were bent over Jeremy's desk, examining

84

the papers strewn all over it. 'Oh,' said Kavanagh as he made to retreat, 'sorry.'

Jeremy, wearing his 'important' expression, looked at him over his glasses. 'Can I help you, Jim?'

'No, no. Nothing important.' As he spoke, he noted that Jeremy's companion was smiling warmly at him. Odd, he thought. Definitely not Jeremy's type. She was probably in her late forties – and looked like the sort of person who would be immune to Jeremy's charms. With an apologetic nod, Kavanagh closed the door behind him – but not before he overheard the woman speaking again.

'The debt-factoring option,' she was explaining to Jeremy, 'could increase an individual barrister's income by as much as five per cent.' Kavanagh didn't hear any more, but had heard enough. Jeremy was up to something.

Sighing, he walked out of the building. Suddenly he no longer wanted that drink. Peter, fair enough, was working. But what on earth was Jeremy up to? As he walked towards his car for the long, slow drive back to Wimbledon, Kavanagh reflected that Jeremy, although down, was certainly not out.

The Lucy Cartwright business had, as everyone at River Court knew, affected Jeremy quite badly. Initially, he had kept the discovery of Lucy's forging of his signature and cashing of his cheques to himself. After a few days, however, he had confided in Julia and then the whole story had emerged. Julia did what she called 'some asking around', and her discoveries had been both fruitful and frightening. Lucy Cartwright was a complete fake: she had taken several men to the cleaners by posing as a wealthy aristocrat temporarily embarrassed for funds. No one had ever pressed charges against her for the simple reason that her victims, all high-profile individuals, would have been laughing-stocks in the eyes of their colleagues and peers.

Yet Lucy had reckoned without Julia Piper. Jeremy, too, was loath to take action, but Julia had egged him on, finally convincing him that he was going to have to stop Lucy in her nefarious tracks. He did so by reporting her to the police and pressing charges against her. His colleagues agreed that it was a brave, potentially hazardous and difficult decision to take – and supported him all the way. For her part, Lucy had been disbelieving. 'You can't prosecute, of course. It'll make you look a complete prat.'

'I can. And I will.' Jeremy had been heartily glad that the conversation was private and that the police were waiting outside his house. Somehow he couldn't bear to look at her any more.

'It'll be awfully messy,' she had replied. Then she had noted Jeremy's impassive expression and realized the game was up. She fled the house – and ran straight into the arms of the police. Yet before she did so, she wounded Jeremy even more. 'For what it's worth,' had been her parting sally, 'you were great fun. A bit of a shit, of course, but the right woman could make something of you.' She hadn't stayed around long enough to register Jeremy's reaction to her barb. He looked, and felt, infinitely sad. He had been wholly convinced that Lucy Cartwright was the right woman.

While Jeremy had tried to brush the whole episode away as a silly interlude, his colleagues at River Court, and especially Julia, were aware that he was hurting inside. Everyone was still being especially nice to him. And now, thought Kavanagh as he pulled up outside the family home, another strange woman was also being nice to him. Yet the scene he had witnessed had been a professional one. He hoped to God that Jeremy wasn't up to some fast-buck scheme to recoup the heavy financial losses he had incurred as a result of his acquaintance with Lucy.

Still mulling over the situation at work, Kavanagh let himself into the house and, because of his preoccupation, committed the cardinal sin: he failed to comment on his wife's appearance. Lizzie, standing at the foot of the stairs, was wearing the time-honoured yet, in her case, uniquely ravishing little black dress.

'How do I look?'

'What? Oh . . . Lizzie.' Kavanagh looked distractedly at his wife and, as he took in the faultless attire, the discreet yet alluring make-up and the newly coiffed hair, he forgot his anxieties. 'Wonderful!' He went up to her and pecked her on the cheek. Then he looked at the dress again. 'Haven't I seen that before?'

Lizzie laughed. 'You bought it – two years ago!'

'Oh. Well . . . it's worn well. Posh do?' he added, as he went into the sitting room and made a beeline for the drinks cabinet.

'Claridges.'

'Wow. I think I could handle that.'

'But could you handle the Association of Women Executives?'

'Ah, well . . .'

'To be honest,' Lizzie continued, as she brushed a non-existent speck of dust off her dress, 'I'm not sure that I can either. But while I'm looking for the right job I've got to keep networking.'

However, Kavanagh had lost interest in Lizzie's even-

ing and was now involved in the beginning of his own
– a hefty slug of malt.

'I'm afraid I didn't have time to make you anything,'
said Lizzie, as she picked up her bag from the sofa.

Oh, good, thought Kavanagh. It's an Indian then.
'No problem,' he said. 'I'll rustle something up.'

I'll bet, thought Lizzie. Since when were you capable
of rustling up a chicken biryani? Moving out of the
hall again, she called through the open door, 'You've
remembered that Matt's friends are coming for dinner
at seven thirty tomorrow?'

'Eh?'

'Matt's birthday!'

Kavanagh went into shock. 'Oh, no. No, of course I
hadn't forgotten.'

Lizzie was chuckling as she shut the front door
behind her.

An hour later Kavanagh was in full non-barrister mode.
Slouched on the sofa watching a TV game show, he
had an empty lager can on the table in front of him,
a full one in his hand, and a vast Indian takeaway at
his side. And then he was rudely interrupted. Frowning,
he reached for the remote control and lowered the
volume of the TV. Unless he was going deaf, the front
door had just opened and closed. He remembered.
'Matt?'

A moment later – and looking oddly shy – Matt
appeared in the doorway.

'I got you a biryani,' continued his father.

'Oh . . . I'm, er, not hungry, thanks.'

Kavanagh didn't believe that for a moment. What
Matt meant, no doubt, was that he wasn't alone. Cran-

ing his neck over the back of the sofa, he looked to see who was loitering with his son in the doorway.

It was a girl. She was peering into the sitting room with great interest. Matt was looking hugely embarrassed – and more so when the girl put her arm round his waist. Then, as Kavanagh frantically tried to adopt a more dignified pose, she stepped forward and held out her hand. 'I'm Miranda Lawson. Matthew tells me you're a QC. That must be fascinating,' she added with a smile.

Kavanagh was feeling as embarrassed as his son. Whatever notions the rather glamorous Miranda Lawson may have had about barristers, he had surely ruined them with the lager and the curry, not to mention the TV show. 'Oh,' he replied as he got to his feet. 'It has its moments.' Then he gestured towards the mess on the table. 'There's enough food for both of you.'

Miranda looked as though she would rather die of starvation than launch into his curry.

Matt rescued her. 'Thanks, Dad, but we're fine.'

With that, Miranda grabbed his arm and then turned to give Kavanagh a distinctly coquettish look. 'We don't want to interrupt you. You must be very busy.'

How, thought Kavanagh as he sat down again, can someone that age make me feel so gauche?

The following day, Tom Buckley was even more distant and abrupt. Seconds after Kavanagh had arrived in chambers, he followed him into his room and unceremoniously dumped an enormous pile of papers on his desk. 'Your Customs brief. Conference is at five.'

Horrified by the size of it, Kavanagh was aghast. 'It's not all mine?'

Tom's expression was answer enough.

'Good God. Just carting that lot about would give you a seizure. No wonder it put Ted Fellows out of action.'

But Tom was not amused.

'Who,' continued Kavanagh, 'is my junior on this one?'

'Miss Wilson.' Tom folded his arms. 'She was the only one available.'

This time it was Kavanagh who wasn't amused. It was more than a little unfair to land Alex Wilson, the youngest and most junior barrister at River Court, with what he knew was going to be a complex, onerous task. 'Tom, do you realize how much work is in this? She's barely been doing the job a year!'

But before the clerk had time to reply, Alex herself bounded into the room. Her gently reproving expression as she looked at Kavanagh told him that she had heard his last words. 'Actually,' she said, 'I've been doing it for fourteen months.'

Kavanagh pursed his lips. He supposed he should be pleased. Fourteen months and she was *still* optimistic.

Much less than fourteen hours later, however, Alex's optimism had been sorely dented. As she and Kavanagh spent the day poring over the brief, it became increasingly apparent that the case was more complicated than even Kavanagh had predicted. Furthermore, the likelihood of securing a prosecution seemed fairly remote.

Just before five o'clock that afternoon, Alex leaned

back in her seat and ran her hands through her hair. 'I think I'm suffering from information overload,' she said. 'Can we recap?'

'Sure.'

'Okay. So the defendant is one Kevin Gregson, arrested on suspicion of importing class A drugs, namely fifteen kilos of heroin.'

'Eighty per cent pure Afghan, no less.'

Alex wrinkled her nose. 'What exactly is the significance of that?'

'If he did buy it, it would have cost him around half a million. It's fairly standard to cut it to five per cent purity, mixing it with glucose. Once refined, its street value would be around five million.'

'Ah. Thus making Kevin Gregson a very rich man.'

Kavanagh indicated the brief on his desk. 'But it seems to me that Kevin Gregson already is a very rich man. Large Surrey house, a yacht, villa in the Algarve, not exactly the trappings of a pauper.'

'And not exactly the trappings of a man whose only sources of income are from a dying nightclub in Dagenham and a haulage contracting firm in East London.'

The latter point was, they both knew, going to be their main problem in the prosecution of Kevin Gregson. The heroin had been found by Customs officers in a consignment of meat transported from the continent by one of Kevin Gregson's lorries to his headquarters in East London. Gregson, however, claimed that he knew nothing about the drugs; that he had no involvement in the day-to-day running of his company, Mainbeam Haulage, and that Patrick Bennett, the man who ran the company, must have been the importer of the heroin. There was nothing in the mountain of paper in front of Kavanagh and Alex to link Gregson

91

directly with the crime. His ownership of the company wasn't hard evidence and neither was the fact that he had been present in the haulage yard when the consignment had arrived.

Kavanagh looked at his watch. 'The Customs officers should be here in a minute, Alex. Want to take a short break before they arrive?'

Alex stood up. 'Sure. Wouldn't mind a quick breath of fresh air.'

Kavanagh also got to his feet. 'Oh . . . Alex, have you noticed anything peculiar about Tom lately?'

'You mean his wife?'

'Eh?'

'Didn't you know? She's in a psychiatric unit. She's having a bad spell of post-natal depression.'

'Oh . . . I'd no idea. Poor chap.'

Alex was incensed. 'What about his wife?'

Kavanagh looked duly humbled. Then, as Alex left the room, an alarm sounded in his head. Something she had said had triggered it. Something about wives.

And then he remembered. Lizzie. She had reminded him that morning, in no uncertain terms, of Matt's birthday dinner. She had made it quite clear that the three-line whip was being drawn; that under no circumstances was he allowed to be late. Groaning inwardly, Kavanagh studied his watch again. Five o'clock. There was no way the conference with the Customs officers would last less than two hours. Given the urgency of the situation – that he had less than twenty-four hours to master a brief that had given Ted Fellows a coronary after two months – there was no way he could cut the conference short. Sighing, he reached for the phone. It was a brief conversation.

'Lizzie . . .'

'I know that tone.' Lizzie's voice, at the other end of the line, was frosty.

'Look,' her husband pleaded, 'it's something completely unavoidable. I'll just be a little late. About nine. Lizzie?'

But Lizzie was no longer there.

Two hours later, Kavanagh knew he was in danger of missing Matt's party altogether. The two Customs officers, accompanied by Clare Ashton, the Customs' solicitor, had arrived an hour late. That had been irritating enough. More galling, however, was the Customs officers' attitude. While both Simon Lloyd, the senior officer, and his slightly hard-nosed deputy Jenny Norris were pleasant enough, Kavanagh had a strong impression that they were not being as helpful as they could be. Lloyd, a good-looking, confident individual, was even a little patronizing towards both Kavanagh and Alex. Odd, thought the former. They were, after all, on the same side.

Rummaging through the photographs that Customs had taken during the seizure of the consignment, Alex looked puzzled as she came across one of an open deep freeze, filled with frozen meals. 'What,' she asked Lloyd, 'is the significance of that?'

'Cutting is a closed operation,' he explained. 'When you're dealing with several million quid you don't want anyone going out of the building until you've shifted it. This amount could take three men several days. They need feeding.'

Kavanagh saved Alex from having to think of a reply. 'How much has Gregson got in the bank?' he asked Lloyd.

'Only a few thousand that we can find.'

'He's clever,' added Jenny Norris. 'The haulage firm does plenty of legitimate business, but we're positive that he has been using it to front a drugs operation for several years.'

'When did he buy Mainbeam Haulage?'

'Five years ago – from Patrick Bennett. He bailed it out, really. It wasn't doing at all well. He kept Bennett on as manager. Six months later,' she added, with a pointed look at Kavanagh, 'Gregson moved to a nice little pad in Surrey. Must have set him back half a million.'

Kavanagh made a few notes and then looked at Lloyd. 'So what was Bennett's role in this operation?'

'He signed the consignment documents. All false. The meat in the back was condemned. The company it was destined for didn't exist.'

'Hmm. And neither Gregson's nor Bennett's fingerprints were on the drugs?'

'No.'

'No evidence at all linking them to the purchase?'

'No.'

Kavanagh turned to the solicitor. 'So the documents only tie in Bennett. We haven't got a lot to prove Gregson was knowingly involved in the operation.'

At that, Clare Ashton looked over to Lloyd.

'Unless,' continued Kavanagh, 'there's something I haven't been told.' He knew perfectly well that there was. Customs and Excise didn't just seize five million pounds' worth of heroin by some happy coincidence. They must have had Gregson or Bennett, or both men, under surveillance for some time. And they must have known where the heroin had come from.

Lloyd, however, remained silent.

'You've got statements from all the investigating officers,' said Clare Ashton.

Kavanagh nodded. 'Yes. But they don't tell us where the drugs came from.'

'They were caught red-handed.'

And I, thought Kavanagh, wasn't born yesterday. Again he turned his attention to Simon Lloyd. 'Juries like to hear the full story. Wouldn't you?'

Lloyd looked at Ashton. Ashton looked at Lloyd. And then Lloyd shook his head. The solicitor, obviously uneasy, said, 'You know how sensitive our sources are, Mr Kavanagh. If we keep them confidential it's for a very good reason.'

Kavanagh gave her a curt nod in reply. This, he thought, was going nowhere fast. Then he turned to Alex. She, too, looked fed up at the lack of progress.

But Clare Ashton suddenly surprised them. As she gathered her papers into her briefcase, she said, 'Kevin was charged with conspiracy to commit armed robbery in eighty-four. The trial collapsed when the main prosecution witness didn't testify.'

'Oh?' Kavanagh was watching her closely. 'Why was that?'

'He was shot on his way to court.'

Beside him, Kavanagh heard Alex's sharp intake of breath. 'Was Gregson charged?'

Clare Ashton shook her head. 'Insufficient evidence. He's still got a clean slate.'

Alex looked even more unhappy. Kavanagh put a comradely hand on her shoulder. 'Don't worry, Alex. If anybody else gets shot it's going to be me.'

Yet despite his jocular manner, Kavanagh was worried. Kevin Gregson was obviously a slippery and deeply unsavoury character. The sort of man who covered his ignoble tracks by employing other, even less savoury characters to do his lethal work.

At exactly the same time as Kavanagh rushed out of River Court Chambers to his car a sallow, thick-set man wearing a cheap shell-suit was ushered into the visiting area of Belmont Prison. Kevin Gregson, betraying no sign of discomfort at his incarceration, looked up as the visitor stopped at his table and tossed a packet of cigarettes towards him. He pocketed it without acknowledgement. He would have preferred not to acknowledge his visitor either. Frank was the most lowly of his sidekicks and a complete contrast to Gregson himself. Gregson prided himself on being smartly dressed, well-mannered and good with children – especially with his five-year-old daughter Mandy. He had never introduced Frank to Mandy – and didn't intend to.

As Frank sat down, he raised a quizzical eyebrow. 'So?'

'The old boy had a heart-attack.'

'What?'

'Yeah. The barrister. Fellows.'

'Damn.' Gregson pursed his lips. Ted Fellows, he had been reliably informed, would have been no match for his defence counsel, the 'Ice Maiden' of the Criminal Bar. Suzannah Dixon would have made mincemeat of Fellows. 'Shit. So who've they got now?'

Frank pulled a notebook out of his pocket. 'A QC called Kavanagh. He defends mostly. Supposed to be brilliant. A working-class lad from up north, apparently.'

Gregson considered. It didn't take him long to decide on tactics. 'Make him an offer.'

Frank wasn't remotely surprised – just unenthusiastic. 'He seems to be pretty tight. Word is, he's not open to that kind of thing.'

Gregson ripped open the cigarettes, lit one and took a deep, contemplative drag. Then he looked back at Frank with a dangerous glint in his eyes. 'Wife? Kids?'

Frank nodded on both counts.

'Well,' continued his boss, 'you know what to do, don't you?'

CHAPTER EIGHT

The trial of Kevin Gregson and Patrick Bennett nearly didn't take place. Suzannah Dixon lobbied the judge assigned to the trial, claiming that there was no case against Gregson. He would, said the frosty Miss Dixon, plead to the importation of contaminated meat. And that was all. Bennett, she suggested, would plead guilty to the charges of drug importation, and a plea of guilty, of course, meant there would be no trial by jury. She forbore to mention that her client, if called into court, would opt for a line of defence of which she herself thoroughly disapproved: he had told her he would claim that the drugs had been planted by the Customs officers themselves. She was still working on him to change his stance on that one: juries, she knew, tended not to swallow lines like that.

Judge Phipson, a genial man in his mid-sixties, was all for saving the Crown money by avoiding lengthy trials. Having listened to Suzannah Dixon, he called all three barristers into his room. Graham Emerton, Bennett's counsel, looked pleased. Kavanagh, however, still hurt by Lizzie's continuing refusal to speak to him because he had missed Matt's party, was worried about the potential ramifications of trying to prosecute a man like Kevin Gregson. While he had affected nonchalance in the face of Alex's alarm over the death of the man who could have incriminated Gregson years ago, in reality he was deeply concerned. He had been around long enough to know that it was not unheard of for alleged criminals – remanded in custody or not – to send their heavies out on little warning sprees to barristers, their wives and families.

But after being called into Judge Phipson's room, Kavanagh's personal worries gave way to professional ones. Although Phipson was skirting around the issue, Kavanagh knew that Suzannah Dixon had planted the idea that there was insufficient evidence to support the trial. Kavanagh was having none of it. At Phipson's loaded questions about whether or not a 'meaningful dialogue' was taking place among the barristers, he saw red. 'If your honour is suggesting accepting a plea from Bennett and not proceeding against Gregson,' he said with a forced smile, 'it's quite out of the question.'

Phipson wasn't surprised by Kavanagh's reaction. He knew that the tough QC was hardly likely to cave in that easily, but, rising to his feet to indicate that the meeting was over, he said, 'I'm sure, Mr Kavanagh, you will be mindful of the pressing obligation to save expensive court time.'

Kavanagh said nothing. He – and Phipson – knew that the way to do that was for both defendants to plead guilty. As if reading his mind, Phipson then addressed the other two barristers. 'Guilty pleas,' he said pleasantly, 'to counts acceptable to the Crown, will, of course, receive the appropriate discount.'

Suzannah Dixon pounced on that one after the judge had left the room. With a sweet smile that failed to reach her eyes, she said to Kavanagh, 'I think that's a pretty clear indication of where judicial sympathies lie. Are you going to make a realistic proposal?'

'Certainly. Gregson can plead guilty to importing the heroin or he can take his case to the jury.'

Adamant that he had nothing to do with importing heroin, Gregson – with the unwilling acquiescence of Miss Dixon – took the latter course. Worse, he had confirmed his decision to claim that the Customs officers had planted the heroin.

'How long did you have people watching Mainbeam Haulage's depot?' Suzannah Dixon glared at the chief Customs officer in the witness box. But if she hoped to intimidate Simon Lloyd with her supercilious manner and steely gaze, she had yet to succeed. Still at ease after gentle questioning by Kavanagh, during which it had been established that the Customs officers had seized fifteen kilos of heroin in the presence of both Bennett and Gregson, Lloyd was as calm and composed as the Ice Maiden herself.

'Thirteen and a half weeks,' he replied.

'Hmm. More than three months. Given that you hadn't come up with a result after that amount of time, might not your judgement have been called into question?'

Lloyd frowned at her. 'I'm not sure I understand what you mean.'

Neither did Judge Phipson. Also frowning, he asked, 'What exactly is your point, Miss Dixon?'

'I'm suggesting these drugs were planted in the trailer by your officers, Mr Lloyd.'

Kavanagh, sitting a few feet away from Miss Dixon, smiled to himself. No wonder she had been so desperate to avoid this trial. Lloyd, too, was smiling. 'I plant flowers, miss, not drugs.'

Everyone in the courtroom laughed at his response – except Miss Dixon.

After a glance at her notes, she resumed her questioning. 'Last year Mr Gregson's income from his two businesses was in the region of a hundred and twenty thousand pounds, wasn't it?'

'Something like that.'

'But even a man of his means would have to dig deep to find half a million pounds to buy heroin.'

Lloyd shrugged. 'I assume so.'

At last Miss Dixon smiled. 'You have to make assumptions, don't you, officer? Because you have absolutely no evidence of my client parting with money to buy drugs, have you?'

'Well . . . no.'

Miss Dixon pointedly snapped shut her notebook and sat down.

Graham Emerton rose and, after a kindly nod at Lloyd, began to question him about his own client, Patrick Bennett. It took him precisely five minutes to establish that there was no evidence of Bennett, who earned twenty thousand a year, buying drugs, or even that he had known of their existence. 'You have told us nothing,' he said, 'which proves Mr Bennett knew there was anything in the trailer other than meat.'

'The facts speak for themselves.'

'Quite so,' Emerton replied. Then he sat down, leaving the jury to contemplate that Lloyd's testimony had revealed very few facts indeed.

Jenny Norris, Lloyd's deputy, was called as the next witness, and Kavanagh wasted no time in getting to the point of her evidence: the photographs for which she had been responsible at the scene of the drugs seizure. Leafing through a bundle of enlarged stills, Kavanagh picked out one and held it up in front of the jury. 'Miss Norris, can you tell the jury what this is?'

'Yes. It's a workshop lined with polythene. The sacks in the foreground contain raw glucose used to cut the drugs to a lesser purity.'

Sensing renewed interest and an element of excitement rippling through the jurors, Kavanagh beckoned the court clerk to pass them the photograph. Then he turned back to Jenny Norris. 'What purpose does the polythene serve?'

'It stops the heroin at a thousand pounds a teaspoon from falling through the floorboards. They maximize their profits in every way,' she elaborated, in her intense, hard voice.

A few moments later, Kavanagh sat down again. He was sure he had established in the minds of the jurors that someone – perhaps several people – at Mainbeam Haulage had been well prepared for a delivery of heroin.

Suzannah Dixon, however, had other ideas. 'Look at the workshop photograph again,' she asked Jenny Norris, the minute she stood up for her cross-examination. 'Do you see the shelves in the far right corner?'

'I do.'

'And the equipment stored there?'

Jenny peered closer at the photograph the court clerk had handed her. 'It looks like a spray gun.'

'Might that not have been used for the perfectly innocent purpose of spraying paint onto lorry panels?'

Jenny looked at the barrister with barely disguised dislike. 'I saw no evidence of that.'

Miss Dixon appeared unperturbed. She turned her

102

attention to the huge file in front of her and opened it at a predetermined page. Jenny Norris also had a file in front of her. Miss Dixon told her to open it at page 853. Several people in the public gallery grinned as she barked out her instructions. Clearly, Suzannah Dixon hadn't got where she was today by being nice to members of her own sex. 'Tell the jury,' she continued, once Jenny had found the page, 'what that is.'

'It's a delivery note for sixty sacks of glucose.'

'To whom is the delivery?'

'Barker's.' Jenny looked up. 'It's a soft drinks company.'

Miss Dixon nodded. 'Would you read out the handwritten instruction on the bottom?'

' "Received sixty. Six returned." '

Again Miss Dixon nodded. 'Would that not explain, Miss Norris, the presence of six sacks of glucose at Mainbeam Haulage? The six sacks that you and your officers claim were going to be used to cut the heroin?'

Jenny refused to be riled. 'It's a possibility. But unlikely.'

Miss Dixon sighed and shook her head. Then she put one hand on her hip, which lent a peculiarly supercilious and arrogant angle to her stance as she eyed the Customs officer. 'The truth is, officer, that for every piece of evidence you say is incriminating, there is an innocent explanation.'

Jenny Norris didn't reply. She didn't have to. Like everyone else in the courtroom, she realized that Suzannah Dixon was speaking the truth.

Alex Wilson was worried that she and Kavanagh were going to lose this case. It was the biggest trial she had yet been part of and she was under no illusions about what a defeat in such a high-profile case would do to her fledgeling career. True, Kavanagh would carry the can, but she was part of the team. One of the main problems, she reflected, was that in all the relevant papers there was nothing about how Gregson managed to have such a lavish lifestyle. If they had even one lead as to what had to be an extra source of income, they would follow it to the bitter end, which would reveal, she had no doubt, drug smuggling. But even Gregson's yacht, seized by Lloyd in Jersey after the Customs raid at Mainbeam Haulage, had revealed no secrets.

At lunch that day Alex decided to tackle Kavanagh. Toying with her salad as Kavanagh plunged into a mountain of shepherd's pie, she took a deep breath and looked him in the eye. 'Look, can't we negotiate on this? We could still get something. I mean, the way it's going . . .' She trailed off with an eloquent gesture that indicated 'nowhere'.

Kavanagh was well aware of where the trial was going. He was also determined that Gregson was going to prison. He paused in the demolition of his pie and told Alex just that.

She didn't look convinced. 'And Bennett?'

Kavanagh smiled. Bennett was the little man. The worm. And worms could turn. 'We'll use him to get Gregson if we can.' Then he remembered Gregson's alleged previous tactics of 'persuasion'. 'That is,' he continued, 'if Gregson doesn't get to him first. Perhaps I'll have a word with Emerton.'

Alex raised an eyebrow. 'The Ice Maiden has him under close arrest.'

That was true. At the other end of the canteen, he and Miss Dixon were huddled together over their own lunch. Alex looked at them. How on earth, she wondered, was Kavanagh going to persuade Emerton to get his client to help sink Gregson? First, that would make him a grass – and you didn't grass on people like Gregson if you valued your life. Second, Miss Dixon really did seem to have Emerton joined to her hip. She didn't look as if she was going to let him get away and jeopardize her own case.

Kavanagh, however, managed to corner Emerton on his own – in the one place where Miss Dixon simply couldn't follow them. 'If your client pleads guilty,' said Kavanagh, without preface as both men stood at the urinals in the cloakroom after lunch, 'I'm willing to accept it on the basis that he played a minor role. The judge will still give him a discount. He might even get away with three years – out in eighteen months.'

Discomfited at being buttonholed while at his most vulnerable, Emerton didn't reply until he turned towards the basin on the other side of the room. 'Three years is rather optimistic.'

'Not,' said Kavanagh, as he doggedly followed his opponent, 'if he helps sink Gregson.'

Emerton was horrified. 'You can't make that a condition!'

Kavanagh's expression was bland. 'Well, you can always put it to him, can't you?'

Emerton did put it to Bennett. His duty, after all, was to do the best for his client, and while this morning's evidence had mainly gone against the Customs officers, he wasn't confident of things remaining that way. He had been up against Kavanagh before, and knew that he had a nasty little habit of coming up with powerful, incriminating evidence towards the end of a trial. Before the court convened for the afternoon session, he visited Bennett in his cell in the basement of the building.

Bennett was unimpressed. 'If I gave evidence for the prosecution that would make me a grass – and do you know what that means inside?'

Emerton did. 'But the prison authorities would ensure you're properly protected,' he reasoned.

Bennett snorted in derision. 'Yeah, but my wife and children won't be. *That*,' he added, as he met his barrister's gaze, 'is the way Gregson operates.'

In the afternoon, Customs Officer Alan Pearson was called to the witness box. It was he, under the supervision of Jenny Norris, who had instructed the photographer to take pictures of the yard of Mainbeam Haulage, the polythene-covered workshop, the prepacked frozen meals and the consignment of meat in which the heroin had been concealed. Kavanagh, who was first to question the officer, asked him about the possibility of the drugs being planted by the officers themselves in the meat carcasses.

Pearson was instantly dismissive. 'Very unlikely,' he replied. 'The heroin was sewn right into the viscera. It would have taken too long.'

'Is there something significant in the way the drugs were concealed?'

'The carcasses must have been specially obtained with the offal still in place to provide a means of concealment.'

Kavanagh screwed up his nose. 'It's enough to turn you vegetarian.'

Everyone in court laughed – except the man who had just slipped into the public gallery. Dressed in an ill-fitting suit, he looked uncomfortable. More at home in a shell-suit, he was also uneasy about being in a court of law. Only when Kevin Gregson saw him and acknowledged his presence with an encouraging nod did he relax a little. Then Gregson smiled. Frank was here. And when the court adjourned for the day, Frank would begin his tactics of 'persuasion' on behalf of his boss.

Suzannah Dixon attacked Alan Pearson in her usual Rottweiler fashion. Yet beside her, Kavanagh, with Alex Wilson behind him, allowed himself the tiniest hint of optimism. Miss Dixon was going hell for leather, but she was failing to establish her client's innocence as she relentlessly cross-examined Pearson about the photographs. Until she asked him to look at photographs seventy-five to eighty. 'What do they show?' she barked.

Pearson dutifully turned to the relevant photographs. 'They show me and Officer Maddox recovering the drugs.'

Miss Dixon nodded in agreement. 'And is there a photograph of the carcasses before you opened them?'

'Er . . .' Pearson flipped through the bundle of stills in front of him. Then, half-apologetic, half-defiant, he said to the barrister, 'Well, there would have been no point photographing every square inch before we searched it.'

Miss Dixon succeeded admirably in making her incredulity seem spontaneous. She had known the answer to her question. Kavanagh, however, had not.

So rushed had his and Alex's preparations been that they had allowed themselves to assume that such photographs existed. Simon Lloyd had not encouraged them to think otherwise. Kavanagh turned slowly to Alex. She, like him, was aghast at the news.

Still feigning surprise, Miss Dixon continued her questioning. 'But there's not even a picture of the drugs sewn into the viscera! What on earth possessed you not to record that? Was your photographer put off by the smell?'

Pearson shrugged. 'We had the drugs, then had them photographed.'

'Perhaps,' suggested Miss Dixon, 'you got to the drugs so quickly that your photographer couldn't keep up?'

Kavanagh raised his eyes. No jury would fail to pick up on what she was intimating.

Again Pearson shrugged. 'It wasn't difficult to guess where they were.'

'Did Officer Lloyd tell you where to find them?'

'No. He did not.'

Next in the witness box was Pearson's colleague, David Maddox. Taking him through yet more photographs, Kavanagh concentrated on the ones of the deep freeze full of frozen meals in the Mainbeam workshop. He concluded his questioning by leaving the jury with the information that there was enough food in the freezer to last several men a few days. Enough food to keep them going while they cut the heroin.

Suzannah Dixon was scathing. 'Is the jury really expected to understand from this that my client was about to spend the next three days turning his business premises into a drugs factory?' She did a convincing job of making the very idea seem laughable.

Maddox glared at her. 'It's part of the whole picture. We also found sleeping bags and camp beds stashed in the lockers.'

Miss Dixon sighed. 'This is a haulage depot. Drivers were arriving at all hours of the day and night, having driven hundreds of miles. You wouldn't expect them to get by on a cup of tea and a biscuit.' Her last sentence was addressed to the jurors as she sank back into her seat.

Significantly, Graham Emerton declined to question the witness. As he shook his head at Judge Phipson, Suzannah Dixon bit her lip. Emerton's reluctance to press on with the defence of his client Patrick Bennett was more than a little alarming.

Immediately after the court adjourned for the day, Miss Dixon followed her client to the cell block and confided her worries to him and his solicitor. 'I think,' she said, as she sat down opposite Gregson, 'that the Crown is trying to make a deal with Bennett.'

Gregson looked only mildly perturbed. 'You mean they want him to turn Queen's evidence?'

Miss Dixon said, 'That's the way I would want it, in Kavanagh's shoes. It's you he's after. If he can get Bennett to testify against you then the Crown will go easy on him.'

Gregson looked at her through narrowed eyes. 'But Bennett's got no evidence to give.'

'He stands to gain a lot from helping the other side.'

'Whaddya mean? I thought we were winning. They've got nothing on me.'

Nothing, Miss Dixon thought, except the unalterable fact that a great deal of heroin had been found in a lorry in his yard – and in his presence. And she knew with a sinking heart exactly what Kavanagh's next line of attack would be. Having failed to secure documentary proof of Gregson's knowledge of the drugs, he would expose the details of his 'high life', which cost a great deal more than a hundred and twenty thousand pounds a year to sustain. This, she thought, was a barrister's worst nightmare: trying to defend someone who maintained their innocence yet who refused to co-operate in giving a believable defence. All he had confided to her about his luxurious lifestyle was that he maintained it by being a 'lucky gambler'. No jury was going to swallow that. Didn't he realize that, despite her seeming success today, he was going to be found guilty? Bennett undoubtedly had something on him – and she was sure he would ultimately testify against him to try to save his own skin. 'Bennett stands to gain a lot from helping the other side,' she tried.

Gregson calmly blew a perfect smoke-ring. 'It won't make him very popular.'

'All I can do,' countered Miss Dixon, with a trace of desperation, 'is seek to destroy his credibility.' Then she tried one last time to make Gregson alter his stance. 'Unless *you* want to offer a plea?'

Gregson merely laughed.

Irritated, Miss Dixon looked at her watch and rose to leave the room. 'I should take any threat of Bennett's more seriously, Mr Gregson. You'll need to give us some pretty heavy ammunition to use against him.'

Gregson gave a slow smile. 'I'll do what I can.'

Dixon felt a chill run down her spine. Suddenly she knew what Gregson was planning.

'Not many miles left in this, is there?'

Startled, Kavanagh slammed shut the boot of his car

and whirled round to see who was standing behind him. He found himself face to face with a thick-set, shady-looking individual in an ill-fitting suit. Behind the man, he noted, were two other similar types. They grinned at him. Fighting back his initial desire to remonstrate with the man, Kavanagh stoically remained silent and walked towards the driver's door. I suppose I knew this was going to happen, he thought. He consoled himself with the knowledge that at least Alex wasn't with him.

Frank followed him round the vehicle. 'You could treat yourself to a little sporty number,' he said. 'A Porsche, perhaps. Now that the kids have grown up.'

Oh no, thought Kavanagh, not the kids. He looked Frank straight in the eye as he opened the car door. 'What do you want?'

'Mr Gregson,' responded Frank, 'can be very generous.' As he spoke, his two friends came a little nearer. 'But,' he added, 'he's also got a very vindictive side. Your address is in the book, Mr Kavanagh.'

CHAPTER NINE

The two defendants were taken back to prison for the night. As was customary, they travelled in separate vans and were put in cells in different wings of the prison. Patrick Bennett, for one, was thankful for the arrangement. He'd always been afraid of Kevin Gregson and, now that the chips were down for both of them, he was glad to be out of his reach. Especially as he had decided to take his barrister's advice and turn witness for the Crown. He was going to grass on Gregson.

But Gregson pre-empted him. A man with friends in high places, he also had a great many contacts in low ones – including Belmont Prison. Two of them, both doing time for GBH, were in the washroom in Bennett's wing as the latter walked towards the showers before being taken to court the next morning. As Bennett went into a cubicle and turned on the jet of water, the men looked at each other and then at the open door, behind which the prison duty officer was just visible. Two minutes later, clouds of steam obscured the officer. A minute after that, one of the men had his hand clasped firmly over Bennett's mouth to stop him screaming. The other held Bennett's left hand against the scalding hot-water pipe. Just to make sure Bennett got the message, he punched him in the stomach and kneed him in the groin.

Not a word was exchanged between the three men. There was no need. Their actions spoke loudly enough.

The same morning, an hour after her husband left for court, Lizzie Kavanagh emerged from Bond Street tube station and hurried along Oxford Street. Dressed in a chic navy suit and contrasting, multicoloured Hermès scarf, she was on her way to her second interview for a job she particularly wanted. So preoccupied was she that it took a few minutes to notice that she was being followed by two men: the same two men who had been with her on the tube all the way from Wimbledon.

A sharp stab of fear pierced her. Last night Jim had told her of the threat he had received and had told her to watch her back. She hadn't paid much attention, assuming that the threats were empty ones. Well-heeled, well-dressed, middle-class women didn't get followed around London by a bunch of thugs, did they? That was the sort of thing that happened in thrillers. For a moment she managed to convince herself that she was being fanciful. If she had taken the tube from Wimbledon to Bond Street, why shouldn't other people? They couldn't be following her. Not really.

To make sure she *was* being fanciful, Lizzie crossed Oxford Street and turned into St Christopher's Place, a tiny pedestrian thoroughfare awash with smart shops. She stopped outside Mulberry, pretending to look at the goods in the window. What she saw were the reflections of the two men. Frozen with panic, aware of her thumping heartbeat, she moved off, cursing the little street for being all but empty. After a few steps she quickened her pace. So did the two men. Lizzie then abandoned all pretence of behaving normally and broke into a run.

Her shoes, however, were not made for speed. Catching one of her high heels in the uneven pavement, she stumbled, wincing from the pain in her ankle as she did so. The fatter of the two men grabbed her arm to prevent her from falling. To a passer-by, it would have looked as if he was just giving her a helping hand. No observer would have noted the vice-like grip in which he held her.

Petrified, Lizzie looked at him.

'Mrs Kavanagh?'

Lizzie groaned.

'Tell your husband,' he continued, as he gave her arm one last squeeze, 'that I was asking after the family.'

In court, Kavanagh watched moodily as Suzannah Dixon relentlessly questioned the medical scientist who had examined the heroin found by the Customs officers. She didn't get anywhere. But neither, a few minutes earlier, had Kavanagh. The doctor was a bit-player in the drama and could only confirm that the substance found had been heroin. He could neither implicate nor exonerate the defendants.

Judge Phipson was looking bored. Kavanagh knew that look. It signalled that he was coming to the conclusion that the whole case was a waste of time and that there was insufficient evidence for a trial. If only, thought Kavanagh, Patrick Bennett hadn't changed his mind about giving evidence against Gregson. With a weary shake of his head, Emerton had imparted that information to Kavanagh just before the court sat. Both men knew the reason. 'It seems that Mr Gregson has powers of persuasion I simply don't possess,' Emerton had said.

Miss Dixon had finished trying to demolish the increasingly alarmed-looking doctor and had turned her attention to the judge. She was telling him that the Crown must prove its case, 'in its entirety', when Alex prodded Kavanagh. 'It's for you,' she whispered, handing him a note. 'From the court usher.'

Kavanagh read it and immediately went white. He handed the note to Alex, muttered, 'Take over. Get an adjournment,' and rushed from the court.

As Alex read the note, Judge Phipson's irritation was plain. He was not accustomed to barristers rushing in and out of his court and didn't take kindly to the commotion. 'Mr Kavanagh?'

But Alex was already on her feet. 'Your honour, a matter of great urgency has arisen. Might we have a short adjournment?'

Twenty minutes later Kavanagh was sitting in the court canteen. He was alone on one side of the table. On the other were the Customs officers, Simon Lloyd and Jenny Norris, and the Customs' solicitor Clare Ashton.

Still breathing heavily from the shock of learning that Lizzie had been approached by Gregson's thugs, he glared across the table. Thankfully, as he had told Alex moments before, Lizzie was unharmed and at home with a policeman. Her voice on the phone, though, had indicated that she was very shocked. And Kavanagh held the Customs officers partly responsible.

'Gregson's heavies just had a go at my wife,' he said to Lloyd in an accusatory tone.

'I'm sorry about that,' replied the Customs officer, as if he couldn't care less.

Kavanagh leaned towards him. 'I think it warrants a little more reaction than that. Any minute now the judge is going to allow Dixon's submission of no case to answer and Gregson will be strolling straight out of that dock.'

Clare Ashton took umbrage at that. 'It's hardly Mr Lloyd's fault—' she began.

But Kavanagh ignored her. 'Your attitude,' he said to Lloyd, 'is probably helping that low-life walk. I know you've got an informant somewhere who could probably put the lid on Gregson.'

Lloyd remained inscrutable.

'Unless,' continued an increasingly exasperated Kavanagh, 'there is enough evidence to put Gregson in the box, we haven't got a hope in hell.'

Lloyd gestured helplessly. 'I want to see him convicted as much as you do.'

But Kavanagh had serious doubts about that. Protecting an informant was one thing; protecting him with the consequence of letting a big-time drugs smuggler go free was quite another. He looked at Lloyd sternly. 'Is that so? But what's the point of protecting your source at the expense of our case?'

Lloyd shifted in his seat. 'You're not responsible for the safety of our informant. I am.'

Clare Ashton, unhappy about the increasing antagonism between the two men, spoke to Kavanagh. 'I don't think you quite appreciate the difficulties of the choices which had to be made.'

'I think I do, Ms Ashton. And I can just about grasp the fact that Mr Gregson is capable of doing a lot more damage outside prison than he is inside.' With those words, and a final, telling stare at Lloyd, Kavanagh got up to leave the room. He failed to notice the look that Jenny Norris, silent throughout the entire discussion, was giving her boss. It was as if she was seeing him for the first time.

Clare Ashton caught up with him in the lobby. Her expression was verging on the contrite. 'Mr Kavanagh.'

'What?'

'I'll . . . er, I'll get the divisional head to review the decision about the informant.'

About bloody time, thought Kavanagh – and probably too late. 'So what do I tell the judge? We're five minutes away from closing our case.'

Ashton agonized for a moment. 'Say we'll get the informant,' she replied, with conviction. 'Ask him to adjourn until tomorrow.'

It was, Kavanagh knew, their only hope. Yet he didn't relish the prospect of waiting until the next day. Lizzie was in a state, he himself was beginning to panic – and Gregson would have more time to get up to his old tricks. And tonight, of all nights, he was obliged to play the genial party-goer. It was that time of year: the annual chambers party.

Lizzie hadn't wanted to go. Still shaken by her encounter with Gregson's heavies, she was also depressed that the subsequent job interview had gone badly. 'I was shaking so much they probably thought I was deranged,' she told her husband. He, however, was determined that she should attend the party – for her own sake as much as his.

'I'm not leaving you alone with an attractive young policeman,' he said, with a nod in the direction

117

of the uniformed officer outside their front door.

Lizzie smiled weakly in response. Kavanagh had arranged for police protection 'until all this is over'. The only problem was, thought Lizzie, would it ever be over? She had quizzed her husband about Gregson, yet he had skilfully deflected most of her questions – mainly because he couldn't answer them. The case now hung on one tenuous thread: the evidence that Lloyd's informer could give. Somehow Kavanagh wasn't confident about it: he was becoming more and more certain that, for whatever reason, Lloyd didn't want Gregson to go to jail. And only in jail would he no longer pose a threat to the Kavanagh family. His hoodlums and his heavies would, Kavanagh knew, melt away when they discovered that their boss was to be incarcerated for a great many years.

When Lizzie got to the party, Jeremy Aldermarten didn't seem to notice that she was looking a little more drawn than usual. The minute she walked into the reception hall at Middle Temple, he bounded up to her and pecked her on the cheek. 'You're looking radiant, Lizzie.' He beamed.

Lizzie smiled thinly. She had always thought Jeremy a complete idiot and had even, she remembered, told him so once. Not, she reflected, that Jeremy had noticed. As she accepted a glass of champagne from a hovering waiter, Jeremy turned back briefly to the woman with whom he had been deep in conversation before the Kavanaghs arrived. Eleanor Foxcott, Peter's wife, had been bombarding him with information about her two favourite subjects – her daughter and her garden – but had now moved on to someone else.

118

Jeremy had been finding it hard work, and thought to his relief that Lizzie would be easier.

'Thank goodness you've come,' he joked. 'Eleanor's spent the last half-hour describing the minutiae of fuchsia cultivation.'

'Fuchsias,' enthused Lizzie. 'My favourite.'

'Absolutely,' replied Jeremy quickly. 'So exuberant.'

Lizzie's tension evaporated. 'So how does your garden grow, Jeremy – professionally?'

Jeremy puffed up his chest. 'I'm currently embroiled in a long-running VAT fraud. Very . . . involving.'

Which is more, thought Lizzie, than I can say for this conversation. Small-talk bored her at the best of times, and this wasn't the best of times.

'Perhaps,' said Kavanagh as he approached, sensing his wife's discomfort, 'we should circulate.'

'Good idea.'

Half an hour, and a glass or two of champagne later, the Kavanaghs, like everyone else, had thawed and were beginning to enjoy themselves. Alex, clad in a stunning cocktail dress that left little to the imagination and probably nothing in her wallet, sidled up to Kavanagh. 'How's Lizzie?'

'Putting on a bold front. She's a bit shaken.'

'Do the police know who it was?'

Kavanagh's face was grim. 'They've got a pretty good idea.' Then he grinned. His own encounter with Gregson's heavies suddenly seemed almost amusing. 'One of them tried to grease my palm yesterday.'

Alex was stunned. 'Good God! How much did he offer?'

Kavanagh gave her a mischievous look. 'Not enough.'

Alex giggled. 'Oh, well, maybe they'll try . . .'

'Alex, what is it?' Kavanagh was puzzled by her sudden silence and change of expression. She was looking towards the doorway.

'Er . . . James . . .'

Kavanagh followed her gaze. 'Oh, God. Oh, no.' The apparition in the doorway, clad in a too-tight tuxedo, was none other than Tom Buckley, clutching a glass of champagne and weaving his unsteady way towards the middle of the room. Like a great number of his colleagues, clerks and barristers alike, at the Bar, Tom was never averse to a drink. Yet this was the first time anyone had seen him plastered in public.

Kavanagh and Alex watched in horror as Tom tottered towards Eleanor Foxcott and Jeremy Aldermarten, together again and now engrossed in a one-sided conversation about Eleanor's daughter's A Levels. Of all the people Tom could have picked on, the wife of the head of chambers was perhaps the least advisable.

Eleanor, however, appeared not to notice the state he was in. 'Such a shame about your wife,' she boomed. 'Is she feeling better?' Her words, though well intentioned, were the last that Tom wanted to hear.

He glared at Eleanor. 'She's bloody well cracking up—'

'I'm sure we all wish her a speedy recovery,' interrupted Jeremy.

That was like a red rag to a bull. Tom rounded on him. 'Bollocks!' he shouted.

Eleanor's mouth fell open and, for an agonized second, there was complete silence in the room. Then Jeremy, for once both speedy and tactful, stepped forward and grabbed her arm. 'Shall we go and look at the seating plan?'

As he ushered her away, Tom looked after him in

disgust. 'You don't give a toss,' he yelled at their retreating figures.

And then Kavanagh was at his side. 'Come on, Tom,' he said, as he put a kindly though firm arm round him and guided him towards the door.

'I haven't finished my drink!'

Kavanagh paid no attention to that. 'You know you don't enjoy these things any more than I do. Why not go home? We've all got work to do in the morning.'

No longer resisting, Tom seemed suddenly lost, defeated somehow. 'Yeah . . . but how long's that going to last?'

'What do you mean?'

'I know you want to get rid of me. Bring in some fancy administrator.'

'Where on earth did you get that idea?'

Tom gave him a pitying look. 'I know everything that goes on in these chambers. That's my job, isn't it?'

Kavanagh still didn't have a clue what he was on about. Steadying the man as he teetered through the doorway, he said, 'No one wants to get rid of you, Tom.'

But Tom's mind was now on other things. After rummaging for a moment in his pockets, he gazed at Kavanagh with the air of a guilty schoolboy. 'You couldn't lend me a couple of notes for a cab?'

Kavanagh couldn't help grinning at his stricken face. 'Sure.' He reached into his pocket and, extracting two tenners, he patted Tom's shoulder. 'There you go. And, Tom, your job's safe. Mind how you go, OK?'

Stumbling down the steps into the street, Tom minded as best he could. Kavanagh watched him for a moment and then turned back to the party. His face was creased with concern. He suddenly had an inkling of why Tom was anxious about his job. The woman he had seen in Jeremy's room the other day. A fancy piece – or a fancy administrator. Suddenly the latter seemed far more likely. Trust Jeremy to try to kick a dog when he's down, thought Kavanagh. He would have a word with his colleague soon – when the Gregson case was over.

The Gregson case looked like being over the next day. Lloyd's informant turned out to be one Dieter Klausen, the driver of the lorry containing the heroin. The written statement he gave was brief: he claimed that Bennett was the one who had organized the importation and that Gregson knew nothing about it.

Kavanagh was not impressed. Yet as Jenny Norris watched him read the statement the next morning in the canteen before the court sat, he betrayed no sign of his disappointment. He merely nodded and then gestured at the photograph that he and Alex had been scrutinizing before she arrived. 'Did Lloyd take this picture of Gregson's yacht?'

She peered at the picture of a sumptuous yacht, which was moored, she recognized from the backdrop, in St Helier. 'I assume so. I wasn't there.'

'Hmm. The only document we've got from Jersey is the yacht's log. Lloyd must have seized more than that.'

'I've no idea.' She was non-committal.

'Oh, come on. You've seized vessels before. You know how much paperwork there is.' His look spoke volumes. Something, it said, is going on here. Someone is trying to hide something.

Jenny Norris didn't quite meet his eye. 'I'll ask him,' she said flatly, and hurried from the canteen.

Kavanagh then surprised Alex. 'We'd better go and

persuade the judge to give us leave to call Klausen.'

'But what's the point? Like Norris said, we know from his statement that Klausen isn't going to implicate Gregson. And he's our witness so you can't accuse him of lying.'

'I am well aware of that, Alex.' Then he grinned. 'But there are other ways.'

There were, indeed, other ways. Judge Phipson reluctantly agreed that the tough-looking Dutchman be called as a witness for the prosecution and, as expected, Klausen stuck to his story that Kevin Gregson had had nothing to do with the smuggling operation; that it had been all Bennett's doing.

Kavanagh, however, was cleverer than Klausen. Steering a fine line that sometimes bordered on the forbidden territory of cross-examining his own witness, he succeeded in sowing seeds of doubt in the jurors' minds about the veracity of Klausen's story.

Klausen, it transpired, supplied Simon Lloyd with information on drug-smuggling in return for money, and had been doing so for years. On this particular instance, he claimed he had alerted Lloyd about the delivery to Mainbeam Haulage – a delivery that cost three hundred thousand pounds. And Klausen said that Patrick Bennett had given him the money, in cash, to buy the drugs.

Kavanagh went into Klausen's long-standing relationship with Bennett. He showed him photographs of Bennett's car, which Klausen correctly identified. Then he showed him several of Bennett's flat, which he also identified. The car was battered and ten years old; the flat was seedy, run-down and had long ago seen better days. Just as Judge Phipson was about to ask Kavanagh exactly what the point of all this was,

Kavanagh pre-empted him. 'Does this,' he asked Klausen, 'look to you like the home of a man with three hundred thousand pounds in his pocket?'

Klausen glared at the barrister.

'Well . . .'

Miss Dixon leaped to her feet. 'Your honour, how can this witness possibly answer that question?'

Judge Phipson raised an eyebrow at Kavanagh, who swiftly moved on. 'Well, perhaps Mr Klausen can help the jury with this. What sort of car does Mr Gregson drive?'

Klausen shrugged. 'How should I know?'

'Perhaps we can refresh your memory. Turn, if you would, to photograph twenty-three.'

With bad grace, Klausen sifted through the file in front of him. The picture showed himself and Kevin Gregson sitting in the latter's car, a gleaming Jaguar.

'You recognize yourself, I daresay,' continued Kavanagh, 'and you recognize Mr Gregson. And the car.'

Klausen stared, appalled, at the photograph.

Again Suzannah Dixon was on her feet. 'Really, your honour, now m'learned friend is cross-examining his own witness.'

'That,' said the judge, in tones of deep disapproval, 'is what it seems, Mr Kavanagh.'

Kavanagh looked wounded. 'Your honour, I'm not cross-examining my own witness at all. It's a perfectly straightforward point, and Mr Klausen can deal with it with me.' He turned back to Klausen. 'Your evidence, Mr Klausen, is, that of the two men we've been talking about, Mr Bennett was the one who gave you three hundred thousand pounds.'

'Yes.'

Kavanagh smiled. 'Thank you very much, Mr

Klausen. Would you wait there?' he added as he sat down.

Klausen waited – for what amounted to destruction at the hands of Graham Emerton. Emerton was delighted. Only now, at the very last minute, did it look as if he was going to make any headway in his task of defending Patrick Bennett. First, Emerton reiterated a point that had been made – but not emphasized – earlier in the hearing. Klausen had made a phone call, had he not, to Mainbeam Haulage to announce that he was through Customs with the delivery? Klausen agreed that he had phoned Patrick Bennett. Emerton begged to differ. He now had in his possession a print-out of the calls made from Klausen's mobile. One of them, made half an hour before arriving at Mainbeam Haulage, had been to Kevin Gregson's car-phone. There was no record of a call to the haulage depot. Klausen offered the staggeringly feeble excuse that he 'must've got the numbers mixed up'.

Emerton stole a glance at the jury and saw that they were looking at Klausen with deep suspicion. 'You know perfectly well,' he continued, 'don't you, Mr Klausen, that my client couldn't even begin to finance a drug deal of this nature?'

Klausen shuffled wearily. 'He must have had some savings.'

'What? On twenty thousand a year?' Emerton all but laughed at the hapless witness. 'Mr Klausen, it's clear to everyone by now that your evidence is absurd. What is it you're afraid of?'

Klausen scanned the courtroom. Whoever he was looking for was obviously not there. 'I'm not afraid of anyone,' he said.

Emerton paused and, with a flourish, picked up the

piece of paper in front of him. 'You have four convictions in Holland for drug-dealing,' he began, 'in a criminal career spanning fifteen years. When caught by British Customs you agreed to exchange information about other criminals for your freedom.' He looked at Klausen with mounting disgust. 'So: the law enforcement agencies don't trust you, and your criminal peers can't trust you. Mr Klausen, why should this jury trust you?'

From the faces of the jurors, as Emerton sat down, it was clear they couldn't think of a single good reason for disagreeing.

Jenny Norris had worked for Her Majesty's Customs and Excise for seven years, the last five with Simon Lloyd. She had always enjoyed working for him: he was both professional and personable and – equally important – had never, in what was still perceived as a macho world, been the least bit patronizing towards her. It was all the more strange, then, that when she related Kavanagh's enquiries about Gregson's yacht to him, he bit her head off. He accused her of telling him how to do his job, and Kavanagh of putting his nose into other people's business.

It was the latter accusation that confirmed Jenny's suspicions about her boss. He must have known as well as she did that Kavanagh, as prosecution counsel, was entitled to see everything seized from Gregson's yacht in St Helier. Jenny herself, although she had not been present when Customs had boarded the yacht, knew perfectly well that registration papers, moorings accounts and bankers' mandates should have been seized when the yacht was taken. Yet Lloyd had never mentioned them and she had never seen them. It worried her – so much that she didn't dare let herself consider the reason behind it. Yet she was a professional to the core and so, for the sake of professional pride, she went behind her boss's back. She phoned the marina office in St Helier and requested them to fax her another copy of all the papers found on Gregson's yacht. She didn't phone from the office, but from a fax bureau to which she requested St Helier to send the documentation. Simon Lloyd never knew what she had done.

After Klausen's testimony, Judge Phipson addressed Suzannah Dixon's question of whether or not there was still a case to be tried. To her extreme annoyance, Phipson declared that Gregson's evident and unsourced wealth, taken together with the phone call from Klausen and the fact that he was present at the depot when the drugs were delivered, established a *prima facie* case against him.

That afternoon, Gregson was sworn into the witness box. Kavanagh, however, was still not overly confident about winning. The case for the prosecution had been closed, which meant that no more witnesses or evidence could be called. If Jenny Norris played ball and came up with any information from St Helier, he couldn't present it to the court. But then there were, as he had earlier said to Alex, other ways . . .

Wearing a shiny Italian silk suit and looking the picture of a confident, self-made man, Gregson created a fairly plausible impression, under Miss Dixon's examination, of the boss wronged by his employee. He claimed to have left the running of Mainbeam Haulage entirely in Bennett's capable – or so he thought – hands. With regard to his income, he confirmed that Mainbeam Haulage and the Dagenham nightclub were his only regular sources, but that he made 'a bit' on gambling. The jurors' eyes widened when he declared that last year he had picked up around thirty or forty thousand pounds that way.

At that point Jenny Norris slipped into the courtroom and handed Alex Wilson a sheaf of faxes. 'Gregson's Jersey account,' she whispered. Alex's heart thumped. Then she handed them to Kavanagh.

Unaware of the transaction, Miss Dixon continued to question her client. 'Would you say things have been going well for you?'

'I had no worries on the financial side. Until,' he added with venom, 'I was arrested.'

'It was suggested to Mr Klausen in questioning,' continued Miss Dixon, 'that you approached him with a plan to import heroin?'

Gregson shook his head. 'I don't know anything about drugs. I hardly know the man.'

'It was also suggested to him that you paid for the drugs.'

'I live well enough without getting into that. But they,' he added with a nod in the direction of the Customs officers, 'thought I was an easy target.'

With a rare smile, Miss Dixon sat down.

Kavanagh was on his feet like lightning. He fired a barrage of questions at Gregson, hoping to destroy the confidence he had radiated while being questioned by his counsel. He began to succeed when he quizzed Gregson about the running of the business.

'I took it over five years ago,' explained the defendant, 'and injected some capital. It was virtually bankrupt.'

Kavanagh then referred to the consignment of putrid, condemned meat in which the heroin had been concealed. 'Was trading in dodgy meat part of your strategy for moving into profit?'

'I didn't know anything about that condemned meat.'

'Really? The smell of it was apparently unbearable – even outside the lorry. Didn't that make you wonder?'

'I didn't notice.'

'Maybe,' suggested Kavanagh politely, 'you've lost your sense of smell?'

'Are you expecting an answer to that?'

'I think we already have it.' Kavanagh looked at his notes. The fax from Jersey lay, for now, untouched. 'So: you said to Miss Dixon that Mainbeam Haulage carried all sorts of foodstuffs for wholesalers.'

'Yes.'

'What are their names?'

'You would have to ask Mr Bennett.'

'Hmm. What are the operating costs per mile on your refrigerated units?'

'That's not a calculation I've done.'

Kavanagh gazed at him in mock surprise. 'So how do you work out what to charge customers?'

'That's Bennett's department.'

'Oh, come on, Mr Gregson. Call yourself a business-man? You must know, for instance, what the business turned over in the last quarter before your arrest?'

But Gregson didn't know. 'I'd have to look in the books.'

'For a man who risked his hard-earned capital on a

bankrupt business, you seem to know precious little about it.'

Gregson sighed impatiently. 'I didn't need to. I had a manager.'

Then Kavanagh went for the jugular. He asked Gregson about his alleged previous year's income of £120,000. He opened the notebook in front of him and, as Gregson answered each question, he wrote down the figures. After three minutes he had established that, winnings from gambling included, Gregson took home around a hundred thousand pounds.

Then Kavanagh started on his outgoings. Again, Gregson was vague but, under pressure, he stated that his mortgage was 'about two hundred and fifty thousand'.

Quick as a flash, Kavanagh calculated repayments of £30,000 per annum. 'And what about your cars?'

Now Gregson was beginning to sweat. 'The businesses own them,' he snapped.

'And you've got a yacht almost as expensive as your house.' A fanatical sailor, Kavanagh didn't need the fax from Jersey to help him estimate the yacht's worth. Yet it helped. 'I presume the yacht is paid for?'

Gregson didn't answer.

'All right, I'll be generous again. Let's assume you're in debt for half of it.' Kavanagh glanced at the fax. 'Two hundred thousand at ten per cent, that's another twenty thousand interest. Seem fair to you?'

Gregson nodded miserably.

'What are the capital repayments?'

'Er . . . about ten per cent a year.'

'So that's forty thousand a year on the yacht plus mooring and maintenance costs. What do they add up to?'

Gregson was silent.

'Mr Gregson, you don't take on that sort of commitment without knowing the costs.' With those words, Kavanagh looked down at the fax from Jersey. 'Is seventeen and a half thousand near the mark?'

Gregson looked as if he had been hit. Every figure Kavanagh had come up with thus far could have been an educated guess. But this one was spot on: there was no way he could have guessed it. Without seeming to notice that all eyes in the courtroom were on him, Gregson turned and looked with pure hatred at the man sitting in the front row of the public gallery. That man was Simon Lloyd.

'We're waiting, Mr Gregson.' Kavanagh's tone implied that he wasn't considering waiting much longer.

Gregson let out a deep sigh. 'Yeah . . . that's about right. Give or take.'

'Good. Now we come to the villa in the Algarve. These classy properties don't come cheap, do they? There's the mortgage, the bills, local taxes, a maid perhaps. And that's before travelling costs. You can't be getting much change out of fifteen thousand.' He glanced up at the now visibly shaken man. 'Would that be fair?'

Gregson glared at him.

Kavanagh drew a bold line on the page in front of him. 'All right. That leaves you with a deficit of about two and a half thousand a year. And that's before your electricity and council tax. It doesn't leave you much to feed a family. Does your wife,' he enquired politely, 'take in ironing?'

A few sniggers greeted that remark, yet the pervading atmosphere was of hushed admiration. It had been quite a performance. And still it continued. Visibly squirming in the witness box, Gregson insisted, through gritted teeth, that the money came from his success at gambling.

'Oh, Mr Gregson. You don't get a quayside spot in St Helier or half a million in loans thanks to a few lucky spins of the roulette wheel. People need to know what you're worth, don't they? With references.'

'There are other ways of persuading people.'

It was entirely the wrong thing to say – and everyone knew it. Kavanagh pounced. 'Oh! So you're accustomed to persuading people, are you? What with?'

'Cash.'

'But we've just accounted for all your cash. You have a deficit of two thousand a year. How else do you persuade people? Force of personality? How, Mr Gregson, do you get what you want?'

Again Gregson had no reply.

'I have to assume you're finding the money from somewhere. Jersey's a good place to hide money from the tax man, isn't it? Is that where you keep it?'

Gregson directed another furious look at the public gallery. 'No.'

But Kavanagh was relentless in his pursuit of an answer. 'In the last five years you have acquired two substantial businesses as well as personal assets probably worth over a million pounds. You've told the court you made it lawfully. *How?*'

Gregson shrugged. 'Talk to my accountant.'

'He must be very good. Persuadable, is he?'

'Your honour,' Suzannah Dixon sprang to her feet, 'this tiresome innuendo is getting us nowhere.'

Judge Phipson reluctantly acknowledged her intervention. Privately, he thought it had got them a very long way indeed. 'Mr Kavanagh!' he admonished in stentorian tones.

Kavanagh inclined his head apologetically and then turned back to his victim. 'You've got an awful lot to lose, Mr Gregson. Up till now you've bullied your way out of trouble. But if you're found guilty and those precious assets are seized, where will that leave you and your wife and child? Right back where you belong.' The tone of his last words left the court in no doubt as to where he thought Gregson belonged.

Angry at the mention of his family, Gregson shouted at Kavanagh to leave them out of it.

Kavanagh took a deep breath. 'You're a drugs dealer, Mr Gregson. That's where your money comes from.'

'No.'

'You knew Dieter Klausen as a man who could fix a supplier. You did a deal and set up your depot to cut down the heroin.'

'Rubbish.'

'You were seen taking personal delivery.'

'I was set up.'

Kavanagh drew himself up to his full height. 'The one thing every gambler learns, Mr Gregson, is that sooner or later your luck runs out. You,' he added, as he stared Gregson straight in the eye, 'are a victim of your own greed.' Keeping his gaze fixed on the man, he lowered himself into his seat. Behind him, Alex Wilson felt like clapping.

Judge Phipson, doing his best to remain impassive, asked Graham Emerton if his client wished to give evidence. The answer was no. Patrick Bennett, after witnessing Kavanagh savaging Gregson, had no intention of letting himself go through the same process. The game, it appeared, was up.

With a nod to the barristers in front of him, Judge Phipson declared the court adjourned. He would, he said, hear the summing-up speeches in the morning.

Simon Lloyd was the first to leave the courtroom after the judge. Kavanagh watched him go. So did Jenny Norris.

Jenny Norris spent a restless night. She knew, in her heart of hearts, that Simon Lloyd had done as much as he possibly could, without arousing suspicion, to thwart the prosecution of Kevin Gregson. And there could only be one reason for that. She, like everyone else in the court, had seen Gregson shooting vicious looks at Lloyd. Yet only she had known what those looks meant. Others might have interpreted them as an indication of Gregson's hatred for Customs officers. Jenny knew otherwise: those looks said, 'You've betrayed me.'

Jenny got up early and went about her day's business. That should have involved going to court to see the dénouement of the trial. Yet today she took upon herself another, even less pleasant task. She phoned a contact at the CID and asked him to meet her at an address in South London later that morning. Then she phoned James Kavanagh. Then she got dressed. In black.

Alex Wilson's nerves were strained to breaking point. She sat in the court canteen alternately drumming her fingers on the table, sipping dish-water coffee and taking bites out of an equally unprepossessing bun. It was on occasions like this that she wished she smoked.

The court had risen and the jury had retired to consider their verdict on Kevin Gregson and Patrick Bennett after Kavanagh, Miss Dixon, Graham Emerton and then Judge Phipson had done their summing-up. Kavanagh had made Gregson look both a liar and an idiot the previous day, which had obviously helped the case for the prosecution, but, Alex thought savagely, idiocy wasn't just the province of people like Gregson. In her short career at the Bar she had seen juries come up with the most extraordinarily lunatic verdicts.

Opposite her, Kavanagh was calmly reading a newspaper. Alex watched him for a bit and then decided she couldn't bear it any longer. 'I hate this wait,' she moaned. 'How on earth can you be so relaxed?'

'I make a conscious effort. Otherwise my ticker would have gone the same way as Ted Fellows's a long time ago.' As he spoke, he looked in amusement at Alex's black coffee and cholesterol-filled bun. 'Just as well you don't smoke,' he added.

They only had five more minutes to wait. Called back into the court, they watched as the clerk read out the indictment to the formidable-looking forewoman of the jury. 'On count one, it is alleged that on the eighth of June this year Patrick Bennett and Kevin Gregson were knowingly concerned in the fraudulent evasion of the prohibition on the importation of drugs of Class A, namely diamorphine, imposed by the Misuse of Drugs Act 1971.' He paused and looked at the woman in front of him. 'On this charge do you find the defendant Patrick Bennett guilty or not guilty?'

'Guilty.'

There was no audible response to that verdict. Everyone had expected it, even Bennett. In the dock at the back of the court, he leaned back and closed his eyes in despair. His barrister Graham Emerton remained impassive.

'And on this charge do you find the defendant Kevin Gregson guilty or not guilty?'

The drama of courtroom processes had obviously rubbed off on the forewoman. She paused until the silence in the court was almost audible. Then she pronounced the verdict.

There was an immediate and appalling noise in the public gallery. Gregson's heavies, gathered *en masse*, were outraged. Gregson went pale. Neither Kavanagh nor Suzannah Dixon betrayed a flicker of emotion. Alex, noting this, tried to wipe the victorious smile off her own.

Judge Phipson ordered Gregson and Bennett to stand up. Bennett's shoulders were slumped. Gregson, although still pale, looked defiant.

'Much as the jury would like to have the satisfaction of hearing the lengthy custodial sentences that you will inevitably receive,' he began, 'the law requires me to remand you into custody pending the preparation of pre-sentence reports. But I warn you now,' he added, with a stern glance at the two men, 'not to expect any leniency from this court.'

Simon Lloyd was waiting for Kavanagh when he emerged with Alex from the courtroom. 'Good result.' He grinned.

Kavanagh gave him a quizzical, piercing look. 'Was it?'

Lloyd wasn't sure how to respond to that. He merely looked at the barrister and then made to walk off.

Kavanagh stopped him. 'Wasn't it a trifle unorthodox to withhold the evidence of Gregson's Jersey account? The one thing which could have put him away without endangering your informant?'

Lloyd squared his shoulders. 'I've no idea what you're talking about.'

'I think you do. You've been trying to trip me up from the beginning.'

'Rubbish. You're getting paranoid, Mr Kavanagh.'

Kavanagh stared at his retreating back. No, he thought, I'm not paranoid – but you should be.

Yet Lloyd had no idea he had been rumbled. And he had no idea, as he walked through the swing doors of the court building, that he was walking into the arms of two detectives and, beside them, Jenny Norris.

Kavanagh knew. He knew that if Jenny's early-morning foray was successful she would bring the detectives to arrest Lloyd as he left the court. He had known from the outset that she would be successful. And he also knew that what she was doing caused her a great deal of pain.

She was almost in tears as she came into the building, minus the detectives. She hadn't been able to stand the expression on Lloyd's face, directed at her, as he was arrested. Seeing Kavanagh still standing there with a rather startled-looking Alex, she went straight up to him. 'I've worked with him for five years,' she said. 'I just . . .'

But Kavanagh wouldn't let her, for her own sake, continue in that vein. He stopped her with a gentle touch on her arm and asked what she had found at Lloyd's house.

'His insurance policy,' she said tonelessly. 'The best part of forty thousand in cash. Two boxes of files relating to Gregson's offshore accounts and a statement from his Jersey account showing a withdrawal of fifty thousand in cash ten days after his arrest.'

'Just about the time Lloyd was in Jersey?'

Jenny nodded. 'Gregson had exclusive authority on the account.' Still incredulous, she looked straight through Kavanagh, as if not believing what she was saying. 'Lloyd took a bribe.'

'Mmm.' Kavanagh shook his head. 'Only fifty thousand. I wonder what they would have paid me?'

CHAPTER TEN

'Any messages, Tom?'

Tom looked up at Kavanagh and Alex. They seemed pleased with themselves. He wasn't to know that their satisfaction was more to do with the cream cakes Alex had insisted Kavanagh buy her than with the verdict. Alex had claimed she needed instant energy to recover from the trial and the subsequent shock of Lloyd's activities. Kavanagh reckoned, imminent heart-attack or no, that she deserved it. It had been a bugger of a trial for someone so inexperienced.

Their goodwill did not, however, pass itself on to Tom. Without a word, he buried his head once more in the paperwork on his desk. Alex and Kavanagh exchanged a look. Tom was obviously having another of his 'days'.

Then he surprised them by announcing that Kavanagh was wanted in Peter Foxcott's room. Kavanagh looked at Alex. Something was definitely up.

That something, predictably, had much to do with Jeremy Aldermarten. As Kavanagh wandered into Peter's room Jeremy, along with other senior members of River Court, was sitting opposite his head of chambers across the large desk. But, unlike the others present, Jeremy was in full flow.

'His language was deplorable,' he was saying. 'In front of Eleanor, too.'

Peter Foxcott grinned. It took more than deplorable language to fell Eleanor.

Jeremy, however, was not to be deflected. 'It wasn't the first time Tom's embarrassed us. It's almost grounds for summary dismissal.'

'Well, the man's under considerable personal stress . . . but I agree we can't let it upset the system.'

Kavanagh made his way quietly to the window and perched on the ledge. 'Ah, Jim.' Foxcott beamed. 'Help yourself to a drink.'

Kavanagh reached over to the cut-glass decanter on the table beside him. As usual, it contained a twelve-year-old single malt. He poured himself a glass as Jeremy, the bit firmly between his teeth, continued his diatribe. 'The man's got no qualifications, yet we pay him an absolute fortune. And in return we get behaviour that quite frankly belongs on the football terraces.'

'And you're a regular at the match, are you, Jeremy?'

Jeremy shot a particularly nasty look at Kavanagh, the source of the remark, but declined to answer. He turned back to Foxcott. 'Is the sort of image Buckley puts out what a modern chambers wants? We have to compete with other sets for big cases now. We need someone with real skill and finesse.'

Again it was Kavanagh who spoke. 'Someone educated, mature, well-spoken? One of us?' The remark, even for Kavanagh, was especially rich in sarcasm. 'Did you have anyone in mind?'

Without a word, Foxcott handed Kavanagh an expensive-looking document. It was a CV with a glossy portrait photograph attached. Kavanagh instantly

140

recognized the face. He knew where he had seen that perfect smile before.

'She looks the right sort,' began Foxcott.

'Mmm. Sarah Lee-Gordon,' read Kavanagh. 'Aged forty-five. Cheltenham Ladies' College, Durham University, chartered accountant . . . Now, where have I seen her before?'

Jeremy glowered at him. 'She's extremely capable.'

Kavanagh threw the CV onto Foxcott's desk with rather more force than was necessary. 'I'm sure she is. A bit too old for you, though, Jeremy.'

Jeremy flushed, with embarrassment and anger. 'She's written an impressive report on how we can increase cash-flow, improve our efficiency and—'

'What other chambers has she turned round like this?'

'Er . . . we would be the first.'

Kavanagh sipped his drink. 'So she's good on theory.'

'She has an excellent pedigree.'

'So has my old man's dog – but I wouldn't drag him out of his kennel to replace a clerk who's spent twenty years building our careers.'

Jeremy had other views of Tom's prowess. 'He's done very little for me.'

'You should try talking to him.'

Sensing that the conversation was in danger of becoming a fully fledged confrontation, Peter Foxcott interrupted. 'Perhaps if we were to discuss this in a slightly more rational fashion . . .'

But Kavanagh was seriously annoyed with Jeremy. 'What Tom's got,' he said to the assembled group, 'is the common touch. What comes with that is a few rough edges. Sure, he made a mistake the other night.

Why not read him the riot act, then give the man a chance?'

Foxcott scanned the room quickly. Everyone – with the notable exception of Jeremy – was nodding their assent. He shouldn't have let himself be swayed by those arguments about money, persuasive though they were. He said to Jeremy, 'Let's keep Ms Lee-Gordon on file, shall we?'

Not famed for his dignity in defeat, Jeremy finished his drink and walked out.

Kavanagh heaved a sigh of relief. He was, he knew, far from alone in resenting the recent drive towards recruiting clerks from other professions. Traditionally, clerks had, as Jeremy had put it, 'no qualifications', but that had never stopped them being among the most successful, and sometimes most highly paid, people within the legal profession. The business of being a clerk was only learned by experience, often passed down from father to son, and as far as Kavanagh was concerned, that was better than most 'qualifications'. Sarah Lee-Gordon, indeed. How well did she think she would go down in the almost exclusively male, chain-smoking, ribald, swearing world of the barrister's clerk?

The next day Tom Buckley was noticeably brighter. Whether that was down to his wife feeling better or to a little birdie imparting yesterday's news to him, Kavanagh wasn't sure. Whatever the reason, he was heartily glad to see the change in him.

'Your case next Monday,' he said as Kavanagh collected his mail in the morning, 'is going to plead . . .'

'Oh, good. Spared a tedious trial.'

'But Mr Aldermarten needs a leader in the Court of

Appeal,' added Tom. To Tom, the concept of an idle barrister was anathema. He liked to see his barristers busy twenty-four hours a day, seven days a week. And even more so now: he was well aware that he had been sailing close to the wind over the last few days. Now, more than ever, he was determined to prove his worth.

Kavanagh, however, had other ideas. 'Sorry, Tom, I'm going sailing.'

'Sailing?' Tom was scandalized.

'Even barristers have hobbies, you know.' He gave Tom an old-fashioned look. 'And holidays.'

'But this case is private!'

Kavanagh shrugged. 'Money isn't the only consideration.'

Tom grinned. That wasn't what Jeremy Aldermarten had said when he'd accepted the case. Then he went back to his desk. 'Oh, well, have a good time, sir.'

'I will.' Kavanagh stopped at the door and glanced back. 'How's your wife, by the way?'

'Coming home tomorrow.' Tom's expression was both relieved and wary. 'We'll see how it goes.'

Kavanagh smiled. 'Give her time. And, Tom, my door's always open.'

Tom's eyes betrayed his gratitude. Then, just as Kavanagh was leaving the room, he grinned broadly. 'I imagine you'll be using your sailing break as a sort of dry run for your next case, sir.'

'Eh?' Kavanagh looked round in surprise – partly because of Tom's attempt at a joke, and partly because he hadn't a clue what he was talking about.

The clerk waved a bundle of paper at him. The pink ribbon round it identified it as a barrister's brief. 'You haven't forgotten, have you, sir? The naval case.'

'Oh, God. No, Tom, I hadn't forgotten.' Sheepishly,

Kavanagh retraced his steps and took the bundle out of Tom's hand. 'Perhaps I ought to do a bit of reading while I'm on the boat.' Tapping the brief with a finger, he looked at Tom and said, 'I sense stormy waters with this one.'

Tom rolled his eyes heavenwards. He supposed he'd asked for it.

Kavanagh intended to keep the brief in the bottom of his suitcase for the duration of his sailing holiday. He had promised Lizzie that he wouldn't take his work with him – and this time he had almost kept his word.

The holiday was meant to be a celebration – partly of Kavanagh winning an unlikely case, but mostly of Lizzie. The board of the hospital trust had given her the job. 'I couldn't believe it,' she had said to her husband after she had heard the good news. 'I really thought I'd scuppered my chances by my behaviour at the second interview. I was shaking like a leaf.'

'Maybe they think you've got a twitch,' Kavanagh had joked, 'and were too polite to mention it. Positive discrimination, isn't that what they call it?'

Lizzie had thumped him and then mooted the idea of the holiday – 'To the Caribbean, perhaps?'

Much to her surprise, her husband had agreed. At least to the holiday part. The Caribbean, he said, was much too hot at this time of year, and anyway, their boat was moored in Hampshire, wasn't it?

Lizzie didn't bother replying that it was *his* boat and that the Caribbean was, as far as she was concerned, perfect at any time of the year. But she was so surprised that he agreed to a holiday that she jumped at the chance to take it. 'Shall we take Matt?'

'Matt? What on earth for?'

'Well, you might not remember this, but he *is* our son . . .'

'Doesn't mean we have to take him on holiday with us. Anyway, he'd be bored. D'you know, I heard him on the phone the other day referring to us as the "old fossils". Bloody cheek.'

Lizzie looked askance at him. 'Good God, I'm only forty-five!'

'Never too young to be a fossil,' said her fifty-six-year-old husband.

'Hmm. Even so, I reckon we should ask him. Poor boy's got a broken heart, remember.'

Kavanagh nodded in sympathy. 'I know – but he'll get over it.'

The prospect of his parents disappearing for a week was almost enough to mend Matt's heart. 'No,' he replied to Lizzie's invitation. 'Thanks, Mum, it's really kind of you, but you and Dad go. You don't want me mooning about under your feet.'

Lizzie put an arm round her son's shoulders. 'I couldn't think of anything nicer than having my two favourite men all to myself.' Then she looked at him closely. 'You're sure, though? I don't want to force you, but . . .'

'I know what you're thinking, Mum.' Matt looked at her through eyes that were suddenly wiser than his sixteen years. 'She was a roaring Sloane, anyway. Not my type. Much better off with chinless Charles.'

Lizzie smiled. 'Chinless Charles' was the dashing and extremely good-looking Viscount Fordham. Miranda, the girlfriend who had caught Kavanagh slumped on the sofa with his lager and Indian take-away, had unceremoniously dumped Matt in favour of the young aristocrat. Lizzie, who had only met Miranda once and had instantly disliked her, hadn't been unduly surprised. Girls like Miranda had the word 'mercenary' tattooed on their foreheads and the fact that Charles's father was an earl put Matt's barrister father firmly in the shade. Privately, Lizzie wondered what Miranda would have done if she had known that Matt's grandfather – Lizzie's father – was a peer with a much grander country house than the Fordhams'. Matt, she suspected, hadn't thought it worth mentioning – thank God.

She hugged her son. He tried to wriggle away. Sixteen, she remembered too late, was the wrong age to be hugged by your mother. But before he had freed himself she patted him. 'For what it's worth I think you're right. Girls like Miranda . . . well . . .'

'Yeah.' Matt grinned. 'I know what you mean. They're wonderful to look at, but it's what's underneath that counts.'

Lizzie wasn't sure whether to be pleased or alarmed by Matt's words. They were surprisingly mature for someone of his age – but they also conjured up a vision she would rather not contemplate. Had Matt been to bed with her? *Did* sixteen-year-olds go to bed with each other? Suddenly beset by visions of yet another offspring with rampaging hormones, Lizzie went upstairs to begin packing. Sometimes she was glad she was a fossil.

'I know you've brought that brief with you.'
'I don't know what you're talking about.'

'I saw it in your suitcase.'

'Oh.' Kavanagh kept his eyes on the road. He knew exactly what he would read in Lizzie's and he didn't feel up to facing it. 'The thing is—'

'The thing is, Jim, you swore blind you wouldn't do any work this week.'

Kavanagh finally looked at his wife. He was grinning, which enraged her even more. And it was her rage that had made him grin in the first place. 'Would you just let me finish, please? I *did* swear blind *I* wasn't going to do any work – and I meant it. Just because I've taken a brief with me doesn't mean I'm going to work on it.'

Lizzie looked at him in outraged disbelief. 'Oh, for heaven's sake, Jim, I wasn't born yesterday.'

Kavanagh held up a hand to silence her. 'I know, I know. I wouldn't believe me either. But this time it's true. I just didn't want to offend Tom.'

'Offend Tom? Tom Buckley?'

'He thinks I haven't done anything to prepare the case. He's wrong, of course, most of it was done ages ago. Harker and I have prepared a pretty good defence.'

'Harker?' The name was familiar. Alarmingly familiar. 'D'you mean Eleanor Harker?'

'The very one. You remember her, don't you? Tall, good-looking woman.'

'Yes. Not an easy one to forget.'

Kavanagh shot a sidelong glance at his wife. Lizzie's lips were pursed, her face set. He opened his mouth to reply, then closed it. Silence descended in the car as they sped towards the coast. Kavanagh's was an amused, contemplative silence. He was rather taken with the idea that his wife was jealous.

A fellow QC, Eleanor was usually to be found prosecuting criminals and not, as was the case in the forth-coming trial, defending them. She and Kavanagh had been professional adversaries and personal friends for a good many years and relished each other's company. But the idea of them becoming more than friends? Kavanagh found it rather funny – and not a little intriguing. Eleanor was, as he had said to Lizzie, a tall, handsome woman. She was also quick-witted with a temper to match and she had an enormous capacity for fun and high-jinks. But she was also happily married. Kavanagh furrowed his brow as he tried to conjure up an image of her husband. He failed, and realized that he had always, albeit unconsciously, thought of Eleanor as a single woman. Single, yet not his sort. Only then did it occur to him why: he had, he supposed, always considered her as one of the boys. Which, under the circumstances in which they were about to find them-selves, was probably just as well.

'So why,' said Lizzie, unable to bear the silence any longer, 'is Harker working with you on this one? She's a QC, isn't she? She can't be acting as your junior.' She had spent the last few moments trying to banish from her mind the image of Eleanor Harker and her hus-band plotting defence strategies over a few bottles of wine. Among Eleanor's many gifts, she remembered sourly, was a staggering ability to hold her own with the boys when it came to booze.

'Two defendants,' replied Kavanagh. 'Mine's an officer – a second lieutenant. Hers is a rating. It's an unusual case.'

'I'm lost already. What's a rating?'

Kavanagh was relieved to see that she was no longer wearing her 'I hate Eleanor' expression. 'A rating, my dear, is someone who isn't an officer. I believe this one is a marine engineering mechanic.'

'And he stands accused along with your sub-lieutenant. What're they accused of? Buggery on the poop deck?'

Kavanagh laughed at Lizzie's attempt at an admiral's voice. 'No.' he said. 'Nothing so mundane – or understandable. They're both accused of arson.'

'*Arson?* Good God, did they sink their ship or something?'

'No.' Kavanagh's voice was quieter now as he reflected on the difficult case before him. 'They set fire to someone's bunk when they were moored in Portsmouth and staying in an accommodation block.'

Lizzie was astonished. 'That seems like a mighty peculiar thing to do.'

'I know. Especially for the son of a vice-admiral. That's why I don't think they did it. But what I *do* want to find out is who did – and why.'

CHAPTER ELEVEN

'Sir, it is perhaps unusual to find an officer and a rating co-defendants on such a charge. However, the association between Sub-lieutenant Kinross and Marine Engineering Mechanic Jones predates, by a good many years, their meeting on board HMS *Merlin*. It is their acquaintanceship – and the division of loyalty it brought about – which lies at the heart of this case.' Lieutenant Commander Hugh Mills, Barrister Royal Navy, paused to take a sip of water. At the desk to his left, Kavanagh nodded to himself. That friendship was indeed, he felt, at the root of this case. Yet Mills would, no doubt, try to shed disparaging light on this alliance of unequal rank: Mills was the counsel for the prosecution or, in the case, the 'prosecutor'. For this was no ordinary courtroom trial: it was a court martial.

To Kavanagh's left, Eleanor Harker was trying her best to look at ease in the unfamiliar surroundings. Like Kavanagh, she had never taken part in a court martial before, and was, on this first day of the proceedings, slightly bemused by it all. The courtroom at the naval base in Portsmouth at least looked like a normal courtroom – but that was where the similarity ended. Instead of a jury there was a board comprised of naval personnel, who sat on a dais at one end of the room. The judge advocate who headed the inquiry sat to their right with the court clerk and recorders. Kavanagh and Eleanor Harker, sitting beside their clients, were opposite them. She found it rather unnerving to be sitting beside Patrick Jones: he was shaking with nerves. Yet what she found most unusual, and a little threatening, was the sword table immediately below the dais. Sub-lieutenant Ralph Kinross's sword was the only object on the table, and it was pointing away from him. Eleanor had been informed that the position of the sword was called 'athwartships', signifying that its bearer was in trouble.

She stole a glance at Kinross. Deprived of his cap as well as his sword, he nevertheless looked composed and dignified as he sat beside Kavanagh. Like Jones, he was in his early twenties, yet he had about him an air of authority that the other man lacked. They made, mused Eleanor as Mills resumed his speech to the board, a strange pair.

'Lieutenant Kinross and Marine Engineering Mechanic Jones had been boon companions as children,' explained Mills, 'their families both coming from Hexham. Indeed, Jones's mother served the Kinross family, in a catering capacity, on numerous occasions.'

Eleanor knew that. She also knew that the two young men had lost contact when, as a teenager, Jones had joined the Navy. It was only after his naval college training and on his first deployment on a ship – HMS *Merlin* – that Kinross had met Jones again. It was hardly surprising, she thought, that they should become friends again. Not surprising – but not practical either. Bloody armed forces, she thought savagely. All they do is perpetrate the class system.

Eleanor followed the rest of Mills's speech with rapt attention, even though she already knew the facts of the case. She and Kavanagh had gone over them again and again. She knew that much of the seventh floor of the accommodation block had been gutted by fire on the night of the seventh of July. She knew there were no casualties as most of the men had been on a regular onshore visit. And she knew that the fire had been started deliberately, with lighter fuel, and had originated in a bunk assigned to one of Jones's fellow marine engineering mechanics, MEM O'Brien. Those facts were not in dispute; nor, unfortunately, were the facts that an empty can of fuel, bearing Jones's fingerprints, was later found in a ground-floor chute and that Kinross's silver cigarette lighter, bearing his as well as Jones's fingerprints, was found on the seventh-floor fire-escape landing. Those discoveries meant that Kavanagh and Eleanor Harker were going to have an uphill job in defending the two men. Neither of them, however, was unduly daunted. The whole thing, as far as they were concerned, was just too pat. And why on earth would an officer help set fire to a mechanic's bunk? It had been an unintelligent crime – and Ralph Kinross was far from stupid.

Both Kavanagh and Eleanor began to make a few notes when Mills stopped imparting proven evidence and regaled the board with testimonies, provided by witnesses, that would aid him in his role as prosecutor. Witnesses, they knew from experience, were far from reliable. 'At 2000 hours,' said Mills, after a glance at his notes, 'Able Seaman Davies saw Lieutenant Kinross entering the accommodation block Hood. He was then seen to take a lift to the sixth floor. It is a matter of record that MEM Jones's quarters were on the sixth floor. Shortly after 2000, Jones and Lieutenant Kinross entered MEM O'Brien's quarters on the seventh floor.'

152

Says who? thought Eleanor with a furious look at Mills. The man, as well as being her adversary, was a pompous ass. And then she wondered, not for the first time, what she was doing here. Why had Kinross and Jones asked for civilian barristers? Wouldn't the board, which consisted of all naval people although they were not acquainted with anyone else in the court, take a biased view? Why hadn't they chosen to be defended by other naval barristers?

'Able Seaman Davies,' continued Mills, 'did not see Lieutenant Kinross leave the block via the front lobby. But,' he added triumphantly, 'he was seen emerging from the ground-floor fire exit at about 2025 by Chief MEM Evans.' Then Mills mentioned, albeit briefly, something that Kavanagh and Eleanor were going to use as part of their defence: that it had been MEM Jones, supposedly one of the perpetrators of the fire, who had alerted Able Seaman Davies to the fact that the seventh floor was ablaze.

'In the opinion of the fire investigation unit which examined the scene,' explained the naval barrister, 'the fire had already been burning for upwards of twenty minutes by the time that Jones told Davies to raise the alarm at 2030.'

Oh, get on with it, thought Eleanor. I want my lunch.

She didn't have long to wait. Mills concluded this opening address by telling the board the reasons that led Kinross and Jones allegedly to set fire to O'Brien's bunk.

Again, both defence counsels knew that they pivoted, as did the reasons for many crimes, around money, cowardice and revenge.

*

'Why is it, d'you think, that the defendants chose civilian counsel?' Eleanor Harker looked up from the lunch she had been fantasizing about. The reality was even better than she had hoped: a delightful seafood salad to start with, followed by, in her case, poached river trout. And two bottles of good Sancerre were already on the table. Officers, she reckoned, didn't waste any effort when it came to creature comforts in the mess.

'That,' replied Philip Driscoll, the judge advocate, 'you would need to ask your client.' He stabbed at a piece of squid. 'Some men, I think, don't feel one of their own would be impartial. An erroneous view, nevertheless.'

But the morning's proceedings had left Eleanor nothing if not belligerent. 'Well, Lieutenant Commander Mills could hardly be described as one of Jones's own. Jones is a rating, after all.'

Driscoll grinned. 'So was Lieutenant Commander Mills.'

Eleanor looked at him, perplexed. Still surprised that both the prosecution and defence teams – and even the judge – were sitting down together for lunch, she was even more astounded by this latest piece of news.

'Worked his way up to us by way of the Bar,' continued Driscoll, 'and he's been a thorn in my side ever since.'

Mills appeared to find that amusing. He winked at Eleanor, which annoyed her. Beside her, Kavanagh grinned.

'So you see, Miss Harker,' continued Driscoll, 'however classbound you might perceive the Service, talent will out.'

'But if they can have civilian counsel, why can't they have a proper judge and jury to go with it?'

'Eleanor . . .'

But Driscoll seemed unperturbed. He was, he pointed out, a 'proper judge' – but for the Royal Navy. 'This was an offence committed by MOD personnel against MOD property.'

Eleanor, now on her second glass of Sancerre, had her hackles up. 'But if a policeman set fire to a section house, he'd be accountable to the Crown Court and—'

'And such is a policeman's lot. Happily, I practise my law in the warm and encompassing bosom of the fleet in which we serve.'

As if on cue, and before Eleanor could muster more invective, the mess steward appeared with their main courses. 'Ah!' Driscoll beamed as the steward hesitated over the orders. Then he gestured towards the fuming Eleanor. 'I believe you'll find that Miss Harker's the trout.'

In London, another barrister from River Court was enjoying lunch, one that by far surpassed anything offered at the Portsmouth officers' mess. Atelier, an award-winning restaurant in Soho's Beak Street, was the favourite haunt of David Lurie, Julia Piper's boyfriend. Julia, too, was beginning to acquire a taste for the place and had dined there several times with him. Lunch, however, was unusual. While Soho was convenient for her, it wasn't in close proximity to David's place of work: the Foreign Office.

Julia had been keeping her romance with David secret from her colleagues since they had all met at a cricket match. Predictably, Jeremy Aldermarten had taken against him, claiming that he wasn't good enough for Julia. Pausing in the middle of her salad of duck confit, Julia thought that the man opposite her, as far as she was concerned, was more than good enough. Tall, blond and with a swimmer's build, he was also great fun and highly stimulating company. Jeremy, of course, was jealous.

'What're you grinning at?'

'Oh . . . nothing. Just thinking of Jeremy.'

'Jeremy?'

'Yes. Jeremy Aldermarten. You know, my colleague.'

'Oh, *him*.' David made a face. 'Wouldn't have thought he was the sort of man who could make you smile.'

'He isn't normally. But you should have seen his expression when I told him I was having lunch with you.'

'You mean he doesn't know about us?' David looked a little put out.

'Well . . . no.' Julia waved her fork in a distinctly unladylike fashion. 'I just thought it was less hassle. Y'know, don't bring your personal life into the office and all that.'

'There might come a time when you won't have much choice.'

Julia gave her companion a playful look. 'Was that a proposal?'

'Yes.'

'*What!*' Julia was so taken aback that she dropped her fork. She had been joking. She had thought *he* had been joking. But his face was serious as he delved into his jacket pocket and extracted a small box. The words Tiffany & Co. were clearly printed on the lid. 'David . . . I . . .'

156

'Open it.'

'But I . . . David . . . I can't!'

'Yes, you can.'

Julia took a deep breath. Yes, you can, she told herself. Of course you can. Stop being so girly.

She opened it. As she did so, she experienced the most peculiar sensation. It was only after a few seconds of looking at the sparkling band of diamonds that she identified that sensation. It was dread.

'Will you marry me, Julia?' David's voice was quiet, matter-of-fact.

'Marry you?'

'Yes.' David smiled at her vacant expression. 'You know – become my wife.' Then, as Julia remained mute, she saw a flicker of doubt cross his features. 'You do love me, don't you?'

'Of course I do. But . . .' Julia looked down at the exquisite ring she hadn't yet touched. 'Well . . . marriage.' Then she looked David in the eye. 'Didn't work for my parents – or yours.'

'We're not our parents.' David made a good job of disguising his hurt at her reaction. And Julia realized that she had been less than gracious. Trying to lighten the atmosphere, she said, 'You don't know me. I'm a slut around the house.'

David leaned forward. 'Slut is good.'

Oh, God, thought Julia. She hated surprises; she hated being rushed. And she hated hurting David. But, most of all, she hated the idea of marriage. 'I'm serious,' she said, avoiding his eye. 'I don't want to . . . to trail after you, picking up your socks. Look,' she added in a brighter tone, 'what if we just cohabited for a sort of trial period? Six months or . . . you know, just see how it goes and . . . What's wrong, David?' He had

157

bitten his lip and turned his head away. Oh, Christ, she thought, he's not going to cry, is he? Julia was all for sensitive men – but there were limits.

'It's the Foreign Office. My posting came through.'

'Oh.' Suddenly she was wary. 'Where?'

'Nairobi. Three years.'

'I see.' She understood – only too clearly. 'And when do you go?'

'Er . . . a month.' He tried to smile. 'Long enough to get the banns read.'

'I don't bloody believe it!' Julia, upon whom several pairs of eyes were already discreetly fixed, attracted the attention of the rest. 'You know full well you're off to Happy Bloody Valley in a month's time and you have the bare-faced effrontery to ask me to—'

'It's short notice, I know, but—'

'Short notice! That's not a proposal, David, it's a game of Beat the Clock. Good God, you expect me to drop everything and follow you half-way around the world?' Julia gestured wildly around the restaurant. The other customers tried to pretend they weren't there. 'Just like that. Well, I've got a career too, David. I've worked damned hard—'

'They do have barristers in Kenya.'

But David's mild, sensible responses only served to fuel her rage. She stood up and threw her napkin on the table.

'Julia?'

'Don't call me!' she fumed. 'Ever. I don't want to see or hear from you again.' After one last killing look at David, she stormed out of the restaurant. Her departure was both frightening and magnificent. No one knew which way to look. It was the kindly manageress who rescued David from his embarrassment by asking him if there was anything else he required. There was. The bill.

The lunch in Portsmouth finished on a rather more civilized note. Eleanor became progressively less antagonistic throughout the meal and even looked as if she was enjoying herself. Kavanagh attributed that to the quantity of wine she consumed. He had always known that she was no slouch when it came to alcohol, but he had never seen her drink on duty before. Neither had he seen her quite so eager to pick a fight. Something, he concluded, was up with Eleanor. His theory was corroborated when, just before they went back into the courtroom for the afternoon session, he saw her emerging from the ladies' looking preoccupied and upset. 'You all right?' he enquired, with what he thought was comradely concern.

'What d'you mean?'

'Well . . . you put a few away at lunch . . .'

Two pink spots appeared on Eleanor's cheeks. 'I don't think,' she replied with a touch of acid, 'that that's any of your business – is it?' With that, she stalked into the courtroom, leaving Kavanagh feeling awkward and slightly worried. Something was definitely bugging Eleanor. He could only hope it wasn't going to interfere with her handling of the defence of Patrick Jones.

First on the agenda as the court reconvened ten minutes later was the evidence-in-chief of MEM O'Brien. Although Mills did a good job of keeping him at his ease as he questioned him about the events leading up to the fire, there was, thought Kavanagh, an underlying nervousness. Whether that was because of the rarefied atmosphere of the court martial or because he was hiding the truth, Kavanagh wasn't sure. But one thing became increasingly clear to him as O'Brien continued: the antipathy between O'Brien, Kinross and Jones had been very real. O'Brien's dislike of the other two stemmed from Kinross having interfered in something that was, as far as the former was concerned, none of his business: namely the loan of three hundred pounds by Jones to O'Brien. 'That wasn't at all usual,' said O'Brien. 'I mean, I know it was the Lieutenant's first deployment and he might've been a bit unsure of the form, but all the same . . .' O'Brien went on to point out that, because of Kinross's interference, Jones began to get bullied by his below-decks companions. The whole thing would never have escalated if the matter had been left in the capable hands of the chief – Chief MEM Jack Evans. According to O'Brien, the chief had told Jones he would have to be satisfied with the money being repaid in instalments. But that hadn't been good enough for Kinross. 'Lieutenant Kinross,' said O'Brien, in tones of disapproval, 'even spoke to the other hands and asked them to leave Jones alone.'

'And how did the other hands feel about that?'

'Well, there was the usual sort of comments, as you'd expect.'

Mills raised his eyebrow. 'The usual?'

O'Brien sniggered. 'Well, the standard sort of "were they at it or what?" sort of thing.'

Mills sighed. 'Yes, I see.'

'It was just the lads being, well, lads. But seriously, whatever sympathy there might've been for Jonesy . . . that was it.'

'How do you mean?'

O'Brien explained that the practical jokes increased,

and that Jones had complained again to Kinross, who warned O'Brien that if things continued he would call in the 'Joss' – the master-at-arms in charge of the ship's security. O'Brien's expression left nobody in any doubt as to what he thought of that. And the actions of the other hands demonstrated that they had also taken a dim view of the affair: they had played even more cruel jokes against Jones, the last of which was to destroy his heavy naval boots.

'How did Jones react to this?' asked Mills.

'He lost the bubble. He came up the galley accusing me of doing it.' O'Brien shrugged. 'There was a bit of a set-to. We ended up before Commander Pilgrim on defaulters. He gave us a warrant fine and ten days' number nines.'

'Sir . . . ?' All eyes in the room turned to Kavanagh as he rose and looked at Driscoll.

'Mr Kavanagh?'

'I'm finding the evidence of this witness somewhat difficult to follow. Warrant fine? Ten days' number nines?'

Driscoll cleared his throat. 'Ah. Yes, of course. He means extra work and musters as punishment.'

'I'm obliged.' Kavanagh sat down, not much the wiser.

On further questioning by Mills, O'Brien claimed that he hadn't been too bothered about the punishment, but that Jones had been livid at losing his 'v.g. conduct' and consequent chances of quick promotion. As for Lieutenant Kinross, within days he had been transferred to another ship under Commander Pilgrim's orders. 'That made Jones even madder,' added O'Brien. 'Said he'd sort me out next time we were alongside.'

'And how seriously did you take his threat?'

'Very. I knew if it came to a dust-up I could handle myself, but someone like Jonesy don't come at you head-on.' O'Brien looked over to Jones, sitting impassively beside Eleanor Harker. 'Know what I mean? Setting fire to your bunk. It's pretty snide. Still,' he added, 'it could've been worse.'

'In what way?'

'I could've been in it.'

Eleanor Harker might have consumed more wine at lunch than was advisable, but her senses remained alert enough to know that O'Brien's evidence did not bode well for her client, and he knew it too. As the court adjourned for the day, Patrick Jones gave her a baleful look. Eleanor said, she hoped reassuringly, 'Very early days, Mr Jones.'

'Yes, ma'am. Yes.'

'Good. Good.'

Jones's persistent politeness, combined with his apparent unease, unnerved her. And her nerves were, anyway, frayed. She picked up her briefcase. 'Well, I'd . . .'

'Yes. Thank you very much, ma'am.'

Eleanor sighed as she walked away, leaving Patrick's solicitor to accompany him to his room. She knew she should have been more forthcoming. She knew she was verging on behaving unprofessionally, yet she could face neither the court nor the naval base any longer.

Kavanagh, hoping to catch up with Eleanor for the train journey back to London, found himself waylaid by the fresh-faced attractive girl he had noticed in the public gallery of the courtroom. She had been sitting between Ralph Kinross's parents.

'Mr Kavanagh,' she said, extending her hand, 'I'm Helen, Ralph's sister.'

'Hello. How d'you do?'

She grimaced. 'Could be better. Look, um . . . my father's not even admitting the possibility and Ralphie won't say, but . . . if things don't work out . . . I mean, would he go to prison? Please,' she added, 'I just want someone to tell me honestly.'

Kavanagh looked appraisingly at the anxious girl. He could just imagine how difficult the Kinross family – and especially Helen – were finding the situation. From his earlier brief meeting with Vice-Admiral Kinross, he had the strong impression that the man would have almost preferred his son to have been killed than to be guilty of the crime. He had grasped that shame was a concept alien to the Kinross parents. He knew from his discussions with Ralph that his father had set high standards; standards that Ralph had always striven to reach and that, with his deployment as Sub-lieutenant on HMS *Merlin*, he had finally met. Now it looked as if it might all crumble away. Helen Kinross was, he concluded, entitled to know that. 'Yes,' he replied. 'He could go to prison. It's a very serious offence he's charged with.' Then he softened. 'But that's not going to happen.'

'Helen!' The stentorian voice from the other end of the corridor made them both jump. They turned to see Helen's father standing with Commander Driscoll. 'Someone I want you to meet.' It wasn't a request, it was a command.

Helen threw Kavanagh an apologetic look. She didn't have to say anything for him to know that she

163

was apologizing for her father – the only way he could cope with the situation was to pretend it wasn't happening. And here he was, deep in conversation with Driscoll, the judge advocate who, if the board reached a verdict of guilty, would pass sentence on his son.

Kavanagh shook his head as Helen went back to her father. 'A difficult man' had been Ralph's only comment to him about the father he had so long tried to impress. Then he had gone on to describe the idyllic childhood he and Helen had spent at the Kinross country house in Northumberland, a childhood he had shared with Patrick Jones, the only son of the widow who helped Mrs Kinross up at the big house. His parents, Ralph had explained, had taken a shine to the young, well-mannered Patrick and his father had been delighted that he had evinced a passionate enthusiasm for all things naval. Yet the subtext of Ralph's talk about his childhood had been clear: it was all well and good for him to associate with someone of a different class while still a child, but not to renew that friendship later on. Especially in the Navy, where the two young men were divided by rank as well as social standing. Ralph's father, reflected Kavanagh, was probably rueing the day he had given his son a silver lighter and cigarette case as a present for passing his naval exams, especially as the former was now a key piece of evidence in the case against Ralph.

Making a mental note not to be too demanding of his own son, Kavanagh walked out of the base and headed for the nearby station. Eleanor, evidently, had decided not to wait for him. Odd, he thought, but she had been in an odd mood all day. Perhaps, on the train home, she would enlighten him as to why.

He didn't have to wait long. As he reached the

station platform, it was to find her scrabbling about on her knees, frantically trying to gather up all the papers from the briefcase she had just dropped. She was also, he was shocked to see, in floods of tears. 'Eleanor!'

'We've missed the train.' She made a token effort to brush away the tears. 'And . . .'

Kavanagh reached down to her. 'Eleanor. That's hardly a cause for tears. Come on. We'll have a cup of tea. And then you can tell me what's really wrong.'

In the station buffet, a few minutes later, Eleanor lit a cigarette with shaking hands. 'It's Neil.'

'Your Neil?'

'Not any more.' Taking a deep drag and then exhaling through pursed lips, she spat out the words. 'Not *my* Neil. *Her* Neil. I'm sorry, Jim, I swore I wouldn't, but . . . he's got someone else.' She looked up and Kavanagh saw the tears once again coursing down her cheeks. 'He left. Last night. He left me.'

'Good God! What . . . I mean . . . just out of the blue?'

'No. It's been . . . the past year.' Now that she had decided to share her sorrow, the floodgates were open. At once angry, devastated and relieved, Eleanor seemed unsure as to which emotion was gripping her most. 'Do you know how old she is?' she raged. 'Twenty-four. When we were saying cheese outside the bloody Chelsea Register, she was eight!'

Kavanagh didn't know how to react to her outburst. Reaching across the table to take her hand would be patronizing, and to say nothing would be cowardly. Floundering in unfamiliar waters, he tried a sympathetic yet, he hoped, sensible approach. 'Maybe it's just a . . . I mean, I don't know . . . men can . . . Perhaps,' he added, with more conviction, 'it's a mid-life thing . . .

crisis. Like you read in *Cosmopolitan*. You know, men have them.'

Eleanor couldn't help smiling. Imagine Jim reading *Cosmo*. 'You didn't have one,' she said.

This time Kavanagh did lean towards her. 'You think the thought hasn't crossed my mind? You hit that age, half-century coming up on the board, youngsters gaining on the rails.' He was silent a moment. 'A man can go one of two ways. He either buries himself in his work . . .'

'. . . or in the nearest bottle blonde.'

'He'll come back.'

But Eleanor recoiled in horror at that one. 'Please! I've got my pride, Jim.'

Kavanagh nodded, in fellow-feeling and in sorrow. 'Yes – but pride costs.' As he said the words, he found his thoughts straying to the Kinross family; a family which was, he felt, about to be torn apart by pride. For if he was correct in his surmise about what had really happened on the night of the fire, none of the Kinrosses would ever live it down.

CHAPTER TWELVE

Kavanagh and Eleanor Harker cross-examined MEM O'Brien the next day. Both barristers adopted the same line of questioning. Like Mills the day before, they grilled him about his relationship with Jones and Kinross, about the feud over money and about the bullying below decks. The picture that emerged was rather different from the one that Mills had painted the previous day. While it was clear that Lieutenant Kinross would have been better advised not to interfere below decks, it also became clear that his real quarrel was with Chief Evans, not with O'Brien. Furthermore, as O'Brien reluctantly admitted under questioning, Evans was well aware of the bullying against Jones.

Eleanor Harker elicited a further admission from O'Brien. Her client Patrick Jones had found out, long before the setting alight of O'Brien's bunk, that O'Brien was not responsible for either the latest spate of bullying or for the loss of the boots. He had apologized to O'Brien and – the three-hundred-pound debt apart – the two men had made up their differences. O'Brien, however, insisted that after Jones lost his v.g. conduct, he once again took against him, and that the fire in the bunk was his way of getting revenge. The atmosphere in court was, as Eleanor had hoped, one of scepticism. Something was not right about the whole story. She knew it; yet she couldn't put her finger on it. She could, however, do a good job of persuading the board of jurors that burning O'Brien's bunk was far too dangerous and extreme a method of exacting any revenge Jones might have felt. She squared her shoulders and fixed O'Brien with an impatient, irritated eye. 'The truth is, you know, that MEM Jones could have chosen any one of a hundred better ways to exact his revenge, if that was his wish, but as far as he was concerned the vendetta was over.'

O'Brien wasn't going to be cowed by a woman he perceived not only as arrogant but also ignorant of naval ways. As far as he was concerned, she had no business at this court martial. She didn't know how the system worked. She didn't know that Chief Evans ruled his engineering department with a rod of iron. She didn't know that he, O'Brien, was scared of Evans. And she didn't know that Evans had had a word or two in his ear before the court martial. 'You can't say what was going on in his head any more than me,' O'Brien retorted. 'It was his fingerprints on the lighter and on the fuel can and no amount of arguing's going to make them disappear. He had it in for me.'

'But it was MEM Jones who raised the alarm and tried to contain the fire, wasn't it? Hardly the actions of someone who'd "had it in" for you?' Eleanor, a mistress of irony, looked witheringly at the witness.

But Mills would have none of that. He jumped to his feet and addressed Driscoll. 'Sir, this witness can't say whether MEM Jones tried to contain the fire.'

'Any more than he can say he started it,' snapped Eleanor.

Driscoll silenced them both with an imperious wave of his hand. 'No. It's accepted from Able Seaman Dav-

168

ies's statement that Jones raised the alarm, Miss Harker, but what action he did or didn't take with regard to dealing with the fire is anyone's guess.'

Eleanor inclined her head towards him, with gritted teeth. It seemed obvious to her that, if her client had raised the alarm, he would hardly have started the fire. If only, she thought as she sat down, someone had seen Jones at the time the fire started. If only he hadn't been, as he had told her, alone in the showers. And if only she wasn't feeling so utterly wretched, she might be able to summon more enthusiasm for the case. Back in her seat, she turned and smiled at Patrick Jones. He tried, but failed, to smile back. He was shaking too much.

That afternoon, it became clear to the court that Chief Evans had been more than just the head mechanic on HMS *Merlin*. He had also been one of the chief culprits in the campaign against both Lieutenant Kinross and MEM Jones. That, however, didn't come out under questioning by Mills. As counsel for the prosecution, Mills had a different agenda, and the answers he elicited from Evans left the court believing that both Kinross and Jones, at the time of the fire, had been antagonistic towards O'Brien. Mills's final questions to Evans were about the movement of Lieutenant Kinross on the night of the fire. Evans answered that he had seen Kinross emerging in a hurry from the accommodation block at 8.25 p.m.

Kavanagh then rose to begin his cross-examination. Evans, he noted, was still looking relaxed and confident. Well, he thought with satisfaction, that's not going to last long.

It didn't. Evans did not enjoy his grilling. A small, wiry man, in his late forties, Kavanagh guessed, he carried with him an air of self-importance. Perhaps his demeanour was his way of compensating for the scarring on his face. Though obviously from old wounds, the scars looked permanent.

No beginner when it came to amateur psychology, Kavanagh reckoned that in reality Evans was riddled with self-doubt and ran such a tough ship, so to speak, in the engineering department to fend off any potential challenger. In short, he was a Little Hitler.

Kavanagh began deliberately with a series of questions that served to bolster Evans's ego. If Evans was surprised he didn't show it, but he did answer with a smirk that, yes, he had been in the Navy for twenty-one years, that he took great pride in running the marine engineering department. On the subject of bullying, he revealed that it was nothing more than a few practical jokes and that, if the target was a bit of a show-off, then it merely served to take them down a peg or two. Kavanagh raised an eyebrow at that one. 'Ah . . . a practice you encouraged?'

Evans didn't flinch. 'From long experience, these things are best left to the boys to sort out among themselves.'

The answer brought Kavanagh neatly to his next question – the involvement of Lieutenant Kinross in the below-decks disputes.

Evans demurred at the suggestion that he disliked Kinross and resented his interference. He claimed that he liked Kinross well enough and that he could excuse his interference on grounds of inexperience.

Kavanagh was not alone in eyeing Evans with more than a touch of scepticism. 'Well,' he said, as he picked up a piece of paper from the desk in front of him, 'you may have liked Lieutenant Kinross, but he had little good to say about you.'

'Sir?'

'In the "Remarks" section of your divisional officer's report for last year, Lieutenant Kinross wrote, "Chief Evans runs the marine engineering department as his own personal fiefdom. Indeed, it is difficult to find any part of the ship into which his influence does not reach. Any rating who questions the more eccentric aspects of his regime is bullied into compliance or ostracized by his shipmates, fearful of Chief Evans's displeasure." '

The expression on Evans's face gave some idea of what he looked like when he was 'displeased'. He looked even more thunderous when he was forced to admit that Kinross's report was the reason why he wasn't promoted to warrant officer, a promotion that would have extended his naval service by a further five years. As it was, he was due to retire in six months' time; and nothing could save him from that. 'So,' said Kavanagh, 'Lieutenant Kinross ruined your chance for a fitting end to an otherwise unblemished career and damaged your financial prospects. Just like that. With a stroke of his pen. And you're asking the court to accept you felt no bitterness towards him?'

'Well . . . I felt a little bit . . . slighted.'

'Slighted. I see.' Looking down at his notes, Kavanagh then proceeded to question Evans about the night of the fire. He established that most of the men had gone to a concert in town, leaving the base underpopulated. Evans hadn't gone, he explained, because he had promised his wife he would go to his quarters to watch a television programme with her.

'Yes. I see. So it was somewhat fortunate that you happened to be passing the accommodation block just as Lieutenant Kinross emerged from the fire escape, wasn't it?'

'It wasn't fortune, it was geography. The block was on my route from the chief's mess to the gates.' Evans looked genuinely puzzled. 'What are you saying? That I didn't see him?'

You know perfectly well what I'm saying, thought Kavanagh. 'I'm suggesting,' he said, for the benefit of the court, 'that you could've been mistaken about the time.'

'No.'

'It wasn't somewhat closer to eight o'clock? Before the fire was started. Say, five past?'

'No.'

'The fact is, the statement you made as to the time at which you saw Lieutenant Kinross was nothing more than a case of wish-fulfilment?'

'What do you mean?'

'Well, here was a young man you had tried to take under your wing and who had repaid your generosity of spirit with a stab in the back, who had cast a blight on your professional and personal life. Are you honestly telling the court that it didn't bother you?'

'I've already said—'

'The truth is,' interrupted Kavanagh, 'that you saw Lieutenant Kinross leave the accommodation block before rather than after the fire was started.'

'No, sir.'

Kavanagh then neatly changed tack, surprising both Evans and the rest of the court. 'The report in which Lieutenant Kinross condemned your way of dealing with the ratings: would his signature alone have been sufficient for that report to go forward, or would his assessment need to be agreed and countersigned by his superior officer?'

Evans accorded Kavanagh a look of intense dislike. 'It, er . . . it would've needed to be countersigned.'

Kavanagh smiled. 'So his findings were upheld, then?' Turning to Driscoll, he nodded and made to sit down. 'No further questions.'

Eleanor, however, had a lot of questions, all of them about Evans's treatment of MEM Jones. Unbeknown to the rest of the court, she had unearthed information that, while it didn't constitute proof of maltreatment, seemed too fanciful to have been invented by Jones. She referred back to a time when the ship had been in equatorial waters and Jones, during a fire drill, had been admitted to the sick-bay suffering from dehydration and heat exhaustion. Although initially taken aback at the mention of the episode, Evans quickly recovered and recalled that Jones had indeed had a 'bad turn' around then. Eleanor suggested that, as Jones had been wearing a heavy all-encompassing fearnaught suit and full breathing apparatus, he would have been hot, wouldn't he? And even hotter if he had been locked in the engine room by Evans.

Evans saw red. 'If you're asking me if I shut Jones in the engine room during that protocol, the answer is no. I didn't. And,' he added with venom, 'if he says I did, he's a lying little shitehawk.'

'Chief Evans!' Driscoll looked at the mechanic in horror. 'I won't tolerate that kind of language at these proceedings. Is that understood?'

Evans bowed his head. 'I apologize, sir, but such a suggestion—'

'Chief Evans,' snapped Eleanor, 'as you know full

well, there was only one person responsible for the practical jokes played upon MEM Jones. And that wasn't MEM O'Brien.' Evans made no reply. 'You resented, didn't you, that Jones had broken rank and gone to Lieutenant Kinross?'

'No . . . sir.' Evans, as Eleanor could tell by his challenging smirk, was egging her on to correct the title to 'madam'. She didn't bother. The look she gave him was far more effective. Evans capitulated. 'Jones,' he elaborated, 'had upset many of the hands. I tried to keep the lid on the situation, but such was the strength of the feeling against him—'

'Oh, I see. You had lost control of your department?' Kavanagh snickered to himself at this.

Evans winced. 'No! I hadn't lost control. But, well . . . a lot of the boys took their lead from O'Brien.'

'But MEM O'Brien has already told the court that he and Jones had called a truce. There had been a cessation of hostilities.'

Evans gazed at her. 'Some of the boys were still hacked off. I mean, I couldn't be everywhere at once. If things happened . . .'

'If things happened, Chief Evans, they did so because you wanted them to.' Eleanor fixed him with a piercing look. 'Not MEM O'Brien. You.'

Kavanagh was awed. Nothing in Eleanor's demeanour betrayed her inner hurt at her devastated personal life; she had let nothing get in the way of her relentless cross-examination of Chief Evans. It had been an impeccable performance. Yet, as she relaxed back into her chair, Kavanagh noticed the signs of strain, the shadows under her eyes and the lines that made her look at once weary and defiant. In spite of his unwillingness and, he knew, gaucheness when it came to discussing other people's personal problems, he made a mental note to do so on the train journey back to London.

Jeremy Aldermarten had no such reservations about the problems of others. And the more personal the better. Not, he told himself as he made his way down the hall at River Court, that he was nosey. *Concerned.* That was it.

Behind the closed door towards which Jeremy was heading, Julia was confiding in Alex Wilson. Alex was, of course, the only other female member of chambers but she and Julia had been acquaintances in their Oxford days. Since Alex had been taken on at River Court, she had become a firm friend.

'It was *awful*,' Julia wailed. 'I behaved so badly. I basically told the whole restaurant that he was a first-class shit and then stormed out. Poor David.'

Alex looked at her friend. She could imagine the scene. With her height, her glossy dark hair and finely chiselled bone structure, Julia always looked imposing. Sweeping in majestic fury out of a restaurant, she would have looked terrifying. Studying her more closely, though, Alex could confirm what she had been beginning to suspect: Julia was having second thoughts about David's proposal. 'And now, of course, you regret the whole thing,' she said.

'Well . . .' Julia looked up. She was smiling. 'It's not every day a six-foot-two cricketer with blond hair and a tan proposes, is it?'

'Proposes to whisk you off to Kenya, you mean.'

'They do have barristers in Kenya, you know,' said Julia, suddenly on the defensive.

Alex grinned. 'So have you talked to Peter about it?'

'He'll implode,' Julia replied with a grimace. 'It was only Jim's lobbying that got me into River Court in the first place. D'you know, Peter gave me five years tops.'

'Well, you're past that.'

Julia reflected on the five and a bit years she had spent in chambers. 'Not by much.' Then, uncharacteristically indecisive, she appealed to Alex. 'I'll set the cause back twenty years in River Court if I throw in the towel now.'

'But if you love him . . .'

'Yeah. There's the rub. I do love him . . . Oh, bugger!' Julia's last words were addressed to the telephone – now ringing, she suspected, with an irate solicitor on the other end. She snatched the receiver and barked a not even remotely friendly, 'Hello.' Her next words brought a smile to Alex's lips, but a thin, set line to her own. 'Look, David, I told you not to call me, right?'

Whatever David's response was, Alex couldn't hear it.

'I'm sorry, but that's it.' The picture of misery, Julia slammed down the phone.

And then Jeremy popped his head round the door. 'Julia, I wondered—'

'Not now, Jeremy. Go away.'

But Jeremy stayed where he was. He looked from Julia to Alex and then back again. 'Something the matter?' he enquired with polite solicitude.

'Go away!' screamed Julia. 'Men! You're all bastards!'

Jeremy recoiled. 'Look, I—'

'Go away!'

Even Jeremy sensed that his presence was not, perhaps, what Julia wanted. He shut the door and scuttled off down the corridor. One of the junior clerks button-holed him on the way.

'Miss Piper in?'

'Wouldn't go in there if I were you. Bit uppity.' Jeremy gave the clerk a knowing, conspiratorial look. 'Got the painters in, I expect.'

While Jeremy failed quite spectacularly in his mission to persuade Julia to share her troubles, Kavanagh, in Portsmouth, had no such difficulties with Eleanor – especially after their train to London was cancelled.

'Cancelled?' She was aghast.

The guard, wary of her after her previous perform-ance on what he regarded as his territory, pointed silently to the sign he had just erected.

'*Suspended?* All of them? Don't be ridiculous.' Eyes blazing, chin set, Eleanor was spoiling for a fight.

Kavanagh stepped forward. 'What's up?' he asked the guard.

Hoping that Kavanagh might at least be sane, the man said, 'Fire outside Petersfield.'

'Damn. So when'll the next one to London be?'

'Eleven tonight?'

'*What?*'

'Come on, Eleanor.' Kavanagh grabbed her arm with more force than was strictly necessary. 'Hotel time.'

'Hotel? *Here?*'

'Well, what else do you suggest? A park bench?'

They took a taxi. 'Where to?' asked the driver.

Kavanagh looked at his companion. 'Nearest good hotel.'

Neither passenger noticed the driver's broad grin in

the rear-view mirror as he turned the ignition and set the ancient vehicle rattling into motion.

'Who was it said, "Better to travel in hope than to arrive"?'

'Dunno, but he obviously hadn't arrived here or he would have included a few swear words. *Look* at it!'

Kavanagh looked. Whether it had been the sheer perversity of their driver or just bad luck, they had ended up at an establishment called the Mirabar Hotel. 'Thirty pounds a night,' the splendidly rouged crone at the reception desk had announced with pride. Then she looked closely at them and grinned. 'Or a fiver by the hour?'

They took two rooms. For the night. And now they were surveying Eleanor's. Kavanagh tried to dredge up something positive to say about it. 'At least,' he tried, 'you've got a view.'

Eleanor stared out of the grimy window. The sea was just visible – if you happened to be a contortionist. 'That, my dear, is not a view, it's a . . . Oh, sod it!' Kavanagh saw that, again, she was on the verge of tears.

He reached out and touched her lightly. 'Come on, I'll buy you some fish and chips.'

Eleanor chuckled unwillingly. 'It just gets better and better, doesn't it?' But the fish – eaten as they sat on the deserted seafront – was about as palatable as their rooms and the chips were infinitely more disgusting. Dispirited, they went back to the hotel where Eleanor surprised Kavanagh by diving into her bag and extracting a half-empty bottle of whiskey. As she rinsed out the toothglasses by the washbasin ('Basins in the rooms. Bathroom's down the hall. Third left,' had been the crone's final words of welcome), Kavanagh gestured towards the bottle. 'This an old habit or a new one?'

Eleanor was drying the glasses on a hand-towel. 'It helps.'

'Does it help MEM Jones?'

'Lock him up and throw away the key, for all I care.'

'You don't really mean that,' replied Kavanagh, as he watched her pour two huge measures.

'No, of course I don't.' Then she paused. 'D'you think they did it?'

'I don't think mine did, no. Yours?'

Eleanor didn't reply immediately. As was always the case, whether prosecuting or defending, barristers never asked their clients whether they were guilty or not guilty, only what they were going to plead. 'No,' she said, eventually. 'I don't think he'd be capable of doing it. Too nervy. But he's certainly keeping something from me,' she added with conviction.

'Don't they all.'

But Eleanor had clearly had enough of barristering for one day. She raised her glass in a salute. 'Oh, well . . . cheers! 'Scuse the glass – servants' night off.' Her humour, Kavanagh saw with a sudden stab of deep sorrow, was forced – and she couldn't sustain it. 'What a waste,' she added, as she stared, unseeing, at the bare wall. 'Sixteen years.' She took a deep slug of whisky. 'I wanted kids, you know.'

'No, I—'

'It was Neil.' Barely aware of Kavanagh's presence, Eleanor continued to stare straight ahead. ' "When we've moved" or "Once I've got the business up and running". And I was working, of course, so—'

'It's not too late . . .'

Aware again of her old friend, Eleanor smiled in

gratitude. 'That's very sweet, but who'd take me on now? Look at me. Bleary-eyed old baggage.' She laughed with – Kavanagh was pleased to note – a trace of genuine humour. 'Half a cat, half a mortgage . . . half a life. But,' she added with ferocity, 'I've still got far more to offer a chap than that – that tart.'

Kavanagh grinned over the rim of his glass. 'Attagirl.'

'I've seen her, you know.' Eleanor was incredulous. 'And all I can say, my dear, is that if he's happy to trade wit, warmth and companionship for a white-stilettoed little scrubber with bad skin and the conversation of Forrest Gump, that's his look-out.'

Kavanagh laughed. 'I think, Eleanor, you're going to be okay.'

'Am I?'

'Yes.' Standing up, Kavanagh drained his glass. 'I can detect the old Eleanor already resurfacing. Thanks for the drink,' he said. 'I'd better go on to my suite. Early start.'

Eleanor studied him. 'You . . . er, you don't have to. Go, I mean.' She took a deep breath. 'You can stay. If you want . . .' She stopped. Kavanagh was staring at her with an expression she had never seen before. She had difficulty reading it.

Then he smiled.

CHAPTER THIRTEEN

The case for the prosecution ended the next morning with a statement from the investigator of the arson attack. As the evidence it contained was not disputed by either Kavanagh or Eleanor, the statement was read out by Mills. It said that Ralph Kinross's silver Dunhill lighter, found on the fire escape and identifiable by the initials engraved on it, was confirmed by the forensic fingerprint laboratory as bearing the fingerprints of both Lieutenant Kinross and MEM Jones. As the statement was read out, Kavanagh allowed his thoughts to wander. The lighter, he mused. There was something Kinross had told him about the lighter that didn't add up; something he wasn't prepared to divulge. And Kavanagh had no doubt that Mills would quiz Kinross very closely about that lighter.

Lieutenant Ralph Kinross was called to the witness box immediately after Mills concluded his statement. He walked stiffly, aware that all eyes were on him – and all too aware that his full-dress uniform was missing two things: his cap and his sword. The latter was still on the sword table at the front of the court. Its absence was a brutal reminder of the accusation against him.

Kinross looked only at Kavanagh as he was taken through his evidence-in-chief. Yet Patrick Jones sat in the corner of his field of vision. He looked dreadful.

As if he already had a noose around his neck. And every time Kinross opened his mouth to reply to Kavanagh's questions, Jones's terror increased. Kinross, on the other hand, conducted himself in the manner in which he had been trained. Every inch the officer, he was immaculately well groomed and scrupulously polite – the sort of young man of which his father should have been proud. Yet his father was sitting stone-faced at the back of the room, and Kinross didn't look at him. Whatever the outcome of the court martial, Kinross suspected that his father would never speak to him again. As he faced Kavanagh, he knew that there was only one way to salvage anything from this fiasco. It would involve sacrifice. It would mean doing something that would take everyone in court by complete surprise. Even, he thought with sadness, James Kavanagh.

With no idea what was passing through his client's mind, Kavanagh continued with his friendly questions. He established for the court that, while on HMS *Merlin*, Lieutenant Kinross hadn't been concerned about the money owed to MEM Jones. His primary motive for intervention below decks had been to stop the practical jokes because, he emphasized, he saw them as a risk to the morale of the ship. As to why he went to O'Brien rather than to Chief Evans, he claimed that the latter had, in fact, been the instigator of the so-called jokes.

'So why,' enquired Kavanagh, 'didn't you challenge Chief Evans directly?'

'He would have denied any part in it. And, anyway, I had no hard proof.'

'I see. How sympathetic was O'Brien to your request?'

'He was not prepared to stand up against Chief Evans.'

'How did you feel about that?'

Kinross shrugged. 'I couldn't blame him – and I certainly didn't bear him any ill will because of it.'

Pre-empting, he hoped, a later question from Mills, Kavanagh then asked Kinross why he hadn't voiced his fears to Commander Pilgrim.

'I did, eventually, after the fight between Jones and O'Brien.' From looking inscrutable, Kinross suddenly looked bitter. 'However, at that time I would have been a lone voice, such was the power wielded by Chief Evans. No one would have dared speak out against him.'

Kavanagh reckoned that Evans had performed badly enough in the witness box for Kinross's statement to ring true with the board. Then he proceeded to ask him about the night in question, about why he had gone to Jones's quarters in the first place.

'I had promised to lend MEM Jones a book. A chronicle of naval battles.'

'What happened when you arrived there?'

'Jones was not in his quarters. I thought he must have gone ashore with the rest of the men. I put the book on his locker and left.'

'What time was that?'

'Less than five minutes after I'd arrived. It was just after 2000.'

Kavanagh paused to let that sink in. 'And how did you leave? Via the lift, or . . . ?'

'No. I took the fire-exit stairs. I'd had to wait an age for a lift when I arrived. I thought it would be quicker to take the stairs.' As Kinross answered the question, he noticed that Mills, partly hidden by Kavanagh, was jotting something down in his notes.

'So,' continued Kavanagh, 'what time would it have been when you left the accommodation block?'

'No later than 2005.'

Again Kavanagh paused. Then he asked his client what he had seen when he emerged from the ground-floor fire exit. 'I saw Chief Evans.'

Kavanagh asked the question then that had been worrying him. He knew the answer Kinross would give. The only problem was, he didn't believe it. 'Lieutenant Kinross,' he began, 'can you tell the court now, please, about your lighter?'

Kinross smiled. 'Well, that's quite simple. I had lost it in a bar earlier in the week.'

'So how do you think it came to be found on the seventh-floor fire-escape landing?'

'I can only imagine,' replied Kinross strongly, 'that someone left it there to implicate me in the arson attack.'

That, Kavanagh thought, was true. He had no doubts on that score. It had been Kinross's response to his earlier question that had set the alarm bells ringing in his mind. Yet as he sat down, he felt an unexpected surge of confidence. If the decision of the board rested on Evans's testimony versus that of Kinross, he knew they would believe the latter. And it wouldn't be because of rank. It would be because, after his performance in the witness box, everyone in the court suspected that Chief Evans was both manipulative and dishonest.

The court adjourned for lunch. If either Driscoll or Mills noticed a tension between Kavanagh and Harker, they chose to ignore it. Eleanor, for her part, tried to ignore Kavanagh. Seating herself as far away as possible from him, she toyed with her food as the others engaged in enthusiastic talk about ships. Kavanagh, of course, was mad about boats and to be at Portsmouth naval base was, for him, a terrific thrill. Eleanor felt differently about it. Not only did she perceive the Navy as archaic and sexist, but she had been miserable since she arrived in Portsmouth. After the night at the Mira-bar Hotel, she was feeling even more wretched. What on earth had possessed her? she wondered. Loneliness and unhappiness, the need for warmth and human comfort, she supposed. But why on earth hadn't she been able to exercise some self-control? Where would her relationship with Kavanagh go now? Would he tell Lizzie? Lizzie, she suspected, was already less than enthusiastic about her: this would put the icing on the cake in that department.

Eleanor stole a look at Kavanagh. What was he thinking? She had managed to avoid any conversation with him that morning. She had failed to materialize at breakfast and had taken a separate taxi to the naval base. Yet she would have to say *something*. Kavanagh wouldn't.

He was a man. All men were cowards. Bastards.

'Something on your mind, Miss Harker?' Jolted out of her reverie, Eleanor whirled round to find Driscoll eyeing her with amusement.

She flushed and said the first thing that came into her mind. 'Oh . . . I'm just thinking, you know. About my client.'

'Mmm.' Driscoll looked more serious. 'Yes. Very nervous, isn't he?'

Eleanor glared haughtily. 'Most people are, on their first time in court. I'm sure he'll be fine once he gets into the witness box.' But Driscoll's words stayed with her as she poked at the slice of pork on her plate.

MEM Patrick Jones had been getting more nervous by the minute. Much more nervous than was normal. It worried her greatly. But it did have the beneficial effect of taking her mind off the events of last night.

After lunch Jones's solicitor, Burrell, who was almost as agitated as his client, took Eleanor aside. 'I've just been to see him, Miss Harker. He's a wreck.' He wrinkled his nose. 'He's been throwing up. I've never seen anyone so petrified. He's like a rabbit in the headlights at the prospect of giving evidence.'

Eleanor frowned. 'Damn! But I've *got* to put him in the box. God knows I don't want to, but without it we haven't a cat in hell's.' Suddenly galvanized into action, Eleanor handed the solicitor her case. 'Here. You'll find half a bottle of hooch in this. Get him coffee – strong, black, sweet – and add about three fingers. No more. I'll talk to the judge advocate. I'll tell him I need to take fresh instruction. Go on, then!' she urged, as Burrell gaped at her.

He went, and Eleanor steeled herself to tackle Driscoll on the subject of delaying the afternoon's proceedings.

Back in judge advocate mode, Driscoll agreed without hesitation and Eleanor went off to the cell to try to boost Jones's confidence.

It was Ralph Kinross, standing chain-smoking beside his barrister and his solicitor, who greeted the news of the delay with alarm. As Driscoll walked off, he turned to his solicitor. 'A conference with Miss Harker? Why now?'

Harris replied, 'Touch of the jitters, most likely. Nothing for you to worry about. It's his problem.'

But Kinross didn't see it that way. 'I don't think there's any need to be so gleeful about it, Mr Harris. We're both in this together.'

'No.' Kavanagh wished Kinross would stop being so infuriatingly solicitous about Jones. 'You're not in this together. You'd left the accommodation block by 20.05. You can't say what Jones got up to after that.'

'But he discovered the fire! He raised the alarm and tried to put the damn thing out.'

Kavanagh was exasperated. 'Yes, but we only have his word for it.'

Kinross shook his head. 'No. I know him. He's a . . . he's a bad liar.'

'So long as he doesn't say anything which damages our defence, I don't care how bad a liar he is.'

'Mr Kavanagh's right.' Harris was also irritated at Kinross's stance. 'It's *you* we're concerned with. If we're being absolutely honest about it, the best thing would be for Mills to crack him in cross-examination. As long as it's clear you weren't involved, that'll be it.'

Kinross was appalled. 'How d'you mean, "that'll be it"?'

'If he makes some admission,' explained Kavanagh, 'something that leaves no uncertainty as to his own guilt while exonerating you beyond reasonable doubt, if Mills gets him to do that, then we're home.'

'You mean you believe MEM Jones is guilty?' Anxiety was written all over the lieutenant's features.

Kavanagh regarded his client. 'I didn't say that. I said Mills might crack him and he may make an admission.'

'But – but – he can't!'

Both Harris and Kavanagh were astonished. Neither was quite sure what to say. And anyway, Kinross was seemingly oblivious of them. He was staring into the distance, wearing an expression of utter horror.

*

In the detention block, Eleanor Harker was likewise trying to calm her client. And, boy, she thought as she looked at him lighting one cigarette from the butt of the last, does he need calming. The Irish whiskey hadn't had any effect. He seemed to have lost it completely, and Eleanor was having an uphill job trying to talk him through his story again.

'I *did* threaten O'Brien,' he wailed. Then he looked imploringly at Eleanor. 'But it was ... heat of the moment. I was very upset at losing my v.g. conduct. I want to get on in the Service and that continued good grading would've been another tick in the box.'

'No doubt, but it's vitally important you get across to the court that you'd no axe to grind with O'Brien. Remember, he has already admitted that the old feud was over.'

Something in her tone made Jones realize that he was making life difficult for his barrister. He attempted to pull himself together. 'Look, I'm sorry. I woke up this morning ... and, well, it's just ... I can't think straight.'

He was a decent person, Eleanor thought. A good friend. Bugger the armed services, she thought savagely. In what other walk of life would every conceivable tactic be used to destroy a boyhood friendship? That was ultimately what this was about. 'That's all right,' she said. 'It's perfectly normal to be nervous, but you're going to be fine. I promise you. I wouldn't let you go into the box if I didn't have every confidence you'd do well.' Christ, she thought. May God strike me down in flames. 'Now, slowly, in your own time, just take me through the events on the evening of the seventh.'

Jones took a deep breath. 'I ... well, I wasn't very popular with the other lads, so I thought it best all round if I gave it a miss – the run-ashore, I mean. I'd just done my weights. Then I thought I'd grab a shower. I suppose I went off about 1945.'

Eleanor nodded. So far so good. 'How busy were the showers at that time of the evening?'

'There was nobody about. It was very quiet.' To Eleanor's mild amusement, Jones lowered his voice in keeping with the atmosphere he was recalling. 'S'pose I'd been in the showers 'bout half an hour. Washing, drying my hair and that. Then I went back to my quarters about 2015. I saw Lieutenant Kinross'd left me a book he'd promised to lend me. I read that for about ten minutes.' Then he looked into Eleanor's eyes. 'And then I smelt smoke. From the next landing. So I went and had a look . . . and when I saw what'd happened, I raised the alarm and tried to contain the fire.'

Eleanor appeared ready to applaud. 'I can't see what you're worried about,' she said. 'Just tell the court what you've told me and you'll be fine.'

But Jones lit yet another cigarette with shaking hands and said, totally expressionless, 'With respect, ma'am, you're not suggesting that what I've told you isn't the truth?'

Eleanor didn't reply.

'Look . . . er, about last night.'

They were making their way into court and Eleanor, feeling that she had quite enough to cope with on the professional front, had decided to gird her loins and tackle Kavanagh about the other problem that had been plaguing her all morning.

Kavanagh stopped in his tracks and bestowed on

Eleanor a beaming smile. 'It's okay. I was ... very flattered.'

Eleanor nearly fainted. Hoping Kavanagh didn't notice, she let out a huge sigh of relief. 'I'm really sorry. I... I didn't mean to put you on the spot.'

'It's all right, Eleanor. Really.'

Eleanor pushed back her hair. 'But, I mean, you of all people. I'm not usually such an old slapper,' she added with a grin.

'Eleanor, we go back more years than I care to remember. You're one of my oldest, dearest, most valued friends.' Then he, too, grinned. 'And if you can't proposition your friends, who can you proposition?'

His words struck a chord with Eleanor: a memory of time wasted. She felt a tinge of regret. 'D'you know, since I took silk, they've been queuing round the block. And I was completely faithful to Neil. Always. Shows what a silly cow I was.'

'No. That's not so. Some things have to count,' Kavanagh said, as if to himself. 'They have to. Otherwise ... what's any of it for? Just because he's a faithless idiot whose brain's in his trousers, that doesn't diminish your constancy.'

Where, thought Eleanor, would she be without Jim? Talk of constancy: he had always been one of her most loyal friends. Then, this time with amusement, she again recalled the previous evening. 'You're the only one of my menfriends who's never tried to get me into bed.'

But Kavanagh looked solemn. 'Bed is easy,' he said. 'Any fool can manage bed. Lovers – good, bad, indifferent – come and go ... but friends?'

Eleanor was pleased. 'My dear, while you breathe, the age of chivalry is not yet past.'

Kavanagh pointed to his chest. 'Guilty as charged.' Then, as they walked in companionable silence into court, he remembered why they were here. They were here for two men who, because they were friends, were determined to stick by each other, come what might. The age of chivalry was indeed not yet past.

'Lieutenant Kinross, when you eventually raised the issue of the practical jokes and the bullying with Commander Pilgrim, what was his response?'

Ralph Kinross hadn't expected to enjoy his cross-examination by Mills, but it was proving even more of a trial than he had anticipated. Each question seemed specifically designed to cast doubt on his story, his integrity and his ability. Then, consoling himself with the knowledge that Mills was only doing his job, he took a deep breath and faced the court – but not his father. 'Commander Pilgrim said . . . he said he would talk to my appointer and get me relieved early.'

'Yes. You were to be relieved early. Hardly a ringing endorsement of your abilities, was it?'

Kinross answered, 'My ability was not in question.'

'Then why should Commander Pilgrim want you landed from his ship?'

'He felt by interceding on Jones's behalf I had somehow compromised my authority.'

'Ah.' Mills consulted the papers in front of him. 'His impression was that you were more concerned with being well thought of below decks than with the proper execution of your duties.'

'He was mistaken.'

'Was he? Well, let's look at that. You were plainly unable to divorce your friendship with Jones from your right and proper duty.'

'My right and proper duty,' replied Kinross, with true officer's bearing, 'was to the ship's company. If anyone of Chief Evans's department had come to me with a just complaint, I should have listened and acted accordingly.'

'Of course.' Mills smiled. The smile carried a hint of disbelief. 'Let's move forward to the evening in question and the entertainment ashore. This was a regular excursion which took place every other Tuesday?'

'Yes.'

'And you were involved with organizing the transport.'

'Yes.'

'What did that involve exactly? Booking coaches – that sort of thing? Making sure no stragglers were left behind?'

Where the hell is this leading? thought Kavanagh as he looked at Mills. Not, he hoped, into uncharted waters.

Kinross, however, didn't seem to mind the seemingly irrelevant questions. 'Yes. That sort of thing.'

'Yes. Now, this lighter of yours. A present from Vice-Admiral Kinross, I understand?'

Unseen by anyone else, Kavanagh gripped his pen tightly in both hands.

Kinross put a hand to his throat in a defensive gesture. 'From my father, yes,' he replied. 'For passing my naval exams.'

Mills went on, 'So it's of considerable sentimental value, then?'

Again the hand to the throat. 'Some, yes.'

'What action did you take to recover it?' The question had a new, harder edge to it.

'How do you mean?'

Mills sighed. 'Well, you've told the court you lost it in a bar earlier in the week in question. Did you go back to the bar where you lost it – ask if it had been handed in?'

Kinross lowered his eyes. 'No.'

'Did you ask after it on the base?'

'No.'

'In the wardroom?'

'No.'

'Put a notice on the noticeboard offering a reward?'

'No.'

'No.' Mills paused to let the information register. 'So, here we have a lighter of some sentimental value, a present from your father, no less, and you make absolutely no attempt to recover it.' Mills curled his lip. 'None, Lieutenant Kinross?'

'No.'

The silence in the court was everything Mills could have hoped for. He wondered what on earth Vice-Admiral Kinross was thinking. He suspected he knew. 'No,' he repeated with emphasis. 'You had not "lost" it in any bar. The truth is, you dropped your lighter on the stairs in your hurry to put distance between yourself and the fire.'

'That is incorrect.'

'Remind the court, will you, why it was you took the fire-escape stairs.'

'Because I'd had to wait an age for the lift when I first arrived.'

'Indeed. For about how long had you waited?'

'Four, five minutes.'

'As long as that?' Mills shot the young lieutenant a surprised look. Then, like lightning, he went back to his earlier line of questioning. 'What time did the last of your coaches leave for the entertainment?'

'Er . . . by 1955.'

'So, by 2000 when Able Seaman Davies saw you arrive, the accommodation block was all but deserted. That's right, isn't it?'

Still not realizing where this was leading, Kinross looked angry. 'Yes,' he replied.

'Yes. You see, a long wait for a lift when the block was full would be understandable.' Mills spotted, at last, alarm on Kinross's face. 'But with it empty?' He shook his head. 'There was no long wait. You left via the fire-escape stairs because you didn't want to be seen quitting the scene of your crime.'

'No.' Kinross's alarm had disappeared. His denial was adamant. But Mills hadn't finished with the lighter. 'Perhaps you can tell the court how it is that Jones's fingerprints were found on your lighter?'

'I can offer no explanation other than that I had handed my lighter to Jones on a previous occasion so that he could light a cigarette.'

'And when would that have been?'

'I don't know.' There was a flicker of something more than uncertainty in Kinross's eyes. 'Around . . . around . . . well, it would've been before I lost the lighter, obviously.'

'Obviously.' Mills's voice was heavy with sarcasm. 'Are you a heavy smoker, Lieutenant?'

'Twenty a day. Something like that.'

'So, you're asking the court to accept that Jones's fingerprints remained intact on that lighter – clear and unsmudged – when it would have been in use perhaps twenty times a day? Is that right?'

'Yes.'

Mills hadn't finished. 'Let me suggest a much simpler explanation. Jones's fingerprints were on your lighter, Lieutenant Kinross, because he had used it to set fire to O'Brien's bunk.'

Kinross stared straight into Mills's disbelieving eyes. 'No.' Again his tone was adamant, confident.

'Your attack,' continued Mills, 'on Chief Evans's good character is nothing more than an attempt to discredit his evidence.'

'No.'

'The only part Chief Evans played in this whole affair was that he happened to see you leave the building.'

'No.'

'As far as you were concerned, the real and only villain was O'Brien. To your mind, he was responsible not only for Jones losing his v.g. conduct rating, but for Commander Pilgrim requesting your transfer. That's right, isn't it?'

'That is not the case.'

'You saw O'Brien as the author of your collective misfortune. And, as such, you and Jones decided to revenge yourselves upon him.'

'No.'

If Mills was slightly disconcerted by Kinross's repeated, positive and convincing denials, he made a good job of hiding it. Then he went back to one of the areas of which Kinross appeared not quite so sure.

'You involved yourself in transporting the men into town for one reason and one reason only. You wanted to know when the coast was clear. You waited for the men to leave and then went across to the accommodation block to tell Jones. How was it? Did you keep watch while Jones set the fire?'

'No!' Again the positive denial. 'I told you. He was in the showers.'

'In the showers?' This was better than Mills had hoped. 'No. That is not what you told the court during your evidence-in-chief. You said you believed Jones had gone ashore with the rest of the men. Now, why would you think that if you were in charge of the transport?'

Suddenly, the atmosphere was electric. Via a convoluted route, Mills had got Kinross exactly where he wanted him: paralysed with indecision. Kavanagh and Eleanor, both sensing danger, looked at the young officer and saw him fighting for an answer. When it came, it was extremely lame. 'I . . . I didn't know where he was . . .'

'But you've just said he was in the showers.'

Kinross reddened. 'You see, he was meant to go into town with the others . . . I remember . . . but when I took – took the book across to him and he wasn't there—'

'So why do you now say you thought he was in the showers?'

Thinking on his feet, Kinross blurted out a reason. 'I . . . I had a look around and I saw him going into the showers.'

Mills greeted that remark with silence; a silence that permeated through the court and drifted back to Kinross, hammering home the complete inplausibility of his statement. And then Mills reminded the hapless lieutenant that he'd made no mention of seeing Jones go to the showers when he was first interviewed about the incident.

'No. It slipped my mind.'

'Yes. Well, that aside, if you saw him on his way to the showers, you could've given him the book then, couldn't you? Your chronicle of naval battles. Why didn't you do just that?'

All traces of the confident young officer had vanished. There was a sheen on his forehead, a wild look in his eyes and, Kavanagh noted with horror, he had begun to shake. The headlights had found a different rabbit.

Then Mills looked up at the accused with a curious mixture of scorn and pity. 'It doesn't add up, does it?'

'I, er . . . I, well . . . no.' Kinross looked as if he was about to try one last valiant attempt to explain – and then gave up. He let his shoulders slump and stared at Mills through dead eyes. 'I saw the lighter fuel on top of Jones's locker. I just saw it when I went to drop off the book and, I don't know . . . All I could see was O'Brien's stupid, leering face.' He saw Kavanagh's face. It was intelligent, furious – and disbelieving. Kinross forced himself to continue. 'I just wanted to pay him back for getting me landed. I only meant it to be his bunk . . . pictures of his kid, something to hurt him, but it got out of control and I panicked . . .'

'Lieutenant Kinross.' Mills's voice was lower, quieter than it had been all day. A whisper would have been enough to penetrate the silence. 'Are you saying you set fire to O'Brien's bunk alone?'

Kavanagh could have sworn he saw a smile playing at Kinross's lips. 'Yes,' he said. 'I thought about warning Jones but then he would've seen me. I'm sorry.' The last words were addressed to the man that Kinross had

197

thus far studiedly ignored: the man sitting ramrod straight in the public gallery, staring at his son through eyes that, for the first time in his life, were wet with tears.

CHAPTER FOURTEEN

'I'm sorry, I was wrong to mislead you.' Back in the detention block, Kinross refused to meet Kavanagh's eye. Exhausted by his ordeal, he sat slumped on his bunk, smoking and staring into space. 'I acted foolishly. It's only proper that I bear the consequences.' Finally he looked up. His eyes were moist. 'Just sorry to have dragged Jones into it. Service means everything to him.'

Still reeling with shock from his client's confession, Kavanagh was further stunned by the irony of Kinross's last statement. 'It's not completely without meaning for you,' he said drily. 'What on earth went wrong? We had a good case. What happened?'

Kinross put his head in his hands. 'There's nothing to be gained from raking it over. Please.'

But Kavanagh was undeterred. The whole thing was incomprehensible to him. 'But we'd been through it all. What was different about today? We were so close to . . .' He was puzzled: they *had* been close. So close.

'There was only Jones's evidence to be heard and . . .' And then it clicked. He cast his mind back to Kinross's increasing alarm about Jones's nerves, about his terror at being in the witness box. *I know him. He's a bad liar.*

When Kavanagh spoke again, his voice was quiet, soft with understanding and sympathy. 'You didn't want him to go into the box, did you? Why?' he prodded, although he knew the answer. 'What would he have said?'

The look Kinross gave him confirmed his suspicions. Jones, shaking with nerves, would have confessed to something far worse, in the eyes of the Navy, than arson.

'When you went to the accommodation block,' continued Kavanagh, 'it wasn't to take a book to him, was it? You were . . . together. When the fire started, you were together.'

Kinross felt a weight fall from his shoulders. Suddenly it was a relief to be able to tell someone; to be able to share the secret. 'I couldn't let him go up against Mills – you do understand that? You saw the state he was in. He's . . . he's a bad liar.' Kinross looked up. Kavanagh recognized several emotions in that look. Relief. Shame. Love recalled. Then, with apparent difficulty, Kinross said, 'If he'd admitted that at the time the fire started he was in my arms—'

'But you had a defence!'

'You can't defend the indefensible,' admonished Kinross. 'In the eyes of some there are worse things than arson.'

But Kavanagh was a barrister, not a naval officer. He stared at the young man in front of him: a man who had knowingly ruined his career to hide a crime that, in Kavanagh's eyes, wasn't a crime at all. 'In certain knowledge of the consequences,' he said, 'rather than reveal you were lovers, you took full blame for a crime neither of you had any part in? Surely the truth—'

'The truth would have meant his career as well as mine.'

As Kavanagh eyed his client with something akin to

admiration, the words of the sentence passed on him rang through his ears.

'*The Court*,' Driscoll had read, '*adjudges the said Ralph Edmund Gordon Kinross to be imprisoned for the term of four years, to be dismissed from Her Majesty's Service, to be put under stoppages of pay until he has made good the sum of three thousand pounds and to suffer the consequential penalties involved.*' And perhaps the worst of those penalties, recalled Kavanagh, had come in the words of Captain Tredinnick, the president of the board. He had eyed Kinross with disgust, accused him of knowingly involving MEM Jones in something of which he was innocent and of being a disgrace to the entire Royal Navy – and to his family. That family, Kavanagh remembered, hadn't waited around to commiserate with their son. Vice-Admiral Kinross had hauled his wife and daughter away from the court, away from the naval base, without so much as a word. He had, by his actions, washed his hands of him.

Kavanagh gazed at the man on the bunk. Hadn't he made a greater sacrifice than most men would ever dream of making? Hadn't he done something that was, in its own way, more honourable than fighting any naval battle? And what had he got out of it? Nothing except disgrace and ruin. Yet there was one man, he supposed, who would be eternally grateful. Kavanagh thought of MEM Jones, now free to pursue the career that meant so much to him. 'Greater love?' he asked Kinross.

'Yeah. Something like that.' Embarrassed, Kinross looked away.

'So who did it?'

'Evans, of course.'

Eleanor sipped her ruinously expensive British Rail gin and tonic. 'You don't *know* that, Jim.'

'I do. He all but told me.' Kavanagh thought back to his last conversation before leaving Portsmouth. Chief Evans had had the effrontery to approach him as he left the base and to taunt him with a half-mocking, 'You can't win 'em all, sir.'

It was one of the few times in his life that Kavanagh had felt hatred for another human being. 'I think,' he replied, without showing his emotion, 'we know who set that fire, Mr Evans.'

'Do we?' Evans was all polite smiles.

'Oh, yes. You see, someone else had been keeping an eye on those fortnightly runs ashore; watching, planning, waiting his moment. He knew that once the accommodation block was empty, Kinross would go to see Jones. And he knew why.'

'Knew a lot, this chap.' But Evans wasn't quite so cocky now.

'He knew Kinross's lighter wasn't lost. He knew that Kinross had given it to Jones as a gift, a token. So that evening, while they were . . . elsewhere . . . he stole the lighter and fuel from Jones's quarters. Having started the fire, he left enough incriminating evidence for the regulators to find. Then he stood outside, waiting to chance upon Kinross leaving the scene of the crime.' Kavanagh recognized the look Evans was giving him. It was that of a criminal relishing tales of his cleverness, of the perfect crime that no one could ever pin on him.

'Why,' said Evans, with a smug leer, 'would *someone* do that?'

'Because he wanted Jones. Physically. For his own gratification.' Kavanagh's eyes bored into those of the chief mechanic. Suddenly Evans didn't want to hear any more. He had never dreamed that the barrister would arrive at that conclusion. He had thought his secret safe.

'And,' continued Kavanagh, 'for a man used to being obeyed, that was more than you could stomach. That's what the bullying was about. Not money. Not breaking rank. Jealousy.' His lip curled with distaste. 'You were jealous of Jones's relationship with Kinross. And to think that you are supposed to stand for honour, courage and decency,' he spat. 'You have none of those.'

At that, and much to Kavanagh's surprise, Evans erupted into a vicious diatribe against 'posh gits' like Kinross; against the Royal Navy, against barristers, and against life itself. Then he held up his hands and pointed to his face. 'Take a good look!' he screamed. 'My face. My hands. You dare say I've no honour. These scars are my honour.' Abandoning all pretence at denying Kavanagh's latter allegations, he glared at the barrister. 'I had a friend once. A sub-lieutenant. We were good pals. Inseparable. He had honour enough to spare. *He* got burned.' Evans shuddered at the memory. 'I was holding him when he died. Couldn't see me, but he knew I was there. They wouldn't even let me join the honour guard to bear him to his rest.' In a feeble attempt at imitating Kinross's clipped vowels he added, in explanation, 'He was An Officer, you see. It was his wife got the medal, the glory. But who d'you think tends his grave now she's married again?' he finished.

Kavanagh felt sick. All that hate. All that secrecy. The warped notions of honour. And the ghastly, misplaced revenge. 'And do you think,' he said, 'that what you've done here honours his memory?'

Evans's reply sent a chill down Kavanagh's spine.

'You people!' he hissed. 'I'd like to see you all burn. All of you. Burn to ashes.'

'Jim?'

'Eh?' Kavanagh blinked, turned away from the window and, with a jolt, remembered where he was.

'You were saying that Evans told you he did it.'

Kavanagh looked at her. 'Yes.'

'But Kinross confessed.'

'Yes.'

'So the case is closed.'

'Yes.'

Eleanor looked forward and patted her colleague's knee. The look they exchanged was one of complete accord. They were friends. Good friends. But just friends. 'It's a tragedy,' she said, with feeling. 'But, mark my words, Evans will get his comeuppance.'

'You reckon?'

'Oh, yes.' Eleanor smiled a strange, humourless smile. 'He'll burn in hell.'

CHAPTER FIFTEEN

'*Leaving?* Julia—'

'Please don't make this any more difficult than it is already, Jim. It's not a decision I've taken lightly.'

'But why?'

'I'm going to get married.'

'*Married?*'

Julia burst out laughing. 'For a barrister you're being shockingly inarticulate. And, I may add, rather rude. You should at least try,' she teased, 'to hide your astonishment.'

Kavanagh exhaled. 'It's not astonishment. It's shock at losing you. And,' he added with a hint of criticism, 'you can't blame me for being surprised. You've been keeping extremely quiet about David.'

Julia shot him a shrewd, appraising look. 'But you knew?'

'Yes. Don't ask me how or I'll start trotting out all those twee clichés about love shining through your eyes. But why does it mean you have to leave? I wouldn't have thought—'

'And I wouldn't have thought,' interrupted Julia with a wry smile, 'that I'd agree to move to Kenya with David.'

'Kenya?'

'Yes. He works for the FO.'

'Oh, yes, I remember. Damn fine cricketer, too.' Kavanagh leaned forward and kissed her. 'I'm delighted for you. It's the best news I've heard all week.'

'So you lost the case in Portsmouth?'

'Oh dear . . . You do know me, don't you?'

'Mmm. And, Jim, I'll miss you. You've been . . . Well, for a start you pushed hard to take me on here. I know Peter had his reservations.'

Kavanagh didn't deny it. Yet he and Julia knew that Peter had long since abandoned those reservations. He'd been Julia's greatest fan for the last few years. Her leaving would have distressed him greatly. 'So how did Peter take the news?' asked Kavanagh.

'Funnily enough, he was the one who made up my mind for me. I, er . . . wasn't very sure at first. In fact, I was really vile to David for springing the whole thing on me. It was Peter who made me see the light.'

'Sensible man, Peter.'

'Mmm.' Peter Foxcott, she remembered, had been surprising as well as sensible. 'Get off the treadmill before you end up like all the rest of us,' he had said.

'The rest of you?' Julia had been completely floored.

'Yes.' Peter, smiling at her over his vast desk, had become almost maudlin. 'When I was up at Caius, I used to write poetry. Doggerel in the main, I don't doubt, but no less valid for all that. Now I write advices.' Then, in his best avuncular manner, he made up Julia's mind for her. 'Don't sacrifice real life on the altar of career.'

'I thought career *was* real life.'

'Real life?' Peter shook his head. 'I prosecuted a boy the other week. He was fifteen. Had four children – each by a different mother. He'd killed the youngest. Terrible, terrible case. But,' he added with a faraway

206

look, 'as he stood there in the dock, shoulders hunched against the sentence, I suddenly realized this shabby, venal, malnourished scrap of humanity had experienced more in his fifteen summers . . . Ah!' Peter stopped. 'You understand? He was more alive than I will ever be.'

'That's not true, Peter. You're—'

But he silenced her with an abrupt hand. 'Going through the motions. But at least I have the Club and Jeremy to keep me amused. D'you know why so many of us are obsessed with music, art, literature?' It was a rhetorical question. 'We've forgotten how to feel. We have these empty spaces which we try to fill with someone else's experience . . . someone else's passion.'

Julia was beginning to feel embarrassed. 'Peter . . .'

'Dear girl, if you decide to leave, then you will go with my blessing.' Fearing that Julia must be thinking him demented, he smiled sadly into her eyes. 'God knows River Court won't be the same without you, but we'll bear the loss all the easier if we know he's the right chap.'

'Peter,' said Julia to Kavanagh, 'was really quite touching about it all. More than I can say for Jeremy.' She grimaced.

Kavanagh chortled. 'What was his reaction?'

'He said that Nairobi was hardly the place for a European woman.' She grinned at the memory. Jeremy had been pompous – and not a little miffed that it had been presented to him as a *fait accompli*. Wildly jealous of David, he had ended up by being rather rude about Julia's 'abandoning ship', as he had put it. She had finally managed to shut him up by hinting that her departure could spell good news for him within chambers. If Peter decided to replace her, she said, then the newcomer would most certainly be junior to Jeremy, and Jeremy would undoubtedly be one step closer to becoming a QC. That, as Julia knew, was rubbish. One applied for silk through the Lord Chancellor's Office, usually after at least twelve years as a practising barrister. Any inter-chambers plotting had little effect. Yet Julia's words had had the desired effect on Jeremy. He had preened himself and – as this year's applications were shortly to be considered – reckoned that he had a good chance of becoming a QC. A much better chance than in the previous five years of failed applications.

Kavanagh, who was well aware that Jeremy had long had designs on Julia, amused himself with visions of a jealous Jeremy. 'Yes,' he said. 'I can well imagine Jeremy being incredibly gracious about it all. I'm glad he didn't dissuade you from going.'

Julia snorted. 'Jeremy doesn't need to dissuade or persuade me to do anything. All I know is that if he says black, I'll automatically say white.' Then she remembered the other reason why she had visited Kavanagh's room, and reverted to barrister mode. 'Jim?'

'Mmm?' Kavanagh looked at her with some suspicion, over his half-moons. He knew that tone.

'I've got something I'd like your help with.' She was aware that his doubt would increase when she told him what it was. 'It's a personal injury case.'

'Good God, I haven't done one of those in years. Twenty years.'

'You're well overdue then, Mr Kavanagh.'

Both Kavanagh and Julia looked round in surprise. Neither had noticed Tom Buckley coming into the room, laden as usual with stacks of paper. He was grinning like the Cheshire cat: partly because he loved butting into other people's conversations but mostly because his wife had now made a complete recovery from her depression.

'Ah, Tom. But I'm not free, am I?' It was, Kavanagh hoped, more of a command than a question.

'Well, actually, sir, you haven't got a lot on at the moment . . .'

Kavanagh looked from Tom to Julia and then back again. Both were grinning. He felt trapped. 'But you have done personal injuries before,' he said to Julia. 'You're much fresher than me.'

Suddenly Julia was intense. 'This one's a brain injury. The claim is seven hundred and fifty thousand pounds.'

'The last one I did involved a rogue Yorkshire terrier.'

'So this would be a challenge.'

Sensing that Julia had victory within her grasp, Tom winked at her, deposited some papers on Kavanagh's desk and left the room as quietly as he had entered.

Now it was Kavanagh's turn for intensity. 'Reading between the lines, I sense that you're trying to get me to lead the case.'

'Well, it's a big one. The clout of a QC would help.'

Kavanagh shook his head. 'It's High Court. Red judge. No jury. Presumably the claim is against an insurance company?'

Julia agreed.

'So they will offer an ostensibly large but inadequate sum, and the claimant will settle. You don't need me. I'm a criminal hack.'

'It could be the last time we'll work together.'

Kavanagh raised an eyebrow. 'Blackmail, Julia, is always a dirty word.' Then he smiled. 'Even when you put "emotional" in front of it.'

'So that's settled, then?' Julia was grinning from ear to ear. 'I'll get you the papers. You can read them at home.'

'Great. Ever heard the sentiment "I'd like to spend more time with my family"?'

But Julia had already left the room.

Kavanagh *had* been hoping to spend more time with his family. He had seen little of Lizzie lately and Matt, as usual, hardly ever appeared at home. Now that term had started again, he had to fit school as well as partying and slothing into his busy schedule. He was also, his parents had been relieved to hear, continuing his swimming training. A talented swimmer, he had recently usurped the reigning school champion and was now set for major local and even national competitions.

As Kavanagh crawled home through the West London traffic, he was surprised to find himself concluding that, despite his neglect, his family seemed to be thriving. During her intermittent and usually fleeting visits home, Kate gave the impression that she had recovered from the Jeffrey affair and, although she remained coy about it, her parents knew she had started seeing a fellow student on what seemed to be a fairly serious basis.

As for Lizzie, Kavanagh was thankful that she had found a stimulating and challenging job. She had seemingly inexhaustible reserves of energy, and her husband knew she was bored with being at home. It left her time to brood, and the last thing he wanted was for her to brood about what he and Eleanor Harker had been doing in Portsmouth. Rather to Kavanagh's surprise, she had barely batted an eyelid when he had phoned the night he and Eleanor had been stuck down there, and had laughed at his tales of the delights of the Mirabar Hotel.

He reached home reflecting that, all in all, life was pretty good. The only shadows on the horizon were Julia's departure and, more immediately, her successful bid to persuade him to take on – and lead – her personal injury case. He couldn't think why he had let himself be bamboozled into doing it. Such cases, in his experience, were often dirty. On one side was an individual, often maimed for life, and his or her family. On the other was a giant insurance company with droves of advisers and lawyers, who thought nothing of spending weeks following the claimant's background, intelligence, family and every move to try to refute either the existence or the alleged extent of the personal injury. And Julia had informed him that the claimant in this case, a student called David Lomax, had suffered his injuries almost a year ago. A lot could happen, he knew, in a year.

Letting himself into the house he was disappointed, although not altogether surprised, to discover that no one was at home. Just as well, he thought, that I haven't got the chance to spend more time with the family. It would be a lonely experience. Ambling into the drawing room, he deposited his case on the sofa and made a beeline for the drinks cabinet. A whisky. Or maybe two. Then he would read the brief on David Lomax.

Half an hour later Lizzie arrived home to find her husband sprawled on the sofa sifting through a bundle of photographs. There was an empty whisky glass on the floor beside him. 'Hi,' she said, as she leaned over and kissed him on his thinning pate. 'Holiday snaps?'

Kavanagh made a face. 'Hardly. Something rather grim, actually.'

'Oh?' But Lizzie was already back in the hall, hanging up her coat. 'Work?' she called over her shoulder.

'Mmm.'

As she came back into the room she remonstrated, 'I thought you were planning to take a bit of time to yourself. You push yourself too hard, Jim,' she said as she perched on the back of the sofa.

'I know, I know. But Julia press-ganged me into taking a case with her.'

'And since when did you let Julia press-gang you into anything?' The question was gentle, affectionate. Lizzie was fond of Julia and had no worries about the amount of time she spent with her husband. Eleanor Harker, of course, was a different story. Lizzie thought she had been incredibly mature about the Portsmouth scenario. Not, she reflected, that Jim appeared to have noticed.

Kavanagh looked up at his wife's smiling face. 'Since Julia announced she was leaving.'

'*Leaving?*'

Kavanagh grinned at Lizzie's expression. Now he knew why Julia had started laughing when he himself had reacted similarly. 'Yes. Leaving.' Kavanagh swung his legs off the sofa. 'Come on, let's crack open a bottle of that rather splendid white burgundy and I'll tell you all about it.'

'I wouldn't have thought that Julia leaving would be a cause for celebration,' said Lizzie.

Kavanagh gave her an old-fashioned look. 'Commiseration?'

'More like.'

Minutes later, as they commiserated over a chilled

Puligny-Montrachet that was indeed rather splendid, Kavanagh told Lizzie the reason behind Julia's impending departure. She was both sad and delighted. 'This David,' she said. 'Is he the chap Julia brought to drinks that time?'

'The very one.'

'Charming.' Lizzie twinkled at her husband. 'And very good-looking.'

'You think? I've never gone for that sort of bronzed six-footer swimming type myself.'

Lizzie smirked. 'Jealousy will get you nowhere.'

'I think that's what Julia tried to tell Jeremy.'

'Oh, God, he's not still after her, is he? That man has the hide of a rhinoceros.'

'Oh.' Kavanagh dismissed Jeremy with a wave of his hand. 'He'll get over it. Anyway, he'll soon have his application for silk to occupy him.'

'Again?' Lizzie looked round in surprise as she idly scanned the photographs Kavanagh had left on the sofa. 'D'you think he'll get it?'

'Oink, flap.'

'I beg your pardon?'

'Pigs might fly.'

Lizzie threw back her head and laughed. 'Very good. But one day,' she added, 'you might have to eat your words.' Then she frowned as she turned over the photograph on the top of the pile. 'This looks rather distressing.'

'Mmm.' Kavanagh followed her gaze. 'It's the personal injury. A young man, also called David, and a brilliant student of marine engineering. Almost crushed between two barge containers at his holiday job.'

'God, how awful. Badly injured?'

'Very, apparently. In a wheelchair with most of his higher brain functions impaired in some way. I expect the insurance company will make some sort of feeble offer to keep it out of court.'

Still frowning, Lizzie flipped through the photographs. As well as the ones of David Lomax, there were others showing some sort of waste-disposal yard on the bank of a river. Huge containers stood in rows while behind them enormous flat barges were waiting to be loaded to take them down the river. In another photograph, a towering construction loomed like a gigantic hand over the quayside. One of the containers was suspended in its giant claws. Lizzie thrust the picture at her husband. 'Don't tell me one of these landed on the poor chap? Nobody could survive that.'

'No. I said he was squashed between them when he was on the barge.'

'Oh. But it all looks automated to me. What on earth was he doing on the barge in the first place?'

'That, my dear, is what I aim to find out. The insurance company is trying to make out that it was a strict no-go area and that he was an irresponsible idiot for being there in the first place.'

Lizzie sat up straight. 'And you're going to tell the judge that irresponsible idiots don't go off and study mechanical engineering?'

'Among other things, yes. Oh,' he added, in an attempt to lighten the conversation, 'the instructing solicitor is an old flame of yours. Sends his love,' he finished, wickedly.

'Oh, yes? And who might that be?'

'Martin Haslam.'

'Heavens above! Haven't heard from him in years.'

'I should hope not. Far too young for you.'

Lizzie swiped at him. 'Toyboys are fashionable.'

'But not Martin Haslam.'

'Oh, I don't know. He's rather dashing, in a tousled sort of way.' Then, remembering, she asked, 'Is he still a Trot?'

'Well, Julia said he was wearing a Paul Smith suit when they met, so I s'pose he must be.'

Laughing, Lizzie stood up. 'Yes, funny how money affects one's principles, isn't it?' Ten years ago, Martin Haslam wouldn't haven't been seen dead in anything other than ill-fitting, second-hand clothes. Still, it was good to see that he was continuing to 'do the right thing'. Acting for the injured boy and his family was hardly the sort of thing that a purely money-motivated solicitor would undertake.

'Hey! What's that?'

Startled, Lizzie looked down at her husband. 'What?'

Kavanagh sprang to his feet anxiously. He had already identified the noise as being that of a motorbike pulling up outside the front door. 'We don't know anyone who has a motorbike, do we?' Kavanagh had a pathological aversion to bikes. He seemed to have forgotten that he used to own one.

Lizzie knew perfectly well who was on the motorbike. She also knew there would be trouble ahead. 'It's Matt. Now don't go spare, Jim. Vanessa's giving him a lift home from the pool.'

'Who is this Vanessa?' Whoever she was, Kavanagh had already decided he didn't like her.

'Someone Matt trains with,' Lizzie said mysteriously. 'Matt says she's "strange".'

This was too much for Kavanagh. This he simply had to see. Glass in hand, he walked out into the hall and opened the front door. He was not disappointed by the sight that greeted him. A huge black bike stood outside, and beside it, an even huger apparition in black leathers and helmet towered over Matt as he struggled to take off his own helmet.

'Matt!'

'Hi, Dad.' Matt grinned at his father. 'This,' he added, 'is Vanessa.'

The apparition held up a gloved hand. Then she took Matt's helmet, put it in one of the bike's panniers, and straddled the machine in one athletic leap. Her farewell to Matt was a tap on the head that, although presumably meant as a friendly gesture, nearly knocked him sideways. Matt rubbed his head and joined his father in the house as Vanessa roared off into the street.

Although amused by the scene he had just witnessed, Kavanagh was thinking about the broader picture: Matt and motorbikes. 'You know what we said about motorbikes,' he remarked to his son as they joined Lizzie in the drawing room.

Before Matt could reply, Lizzie leaped to his defence. 'Jim! It's only a two-mile ride from the pool.'

Kavanagh, stunned, turned to Matt. 'She's a swimmer?'

'Diver.' Matt chuckled at his father's expression. 'She lives on nuts and seeds.'

'She's done very well on them,' said Lizzie in awe. Vanessa, she reckoned, had to be at least six feet tall.

'She wants to be a stuntwoman.'

'I'm sure she'd be very good at it,' said Kavanagh drily. 'I can't imagine she'd let much get in her way. Interesting-looking girl,' he mused, thankful that he'd only had one brief glimpse of her.

'She's strange, Dad.'

Kavanagh relaxed. Romance, then, wasn't in the air.

216

Thank God. Feeling altogether warmer about Vanessa, he made an admiring remark about her motorbike.

Matt looked speculatively from one parent to another. 'Well,' he said to his father, ''s okay. But you've had bikes, Dad, you know how draughty they can be . . .' He let the statement drift, yet his expression was anticipatory. Hopeful, even.

Lizzie sensed danger. 'Don't worry . . .' she began.

But Kavanagh knew exactly where Matt wanted the conversation to lead and was having none of it. He picked up his case. 'Well, I'll just go back and finish reading about a young boy with his head bashed in. And my son doing ninety on the back of a bike with a herbivorous leather-clad Amazon will not cross my mind,' he concluded severely.

Matt stared after his father. Lizzie stared at Matt. Her expression said it all. The subject was obviously not worth pursuing.

CHAPTER SIXTEEN

David Lomax would never be able to ride a motorbike. Neither would he be able to walk again. Resuming his degree in mechanical engineering was an impossibility and work, of any kind, out of the question. His elderly parents, who had been in their forties when he was born, were going to have to spend the rest of their lives caring for him. And the enormous amount of time and energy they spent caring for him meant that their lives would, through sheer exhaustion, be cut short. Unless they secured a fitting sum in damages to pay for David's care.

As the Kavanagh family sat down to dinner in their large, well-appointed Wimbledon house, the Lomax family, miles away in an ex-council house in Norwich, embarked upon a rather different meal. The Kavanaghs enjoyed *boeuf bourguignon*, red wine and lively conversation, marred only by the unmentionable word 'motorbike' hanging over them. The Lomaxes had cold ham and salad, but Sam and Gina, David's parents, hardly noticed what they were eating. They were too busy trying to make sure David got his food into his mouth. At nineteen, he was far more of a handful than he had been at nine months.

Gina looked across the table at her husband. He was, she thought, even more exhausted than she. Perhaps it wasn't surprising. After David's accident they'd moved to Norwich to be near the best specialist care. Sam, however, hadn't been able to move his job and still drove to London every day. It was too much, she thought, for a man in his early sixties. Wearily she ran a hand through her hair. Her hair. Once, she thought, I used to care about my appearance. Now I don't have the time. Or the energy.

David's dark head was bent over his plate as he concentrated on the food. It was already cut up into small pieces, but it was touch and go whether or not he would lever the spoon to his mouth or hurl the whole lot at the wall. That wall, like every other in the small house, bore traces of David's accidents – and his rages.

He looked up. Gina could tell he was almost in tears, but she had learned not to acknowledge that. It only served to turn his frustration into anger. He hated being pampered. He always had. But now her robust, good-looking son, who used to have a twinkle in his deep blue eyes, had no option.

The people at the hospital had been kind, sympathetic and hadn't tried to pull the wool over their eyes. Personality change, problems with short-term memory, loss of initiative, occasional extreme emotional distress were only some of the problems arising from his brain injuries. Retrograde amnesia was another, an amnesia that was all the more tragically poignant as it had left him with absolutely no memory of the accident. His three colleagues at East Bankside Recycling Centre had been no help on that score: none of them, they had claimed, had seen him on the barge. They had no idea he had been there. Jim Dale, the site administrator, had gone so far as to say that David had been stupid and irresponsible to go there. Gina had disliked the man on sight. Flashy, he had been. Much more interested in his Mercedes than in his employees. And those employees, she reckoned, had been cowed by him. It had been Dale's intractability that had made her all the more determined to sue the company for compensation. She knew her David. Stupid he was not. And he had always taken his responsibilities seriously.

Suddenly David shoved his food violently from his plate. Sam automatically tried to put it back again. Instinctively, Gina stood up and fetched a cloth from the draining board. But David had had enough. Pressing the reverse button on his wheelchair, he tried to get out of his place at the table, but was thwarted by the proximity of the wall. Undaunted, he moved his chair forward and back, forward and back. Sam reached to steady his beer – but too late. It spilled all over the tablecloth and onto the floor. At the sight of the liquid, David stopped struggling. For a moment, the three were frozen into the immobility of inertia. The only sound in the small room was the steady drip of the beer onto the linoleum floor.

'The care costs are astronomical,' said Kavanagh in surprise. 'How on earth can a wheelchair cost seven thousand pounds?'

Julia looked up from the solicitor's brief. 'I don't know, Jim. I haven't bought one recently.' It wasn't an attempt at a joke; it was an indication of her irritation. Kavanagh had come into chambers that morning and had done little more than reminisce about his days as a biker. He wasn't taking the Lomax case seriously enough, she felt. And given that the Lomaxes themselves were coming to see them later that day, she felt he damn well ought to be. 'Jim,' she asked, 'how do you feel about this case? I mean, generally?'

'Like a criminal hack doing a personal injury case.'

'A good advocate,' said Julia, 'can handle anything.'

'Who told you that?'

'Oh . . . some old criminal hack.'

Kavanagh laughed. 'Point taken.'

'Good.' Julia went back to her task. 'We have to add "respite care" for the parents as well. And these claims for architectural conversion of their house. There's three different quotes. Which one d'you reckon?'

'Cheapest. I'm going to have to stand up and argue for every penny. And, of course, we don't have the other side's medical reports.'

'They haven't been completed anyway. They couldn't finish them last time.'

'Oh? Why?'

'He kept ramming people.'

'Ah. Quite a handful, then, this boy David?'

'You'll find out soon enough.'

They found out five hours later when David, his medical appointments over, arrived at River Court with his parents and Martin Haslam. The arrival itself was fraught. River Court had not been designed for wheelchair access and, once out of the taxi, David had to be taken in via a back entrance, along several dingy passageways and up in the goods lift to get to Kavanagh's room. Out of politeness, Kavanagh accompanied them. David, however, did something less polite. He fixed his gaze on Kavanagh the minute he met him and refused to look elsewhere. It made Kavanagh feel uncomfortable yet he wondered if, perhaps, he should

221

be flattered. David's eyes were piercingly intelligent. And the message they sent out was one of complete faith. They said more than the boy's words, even though, as Haslam had whispered, today was one of his lucid days. His speech was gruff; covering, Kavanagh suspected, his embarrassment.

Formal niceties over, Kavanagh explained to the family that, arguing the case for the prosecution, he had two separate areas to deal with. 'The first,' he explained, 'is liability. The defence will try to prove that David was responsible for his own injuries because he acted irresponsibly, undirected, on his own initiative.' He smiled at the Lomax parents. 'We do not accept that. We begin with the simple contention that accidents such as these simply should not happen. After that, we look for inconsistencies in the statements of their witnesses.

'The second area of the case,' he continued, 'is "care claim", exactly what David needs and how much it costs. I must emphasize that proving liability does not necessarily mean you will be awarded the full amount of the claim. The defence will bring in medical experts who might contradict ours. They will try to prove that David is a charlatan, and that you are over-protective, greedy parents.' These parents, he noted, seemed shell-shocked. Yet it was as well, he knew, to prepare them for what might turn out to be a messy, hurtful battle. 'We have to show the need,' he ended, 'for every penny we are claiming.'

The Lomaxes remained silent as they contemplated the enormity of the task they had taken upon themselves. Kavanagh thought he detected an element of doubt on Gina's face. He sought to dispel it. He said to her, 'I understand that the insurance company has made an offer of fifty thousand pounds, which you have quite sensibly rejected.'

Gina nodded. Intimidated both by her surroundings and by Kavanagh's easy eloquence, she was frightened to say anything. 'Mrs Lomax,' Kavanagh said encouragingly, 'if you have any questions, please don't hesitate to ask.'

'Well,' she began tentatively, 'if they offered money, doesn't that mean they think . . . well, that they're going to lose?'

'I'm afraid not. They think they *might* lose. So do I. And if they do, their costs will be a lot more than fifty thousand. They are an insurance company. That offer is almost like a policy against losing. But they may improve that offer, and it's up to you to decide whether any new offer will be acceptable.' He leaned back in his chair. 'I act on your behalf, but I can't make that decision for you.' His last words were addressed to David, whose eyes had not left Kavanagh's face all the time he had been speaking. It was apparent that his parents, worn out by the demands of looking after him and bewildered by the legal process they had entered into, would leave any decision to David.

Sam, his face creased with worry, shifted uncomfortably in his chair. 'What are our chances, Mr Kavanagh?'

'At this stage, I think, fifty-fifty. But I can't predict that the judge will see it like that,' he said, as he saw the worry deepen. What he didn't tell them was that the judge was liable to go either way: some judges were notorious for their unsympathetic approach to such cases.

Anxious to press on and avoid any speculation on that score, Kavanagh changed the subject. 'Let's look at what you might be saying in court, Mrs Lomax.

Perhaps you could tell us what your days are like. Your normal routine.'

Gina didn't have to give that one much thought. Every day was the same: the hard, relentless grind. 'We get up,' she began. 'Then we clear up what David has broken in the night – he doesn't really sleep. We . . . er, pick up what he's thrown out of the window.' Slightly apprehensively, she looked at her son. He was nodding in agreement. 'Then we wash him. Dress him.'

'I can dress myself!' David was outraged.

'Sometimes you can.'

'Always! I dressed myself this morning.'

'You had your socks on your hands,' interjected his father.

David didn't disagree. His sudden passion spent, he lapsed into silence. Kavanagh, along with Julia, and Martin Haslam, was beginning to get a picture of everyday life in the Lomax household. It was not a pretty one.

'I take David off to the Harwell Centre for four hours,' continued Gina, in a monotone. 'Sam sets off on his three-hour drive . . .'

'I still teach in Enfield,' explained her husband. 'We had to move to Norfolk. The Harwell was the closest treatment centre that had a place.'

Gina went on with the story. Without a trace of self-pity, she explained that the day really depended on David's mood; that it was exhausting and unpredictable. They never questioned their plight: David was their son, and they would do anything for him.

But for how much longer? thought Julia as she looked on in sympathy. Their energy and their lives were not infinite. Then, prompted by Kavanagh, Gina admitted that they hadn't had a holiday, or even a short break, in the last year; that they were short of money and that, no, they had no relatives in the country. David's grandmother had been the only one, and she had died three years previously.

Although deeply sympathetic, Kavanagh knew it would be undesirable to express pity. They had not come here for emotional support. They had come on business. 'Perhaps,' he said, as he extracted some photographs from the manila folder in front of him, 'we can look in detail at the geography of the site.' He handed out copies of the photographs to everyone in the room. David, however, made no attempt to take one. He suddenly seemed distant, as if his thoughts were elsewhere. 'All three defence witnesses,' said Kavanagh, 'will say that they were inside the main building when David went out onto the barge. As you can see from the photographs, it is not possible to see the barge from that building. So, when the machinery—'

'Nana died?'

Everyone's attention was suddenly on David. He was looking at his mother with a pained, uncomprehending expression. Gina stroked his hand. 'Yes. We told you that, remember?' But David looked blank.

'Er . . . when they switched the crane apparatus on—'

'Why didn't you tell me she died?' This time it was a shout. Flushed and angry, David glowered at his mother.

'Darling . . .' Gina stood up and tried to comfort her son. For a second or two it looked as if he was going to let her. Then, in a gesture that shocked Kavanagh and his team, he lashed out at her. Sam, on his feet like lightning, tried to calm David, but only succeeded in further enraging him. David lunged forward in his chair, sending papers and photographs flying. Flicking the switch on his wheelchair, he then sent the machine forward – straight into Julia's legs. She gave a yelp of pain and leaped up to avoid another blow as David, seemingly determined to get out of the room, rammed his chair against the doorway. Martin Haslam looked on in horror. It was Kavanagh who, determined to spare Sam and Gina any further agony, overcame his own shock and declared that they all ought to take a break. 'I'll get Tom to send in some sandwiches,' he said, with what he hoped was a smile of reassurance and acceptance.

The break proved a good idea. David calmed down almost as quickly as his fury had erupted and, much to everyone's relief, seemed to have no recollection of the drama. Moreover, he spent the rest of the meeting making clear, incisive remarks about the forthcoming hearing. Kavanagh was impressed by his mental acuity, and told him so as the two of them left the room slightly ahead of the others. But the remark only served to distress David again. He looked down at his useless legs and then up at Kavanagh. 'Why do I have to do this?' he asked quietly.

'You know the answer to that.' Kavanagh was unemotional, matter-of-fact.

'I love my mum and dad. What's going to happen to them?' he said, pleadingly. 'I don't remember anything, Mr Kavanagh. How on earth can we win?'

'We have one major advantage – the fact that they have three witnesses.'

But David couldn't see how that could be an advantage.

'It means,' explained Kavanagh, 'there are three different perspectives of what happened. Three chances to make a mistake. But it won't be easy, David, and you have to help.'

At exactly the same time as the meeting in River Court was ending, another, in a nearby office, was just beginning. The offices were those of the Sanctuary Insurance Company PLC, insurers to the East Bankside Recycling Centre. Jim Dale, the man who had been David Lomax's boss, was sitting with his solicitor Clive Gosling across the table from three representatives of the insurance company. On Dale's other side sat a thuggish, bored-looking young man dressed in jeans and a denim jacket. He answered, when he could be bothered, to the name of Len Baxter and he was a permanent and lowly member of East Bankside's staff. He was also scared of Mr Dale. Like Bob Pearson, the site foreman at East Bankside, he had been on the receiving end of Dale's temper. It was best, in his experience, never to disagree with Dale.

Bob Pearson was the reason why the three men were waiting, with increasing impatience, for the meeting to begin. 'He's always late,' Dale had snapped to the men from the insurance company. What he had failed to add was that Pearson was invariably late because his wife, bedridden at home, was in the final stages of terminal cancer. But that tragedy was, to Dale, merely a source of irritation.

Twenty minutes after the meeting should have started, Pearson arrived. He looked strained, and his already lined face was further creased with worry. A few years short of retirement age, he looked much older. Short and stocky, he was hunched as though he carried the weight of the world on his shoulders. He let himself into the room and, while pointedly ignoring Jim Dale, apologized to the solicitor for his tardiness. But he had forgotten that Clive Gosling was cast in the same mould as Dale. Gosling looked at him with undisguised distaste. 'Not quite in synch with the rest of us, are you, Mr Pearson? A bit like your witness statement,' he added as he brandished a sheet of paper. 'But now that you're here, let's have another go, shall we?'

Pearson looked at his boss. Dale looked straight back at him and smiled his predatory smile. 'The point is, Pearson,' he said, 'you don't tell them any more than you have to. Right?'

Pearson retained his composure with difficulty as he sat down. He knew what the men from the insurance company did not, and he also knew that his livelihood was at stake. That morning Dale had made that perfectly clear on the phone. 'This is much more than an insurance claim,' he had said. 'If they sus us, we'll all go down.'

CHAPTER SEVENTEEN

The following day, while Kavanagh went to the Harwell Centre to talk to David's consultant, Julia, accompanied by Martin Haslam, paid a visit to the East Bankside Recycling Centre. Jim Dale and Clive Gosling, who both made it quite clear that they had better things to do, showed them round. They were, however, scrupulous about making them wear hard hats in designated areas, and Dale in particular was at pains to point out the many prominent signs warning of dangerous machinery in operation. The import of his words and actions was not lost on Julia: David Lomax had only himself to blame for the accident that had maimed him for life. After examining the layout of the exterior part of the site, and in particular the giant 'spreader', which transported the containers in its claws from shore to barge, they went back into the main building.

'This,' said Gosling, as they paused at the entrance, 'is the main power box. This lever,' he explained, 'turns off all the power and it also trips the power in the cab of the spreader.' Then, walking forward past a shelf of hard hats and stopping beneath a prominent 'No Smoking' sign, he gestured towards a control booth in the corner of the building. 'That's the booth where Mr Pearson and Mr Dale were when Lomax was on the barge.' His attitude when he said this was at once smug and challenging.

Julia retraced her steps to the shelf of hard hats. Like a shop assistant displaying her wares, she held one out to Haslam. 'Nice and shiny, isn't it?'

'Mmm,' Haslam responded. 'Just like all the others.'

'And all those warning signs about dangerous machinery look new as well, don't they?'

Again the solicitor agreed. 'Doesn't prove anything, though.'

'No. But grist to the mill, and all that.'

Haslam was doubtful. To his mind, they had an uphill task ahead of them. Gosling's expression told him that Dale, Baxter and Pearson were adamantly sticking to their guns about their ignorance of David Lomax's whereabouts – and about the stringent safety procedures adhered to by all.

'I thought,' said Jeremy with a smirk, 'that you'd like it here. One of my favourite places.' He leaned over towards Julia. 'And they do give me rather special treatment, you know.'

Julia didn't know. She looked around her. Should she tell Jeremy? Probably not: it would be cruel to ruin his fantasies. And fantasies they undoubtedly were.

Their surroundings were in sharp contrast to the industrial wastes of East Bankside from where Julia had had to rush to get to lunch on time. They were also familiar to her. She and Jeremy were lunching in Atelier, the scene of David's memorable proposal and Julia's equally memorable reaction. The manageress, although she had greeted Julia with her customary charm, was clearly surprised to see her back so soon –

and with another man. A man whom she quite patently didn't recognize. If Jeremy thought he was given 'special treatment', it was testament to the quality of the service, not to the familiarity of his face.

Julia had been more than a little surprised at his invitation to lunch. 'It would be nice for the two of us to be together, to have one last chat *à deux* before all your leaving celebrations,' he had said. 'Please, it would give me great pleasure.'

Put like that, it had been difficult for Julia to refuse. Yet she was still wary. Jeremy never did anything without an ulterior motive – especially things that cost him money. She suspected that he was going to milk her for information that would further his quest for silk.

'It's that time of year, isn't it?' she had said to Tom Buckley, after Jeremy had issued his invitation.

'I beg your pardon, Miss Piper?'

'His nose starts twitching and he can't stop shrugging. He's applied for silk again, hasn't he?'

Tom made an unconvincing attempt to look pompous and affronted. 'I couldn't betray Mr Aldermarten's confidence, Miss Piper.'

'But if he had – and of course you couldn't betray that confidence – what sort of odds would you be offering against him getting it?'

'Hypothetically?'.

'Of course.'

'Well, hypothetically of course, six to four on. I'm afraid that Mr Kavanagh took the last of the even money,' said Tom with a quirky smile.

Jeremy was now perusing the wine list. Heaven knows, Julia thought, why on earth he thinks I can possibly influence his bid to become a QC. I'm a woman, for a start.

231

The selection process for QCs was arcane and, in the eyes of the Association of Women Barristers, subjective and sexist. The Lord Chancellor's Office, in considering applications, approached eminent judges and QCs about the personal and professional reputation of the applicant. No specific questions were asked and there were no set selection criteria. To Julia's mind – and she knew she was not alone in thinking this – it left the system dangerously open to subjectivity and to the influence of the old-boy network. If an applicant had been to the same school as one of the judges or QCs approached, if they had been to the same university or belonged to the same club or were simply 'a good egg', then these factors could influence, however unconsciously, the final decision. As there were fewer women in the profession, and many public schools and London clubs were all-male establishments, Julia felt that selection was consequently biased towards men. Jeremy, no doubt, thought differently.

Why on earth he thought she could be of any use to him was, therefore, a complete mystery. As she read through the menu she found herself forced to contemplate the alarming notion that he had asked her to lunch simply because he enjoyed her company.

'I think,' said Jeremy, interrupting her thoughts, 'that we ought to have champagne, don't you?'

'Oh! Well . . . yes, that would be very nice, Jeremy. Very decent of you.'

'It's the least I can do.' Jeremy beckoned to the manageress and asked for the 'finest champagne'. Julia cringed. The manageress tried her best not to look surprised. She well remembered the commotion Julia had caused last time. She hoped another proposal wasn't in the offing.

'To be truthful,' said Jeremy, as the champagne arrived, 'I did have an ulterior motive for this invitation.'

'And I thought,' lied Julia, 'you just wanted to say goodbye in style.'

'Well, that's partly it.' Jeremy, noted Julia with delight, was beginning to squirm. 'The thing is,' he continued, 'I've been thinking . . . and I'm sure it's the right thing . . . Well, the thing is, Julia, I want you to marry me.'

Julia nearly dropped her glass. She froze. Then she burst out laughing. 'Jeremy! I'm marrying David!' This man, she thought, had taken leave of his senses. The idea was preposterous. Then she saw his expression. 'Oh, my God, you're serious.'

'Deadly.'

'But I'm going to marry David.'

Jeremy waved that one away with a dismissive gesture. Presumably he considered it an irrelevant detail. 'I think we both know you're not serious about that.'

'*What!* Jeremy, I – for God's sake, Jeremy.' Then, intrigue taking the place of shock, she leaned over the table. 'Why on earth would you want to marry me anyway?'

'Because, despite appearances, deep down we're right for each other.'

That, again, was shocking. 'But we're total opposites! We don't agree about anything. We're utterly, completely and hilariously mismatched.'

'But don't you see? That's just the point! We've suppressed what we really feel beneath a façade of bickering and hostility.'

Julia could hardly believe her ears. Jeremy was mad. She decided to set the record straight once and for all.

'It's not a façade, Jeremy. We genuinely don't like each other.'

'Nonsense.' Jeremy sipped his champagne. 'God,' he said, 'I could scream when I think of the years I've wasted with ghastly debs and brain-dead upper-class bimbos. What I needed all along was someone with spirit and backbone and guts. Someone like you.'

Julia took a deep breath. Never, she thought. I am never coming back to this restaurant. 'Well,' she began, 'I can honestly say you've surprised me, Jeremy. No, that doesn't quite do it. I think astounded might be the word.'

Jeremy was delighted. 'So what do you say?'

'Absolutely, unconditionally, irrefutably – no.'

'I don't want you to rush into a decision.'

'Jeremy . . .'

'No. Not another word.' Jeremy went back to the menu. 'Take a while to get used to the idea. I think you'll find I'm right.'

What is it with this man? thought Julia, in amazed disbelief. And then, after agreeing that the only way of getting through lunch was to drop the subject, she reflected that Jeremy had just done her the most enormous favour. He had made her realize just how much she wanted to marry David.

After they ordered, Jeremy embarked on an enthusiastic monologue about QCs. Nodding occasionally, Julia found her thoughts drifting from her David to another David: David Lomax.

Back at River Court, after a morning spent with Diana Walsh, the somewhat severe consultant who looked after David at the Harwell Centre, Kavanagh found himself in something of a quandary. Two things had caused it. The first was Tom Buckley's announcement that the judge for the David Lomax case was to be Mr Justice Swarbrick. 'Oh, God.' Kavanagh greeted the news with distaste.

'He's not that bad, is he?' countered Tom.

Kavanagh gave him a withering look. 'Remember the story about King Solomon and the two women fighting over the baby? Swarbrick would have chopped the kid in half first to save court time.'

'Ah.'

'And that's not all,' he continued. 'George Crosby is leading for the defence.'

'He a friend of the judge?'

'Well . . . Eton's a big place. There's a chance they never met,' Kavanagh said sardonically.

But Kavanagh's second dilemma was more pressing. The solicitors acting for Sanctuary Insurance had just phoned with a new offer of compensation. At two hundred and fifty thousand pounds it was a vast improvement on their original, derisory offer. Yet at a third of the claim Kavanagh was making, it was still far short of what he considered reasonable. He wanted to reject it out of hand – but couldn't. David was the plaintiff and only he could make a decision.

Kavanagh phoned the Lomaxes at the London hotel where they were now ensconced for the duration of the trial. It was Gina, sounding tired and on edge, who answered his call. David, she explained, had only slept for twenty minutes the previous night – which meant that she and Sam had managed ten.

'Can I have a word with David?' asked Kavanagh, after expressing genuine sympathy at Gina's plight.

'He's gone out to Covent Garden with two friends.'

Gina sounded relieved. 'It's not often that his friends are prepared to look after him.'

'Ah. Well, I'm afraid it's a matter of some urgency that I speak to him. They've made another offer.'

After hearing the amount, Gina was adamant. 'I want to take it.' As gently as he could, Kavanagh explained that only David could take the decision to accept.

'What if we end up with nothing?' wailed Gina over the line. 'Are you going to come and wipe his backside?' she added with sudden ferocity. 'I don't think so.'

'I hope I can win your case, Mrs Lomax.' Kavanagh hated doing this – especially over the phone. But Sanctuary's solicitors wanted a response before they closed for business. And this being Friday, they rather inconveniently closed at three o'clock. Monday would be too late: the case was scheduled to begin that day. Kavanagh needed an immediate answer. 'David could live another fifty or sixty years,' he said in a low, unemotional voice. 'What happens when you're not there to look after him?'

Obviously distressed by that harsh reminder, Gina was silent for a moment. Then she said, in a small defeated voice, 'What did we do to deserve this torture?'

'Nothing. Bad things happen to good people all the time. Look,' went on Kavanagh, after a pause, 'I could get a cab if you tell me where he is in Covent Garden.'

'There's no point.' Gina's mind was made up – against, as it turned out, her better judgement. 'I know what David would say. He's developed this unshakeable faith in you, Mr Kavanagh. He thinks we can't lose.'

'I hope he's right.'

'But you're not certain, are you?'

Kavanagh didn't reply. Gina's latest sacrifice for her son was the greatest she had yet made. She knew full well that they could end up with nothing. So did Kavanagh.

Try as he might, Kavanagh found himself unable to think of anything else all weekend. His preoccupation, for once, suited Lizzie. She had a plan, and her husband's distracted state of mind made it easier, she hoped, to get him to agree to it. Although he was unaware of it, he had already paved the way for her: he had let himself be duped by Lizzie and Matt.

'You are not having a motorbike,' he had said, when Matt had broached the subject. 'I don't care how much of your own money you've saved.'

'The insurance wouldn't be—'

'We can't insure your brain.'

Matt's next remark had greatly amused his mother. 'You had an AJS 650. That's a precedent, isn't it?'

'Yes.'

'That's how the law works, isn't it?'

'Ye-s.'

Matt grinned. 'I rest my case.'

Kavanagh was not amused. 'A precedent does rule . . . until a better one comes along. You have the privilege of remoulding family law. You are that new and improved precedent. You cannot have a motor-cycle. Goodbye.'

What Kavanagh hadn't noticed as he strode out of the house was that Matt and Lizzie, far from being disappointed, had exchanged a conspiratorial wink behind his back. Plan A had worked.

And now it was time for Plan B. 'I was thinking,'

237

began Lizzie as they strolled on Wimbledon Common on Saturday morning, 'that . . . well, Matt will be old enough to drive a car in a few months.'

'So?'

'So it's the lesser of the two evils.'

Kavanagh snorted unpleasantly and stomped off.

Lizzie sighed. This was not going to be easy. 'Look,' she said as, slightly breathless, she caught up with him, 'you think every problem with our children is going to be "the big one". The final catastrophe. Matt talks about motorbikes and you see him dead in a morgue.'

'I worry about him.'

'You can't worry about him for ever.'

But Kavanagh was unimpressed. 'That's what the Lomaxes have to do now.'

Lizzie shoved her hands into her pockets. Why, she thought, must he always bring his work home? She had every sympathy for David Lomax − but Matt wasn't David. Tackling her husband in his present mood, she realized, was probably not such a good idea, after all. 'Matt,' she said carefully, 'has more choices than David Lomax. And the right to exercise them.' Kavanagh didn't reply. They walked on in uneasy silence. 'What's he like,' asked Lizzie after a few minutes, 'this David?'

'Opinionated. Difficult.' Kavanagh knitted his brow. 'Proud . . . not arrogant. A fighter.'

Lizzie smiled. 'Oh, we've got one like that.'

Again Kavanagh lapsed into silence. When he finally spoke, his tone was severe, yet his eyes told a different story. 'A sensible car,' he said. 'Not a joke. Nothing trendy.'

In the deep pockets of her coat, Lizzie uncrossed

her fingers. Kavanagh, though, suddenly looked pensive. Once again, his thoughts had strayed. His own son would be delighted with him but, the following week, would Gina Lomax's son feel the same way?

CHAPTER EIGHTEEN

'May it please your lordship, in this matter I represent the plaintiff, along with my learned friend Miss Julia Piper. Mr Crosby and Mr Manzy represent the defendants, Sanctuary Insurance PLC.' Kavanagh looked up. 'I trust your lordship is familiar with the pleadings and particulars in this case?'

'I am.' Judge Swarbrick was tanned, healthy and evidently rather bored. 'And I trust you'll stick to them, Mr Kavanagh.'

'Certainly, my lord.' Kavanagh gave a sideways glance at David. The High Court differed greatly from a Crown Court and resembled the House of Commons in that the two parties sat on opposite sides of an aisle, with the judge on a dais at the end of the room. As prosecution counsel, Kavanagh sat in the same row as his clients, as did the defence counsel opposite him. David, he noted with a certain unease, was alert and seemed belligerent. His consultant had warned Kavanagh that, as he responded well to stimulation, he would probably be firing on all cylinders in court. Or, at least, on all the cylinders he possessed. It was a bitter irony that Kavanagh would have preferred David to be at his worst.

He picked up the notes that formed his opening address. He had worked hard on this speech. It was long, but eloquent and moving. 'My lord,' he began, 'this case centres on two issues—'

'We don't need lengthy opening statements, do we?' interrupted Swarbrick. 'However eloquent. Let's just press on.'

Kavanagh did his best to hide his disappointment. He put down his notes and looked across at his opposite number. Crosby, the Old Etonian contemporary of Swarbrick, was grinning. Fifteen–love: and they hadn't even begun. 'As your lordship pleases.' Then, forced into a new beginning, he began, 'I understand that one of my learned friend's expert witnesses has a pressing appointment tomorrow, so perhaps we can take medical testimony first. Subject,' he added with a sarcasm only detectable to Julia Piper, 'to your lordship's approval.'

His lordship graciously inclined his head and, two minutes later, Diana Walsh was on the stand. She was Kavanagh's witness, and he had every confidence that, as David's consultant, she would establish to the judge the severity of her patient's condition. They both knew that Dr Marsh, the expert witness to the defence to whom Kavanagh had just referred, would try to contradict Dr Walsh's findings.

This was not the first time Diana Walsh had been called upon to give medical evidence, and her answers to Kavanagh's questions were quick, succinct and unemotional. She listed the damage to David's spinal column, resulting in lower body paralysis, and the traumatic assault to his brain. But the main culprit, she stated, was a haematoma that caused severe pressure on the frontal lobe. Although it was removed in hospital after David's accident, it had caused damage in the brain tissue. The condition of the patient, she stated unequivocally, was chronic and, no, there was no chance of his mobility ever improving.

So far, so good, Kavanagh thought. 'Can you briefly remind the court,' he went on to ask, 'of the psychological effects David has suffered?'

Again Dr Walsh was quick and confident. Her words matched the severity of her appearance. 'Personality change, problems with short-term memory, some retrograde amnesia, loss of initiative, occasional extreme emotional distress. Cognitive impairment. Most of the higher brain functions are affected in some way.'

Kavanagh paused briefly. 'David was a university student of marine engineering,' he said, as he addressed her again. 'Would you judge it likely that he might be able to resume those studies?'

'No.'

'Would you judge him capable of any kind of productive work in the future?'

Dr Walsh considered that. 'He has trouble concentrating on the simplest tasks . . . so, no, I wouldn't.'

'Thank you, Dr Walsh.' Kavanagh sat down as Crosby got to his feet.

'Dr Walsh, Mr Lomax recorded perfect scores in the reading and comprehension tests, didn't he?'

Dr Walsh looked annoyed. 'In those tests on that day—'

'In those tests on that day,' persisted the barrister, 'he displayed no indications of cognitive impairment. Correct?'

'Yes.' Dr Walsh was furious. Two hours of tests on one day was not, in her book, adequate for a diagnosis.

'Dr Walsh, you said David suffered a personality change. How is that manifested?'

'He has rages. Fits, almost. He can be rude and

abusive. Quite suddenly, unpredictably. And he needs constant stimulation—' She broke off. She knew this must be hurting David, but he was, as she had suspected, looking stimulated. 'If . . . er, if he doesn't get the stimulation, he can just lapse into a kind of . . . torpor.'

'Hmm.' Crosby looked distinctly unimpressed. 'Depression is common in people who've suffered debilitating physical injuries, isn't it?'

'Yes.'

'So the torpor could be depression.'

'It's a kind of depression, yes.'

'But he can read?'

Dr Walsh looked surprised at the sudden change of subject. 'At times, yes. He can read perfectly.'

'So he could have read about the psychological effects of brain injuries, couldn't he?'

'He has.' Dr Walsh stared Crosby in the eye. 'I encouraged him to.'

Crosby hadn't expected that. 'You don't know,' he continued, after a brief flurry with his papers, 'that David Lomax wasn't a rude and offensive young man before this accident, do you?'

'His parents said—'

'You believed them?'

'Why would they lie?' Dr Walsh was equally quick to rise.

'I don't know. Can you think of a reason?'

'No. I cannot.'

'David Lomax could be making up most of these "psychological" problems, couldn't he?'

Dr Walsh's expression spoke volumes about her feelings for Crosby. 'He doesn't have that much control,' she said. 'I wish he did. I wish all my patients did. None of them have enough control to lie that effectively,' she finished.

There was complete silence in the court as Diana Walsh left the stand. An awed silence.

Dr Marsh had the unenviable task of succeeding her as a witness. Some doctors were wary of contradicting their peers. Dr Marsh did not seem overly concerned although during his brief questioning by Crosby, he agreed with Dr Walsh about David's physical injuries. 'But his cognitive powers,' he said, 'seemed perfectly normal. His communication and comprehension skills were quite adequate, and I judged him to be aware and capable of perceiving threat to his physical being.'

'Thank you, Dr Marsh.' Crosby sat down.

'I won't take up too much of your valuable time, Dr Marsh,' said Kavanagh, with a deliberately patronizing smile. 'Get you away in time for your pressing appointment tomorrow.'

'Thank you.'

'More litigation, is it?'

Dr Marsh frowned. 'Yes.'

'For the same party? Defendant?'

'Yes.' Dr Marsh's face was stony. 'By coincidence.'

But Kavanagh's ensuing, albeit short, silence indicated that he thought it no coincidence. He thought that Dr Marsh was Sanctuary Insurance's resident expert medical witness and therefore not impartial in the Lomax case. 'Why did it take you two days to complete your tests on David Lomax?' he asked.

'We couldn't complete the tests on the first day because Mr Lomax became uncooperative.'

'How?'

'He was verbally and physically abusive.'

'How was he physically abusive, Dr Marsh?'

Marsh grimaced. 'He ran over my foot.' His remark was greeted by a few sniggers around the court. Swarbrick silenced them with one majestic, withering look.

Kavanagh allowed a smile to play at the corners of his mouth. 'That must have been . . . uncomfortable for you. You've heard Dr Walsh state that the extent of David Lomax's cognitive impairment fluctuates—'

'I can't confirm that,' interrupted Dr Marsh. 'His manner seemed quite calculated and consistent most of the time.'

'Most of the time?'

'Er . . . all of the time. You don't have to be brain damaged to be rude.'

'How long did you spend with Mr Lomax?'

'I've already told you. Two days.'

'Forty-eight hours?' In the row behind Kavanagh, Julia Piper wondered how many years it would take her to emulate Kavanagh's knack of sounding truly hostile while being conspicuously polite.

'Certainly not,' replied Dr Marsh. 'I saw him on and off throughout the two days.'

'On and off. These tests took a total of about two hours, didn't they?'

'The actual tests.'

'So you are only in a position to state that David Lomax displayed no cognitive impairment for two hours on the eighth and the nineteenth of April? Yes?'

But Dr Marsh refused to be intimidated. 'He completed standard cognitive tests satisfactorily.'

'But if he was so "calculating", why didn't he fail them?'

Marsh shrugged. 'I don't know. I'm not a mind-reader.'

'Thank you.' Sitting down, Kavanagh sent up a silent

prayer of thanks. The medical evidence had definitely favoured the plaintiff.

But then the bombshell hit. A slight disturbance on the defence benches was followed by a smug-looking Crosby rising to his feet. 'My lord, the defence has new evidence that it wishes to submit.'

Kavanagh whirled round to Julia.

Judge Swarbrick, however, looked annoyed rather than alarmed. The last thing he wanted was a delay; a waste of valuable court time. 'In what form is that evidence, Mr Crosby?'

'A videotape, my lord.'

Swarbrick asked, 'Have you seen this, Mr Kavanagh?'

'I have not, my lord.'

Swarbrick had feared as much. Much against his will, he was obliged to adjourn the proceedings until Kavanagh and his client had viewed it. Yet more court time wasted.

Kavanagh, Julia and Martin Haslam watched the film with David. The lawyers were more than a little surprised by its contents. They were even slightly shocked. David betrayed no emotion whatsoever. Kavanagh turned to him as soon as the short tape was finished. 'Were you set up, do you think?'

David shook his head. 'No. I wanted it. But it's not how it looks.'

But to the three lawyers, it looked pretty bad. 'And will you be able to explain that?' asked Kavanagh.

'Yes.' David seemed confident. The others most certainly were not.

'It will be shown in court,' said Kavanagh, as he rose and moved to the door behind which David's parents were waiting. 'In front of your parents. I suggest you warn them.'

The parents were already agitated. 'What's on the tape?' asked Sam, as soon as Kavanagh opened the door. 'Can they do this? Have they been spying on us?'

Kavanagh looked grave. 'They can and they have. I'm afraid the defence will have been watching David for weeks.'

To Gina, that news was almost worse than anything that had gone before. 'What do they want to see?' she wailed. 'Him crawling in the dirt and messing himself like an animal? He's not like that. What have they filmed?'

Standing aside, Kavanagh gestured towards David and then left the room. There were some things he couldn't do for the Lomax family.

Fifteen minutes later the court reconvened and David, in his wheelchair beside the witness stand, was given a copy of his statement, at Kavanagh's request. His useless left hand hung by his side while he tried to grasp the file in his right, managing to do so for long enough to answer Kavanagh's one simple question. 'Are the contents of your statement true?'

'Yes.'

'Thank you.' Kavanagh turned to Swarbrick. 'Nothing further, my lord.'

The judge beamed at him. At this rate they would soon make up for any lost time. Crosby, however, was surprised to be called so quickly. He had assumed that Kavanagh would take his client through the contents of the tape and formulate some explanation. Instead he had done precisely nothing. 'Could the witness's statement,' he said as he rose, 'be opened at page sixteen?'

The court usher made a move towards David but, with the statement now in his lap, he turned the pages himself. He looked expectantly at Crosby.

'Can you read the first sentence of the second paragraph, David.' David did so. 'I have no sexual function,' he read.

'Thank you.' Crosby turned to the usher. 'Perhaps we could now run the videotape.'

Two minutes later the one, extremely junior, member of the press who was covering the trial had decided that this seemingly mundane hearing could, after all, be a sensation. His editor would be delighted. Especially after he had gilded the lily and embellished the truth.

The tape was of David's visit to Covent Garden the previous Friday. At first it showed David with his two friends, sitting at a table outside a pub. Their activities – drinking several pints of lager – were innocuous and the few audible snatches of their conversation proved it to be desultory. But later, when the trio moved on to Soho, the action became far more exciting. Even though whoever had taped the scene had done so clandestinely and through a window, there was no doubt what was going on in the grubby, dingy little room.

'Can you explain what was happening there, Mr Lomax?' asked Crosby, the minute the tape finished.

'She was called Mandy, and she was from Raynham. She was twenty-five.' David's tone was supremely confident; his bearing haughty. He was undoubtedly spoiling for a fight.

'You met her,' continued Crosby, 'on Friday afternoon in Soho. And you paid her for sex?'

'I paid her for half an hour. Seventy-five pounds.' In the press gallery, the reporter scribbled frantically on his pad. Things were definitely looking up.

'You paid her for sex?'

David shook his head. 'For wishful thinking. Haven't you ever thought you could do it when you were drunk?'

Crosby ignored the taunt. 'But she was removing her clothing, wasn't she?'

'I'm not blind.'

Crosby sighed. 'So you paid seventy-five pounds for half an hour of . . . of unclad chat?'

David grinned. 'I was ripped off. She didn't have much conversation.'

Oh dear, thought Kavanagh. He's not doing himself any favours. None at all.

Crosby was dubious. 'And you still claim you have no sexual function?'

'Desire is bloody inconvenient. The plumbing's not much good if you can't turn on the tap. You must know that, Mr Crosby.'

Again Crosby ignored the jibe. He knew as well as Kavanagh that, with every sharp, barbed or intelligent remark, David was weakening his case. 'But you obviously thought,' he continued, 'that the tap might get turned on that afternoon?'

'I live in hope.'

'You speculated seventy-five pounds.'

'It was almost worth it.'

'Was it?'

David stared at the barrister with intense dislike. 'I didn't buy sex. I bought the company of a woman. For seventy-five pounds I bought half an hour of somebody's attention.' He contemplated his useless body. 'It was almost worth it,' he went on. 'Most people give me five minutes.'

Sensing that the tide was beginning to turn against him after David's poignant words, Crosby changed tack. 'You get lots of attention at the Harwell Centre, don't you? Lots of attention from Mum and Dad?'

David stared at the barrister. Something in his expression had changed. 'I have very little function,' he replied in a flat monotone. 'I used to work at a recycling centre. Now I just recycle air. Breathe in, breathe out. That's my function.'

'But you'd like to do more, wouldn't you?' Crosby said.

'Yes.'

'Like to be a bit more independent?'

'Yes.'

'You can dress yourself, can't you?'

'Yes.'

'Wash yourself, read, write. You're capable of some productive work?'

'Five minutes, usually. Then I see them looking for excuses to get away. They think I don't notice . . .'

'There's lots you could do if Mum and Dad didn't worry so much, isn't there? If they didn't insist on doing it all for you.' Crosby leaned forward. 'You don't want that, do you?'

'No.' David looked across to his parents and smiled. Even though they were aware that he was undermining his own case, they smiled back. They always smiled when David was on form. It made them forget what it was like ninety per cent of the time.

'What sort of thing,' asked Crosby, 'do you think you can do?'

But the light had suddenly gone out of David's eyes.

He appeared not to see Crosby. 'Breathe in,' he said. 'Breathe out. Breathe in, breathe out. No one pays you for that.' Then, as if suddenly remembering something, he blinked several times. 'I can make people cry. I'm sorry,' he said, as he turned to his parents with tears in his eyes, 'that I make you cry.'

An embarrassed silence descended on the court. David, it was clear, was no longer with them, and Crosby knew he had lost him. He considered battling on and then, shaking his head at Judge Swarbrick, he sat down. Swarbrick called the court to adjourn for lunch.

Gina Lomax was called as the next witness. Standing in the box, she looked like a woman at the end of her tether. There were deep shadows under her eyes; her face was lined with worry and anxiety. She was exhausted. Sleep was a luxury now largely denied to her, and her waking hours were consumed by David.

Julia Piper, taking over from Kavanagh, was the first to question her. She asked Gina to outline, for the benefit of the court, the pattern of her days. Gina did so. Even the reporter in the press gallery, who had been annoyed by the collapse of his sensational sex scoop, looked appalled as Gina described, without self-pity, her daily grind.

'Dr Walsh told us that David may lose his place at the Harwell Centre quite soon,' said Julia, after she had finished. 'Are there any aspects of his care that you feel unable to cope with on your own?'

'Too many.' Gina sighed. 'I try to be patient but . . .' She fell silent as she tried to find the right words. Then she looked up and straight at Julia. 'There is a light in people's eyes. I watch it go on and off in my son.

And sometimes it just dies and he disappears into the darkness and . . . and then someone else comes and sits in his seat and . . . he's horrible. It's like,' she bowed her head, 'having a stranger in the family.'

'Thank you, Mrs Lomax.' Julia sat down and immediately buried herself in her notes. She was trying to fight back the tears.

Crosby, however, remained unmoved by Gina's distress – and therein lay his mistake. He began, and continued, his cross-examination by firing a barrage of questions at her. Questions about her being overprotective of her only, late-born child. Questions about how she and Sam had always indulged David, about how he had never left home, about his supposed lack of initiative. Questions that, in the end, reduced Gina to tears of frustration and anger. Seemingly unaware that even Judge Swarbrick was beginning to squirm, Crosby refused to let go. 'He's like a child again,' he all but shouted at her, 'and you want to keep him like that!'

But Gina had had enough. 'I don't want him like this!' she screamed. 'I look at him sometimes and think: "Why didn't you die?" Sometimes,' she shouted through the shocked court, 'I still hope he'll die!'

Even Crosby realized he had overstepped the mark. Horrified, Judge Swarbrick leaned forward to admonish him – but it was David's voice that echoed through the court. 'Leave her alone!' he yelled at Crosby. 'Leave her alone!' In great distress, he tried to set his wheelchair in motion, to tackle the stunned barrister. His mother, now in floods of tears, looked on helplessly from the witness box while Sam, equally upset, rose from his seat and ran to David.

Pandemonium ruled. It was the first time, and, he

hoped, the last, that Swarbrick had presided over such a scene. Finding his voice, as Julia, breaking court etiquette and not caring about doing so, rushed over to help with David, he said, 'Mr Kavanagh, if that is your case, I will rise.'

Kavanagh stood up. Originally he had planned to call Sam to give his testimony, but now there was no need. He knew that he had won the first part of the battle: no one was in any doubt that David Lomax needed constant care. But the next part would be more difficult to prove: the question of liability. He faced Swarbrick. 'That is my case, my lord.' Then, as he gathered his papers and prepared to leave the room, he looked towards the public gallery. The people there, he knew, were David's ex-colleagues at the recycling centre. One of them, a short, wiry, middle-aged man, was staring at the place where David had been. Lost in thought, he bore an expression of infinite sadness. He seemed not to want to leave the room, and only did so when another man, sharply dressed and looking irritated, grabbed his arm and urged him out. Kavanagh couldn't hear what they said, but he could tell that there was no love lost between them. Had he heard the words, his impression would have been confirmed. 'Come on, Pearson,' said the younger man as they left the room. 'I want you to rehearse your statement. Again.'

CHAPTER NINETEEN

The following morning, while the court sat for what Judge Swarbrick fervently hoped would be the last day of the Lomax hearing, Jeremy Aldermarten went shopping. Although he knew that, for today at least, he would have to confine his activities to window-shopping, he felt it was best to be prepared. He had known other men to get in a complete panic just before the big day. Not for Jeremy an undignified scramble at the last minute. Turning into Chancery Lane, he cast a furtive glance around him. Today's business was strictly private, and he didn't want to be seen by anyone he knew.

A minute later, he had reached his destination. Ede & Ravenscroft was a Dickensian-looking establishment that had indeed been established in the previous century, specifically for people like Jeremy. It was London's leading supplier of barristerial outfits and accoutrements.

After another quick look up the street, Jeremy nipped into the shop and made a beeline for the rows of black suits in one corner. His hope of being left alone to browse among them was immediately dashed.

'Can I be of any assistance, sir?' The smartly dressed assistant was smiling in a manner at once unctuous and patronizing.

'Oh! Er . . . yes. Um . . . these suits . . .'

'Yes. They're for silks, sir.'

Jeremy squared his shoulders. How did this callow youth know that he wasn't a silk? 'Yes. Yes, of course they are. And how much . . . would . . . would . . . ?'

Without a word, the assistant reached forward and turned over the price tag on the sleeve of the nearest suit. Jeremy's eyes nearly popped out of his head. 'My goodness.'

'Taking silk *is* an important occasion, sir.'

'Of course it is. Quite right and proper too. And how long would it take to . . .'

'Alter them, sir? There are only two weeks between the announcement of new silks and the ceremony. We have some experience in altering them quickly. Is sir,' he added as he savoured Jeremy's discomfiture, 'expecting elevation?'

'Me? Er . . . well, you know,' Jeremy faltered. 'One makes an application out of obligation almost. Who can predict what criteria are used to decide these matters?'

'Skill,' replied the assistant, with a thin smile. 'And experience, I believe, sir.'

Funny, thought Jeremy. Tom Buckley had said exactly the same thing. 'Well,' he said. 'Perhaps I'd better try one on. Best to be prepared, don't you think?'

'Indeed, sir.'

None of the suits fitted. Jeremy, however, was unperturbed: that discovery was merely confirmation that he had done the right thing. Leaving his measurements with the assistant – 'just in case' – he made his way back to River Court with a new spring in his step. As he walked through the front door, he looked at his watch. Then he went into Tom's room.

'Post arrived yet, Tom?'

'Yes.'

'Er . . . anything for me?'

Tom suppressed a smirk. Mr Aldermarten was so transparent. 'Would I hide it from you?'

Jeremy's face fell. 'Nothing?'

'Mr Aldermarten, when it comes it will be in a great big white envelope with the stamp of the Lord Chancellor's Office on the front. Unless, of course, you don't get it. In that case, it'll be in a tatty little brown envelope with a second-class frank.' Which, he felt like pointing out, you should know full well by now.

'You wouldn't leave that sort of thing just lying around, would you, Tom?' said Jeremy anxiously.

Tom grinned. 'Am I likely to expose you to public ridicule, Mr Aldermarten?'

Jeremy felt silly. 'Just a little nervous,' he explained as he started to leave the room. Then, realizing what Tom had said, he turned back. 'Ridicule, did you say?' The only way he could be exposed to ridicule was if the little brown envelope . . .

But Tom, now bent over his paperwork, appeared not to have heard him.

Jeremy made his way to his room. This was all becoming a little stressful. Waiting for other people to make decisions was simply not good for one. Which reminded him that Julia had not yet come back to him with her decision about marriage. No doubt she wanted to mull over it a while longer.

Jeremy's proposal was the last thing on Julia's mind as she sat in the High Court. In fact, she had done her best to obliterate the entire episode from her memory. Jeremy, she decided, had been jealous of her fiancé.

And, more topically, he had no doubt decided that, as a QC-to-be, he needed a wife. A ridiculous man, but harmless.

The man on whom Julia was currently focusing her attention, however, was a different kettle of fish. He cut an unimpressive figure in a too-tight suit and a tie that had seen better days and fewer stains. She suspected that he was an unpleasant individual. Clearly not very bright, he tried to hide this by employing a certain pugnacious arrogance as he answered Kavanagh's questions. Len Baxter, his responses implied, was not a man to be messed with.

Prior to Kavanagh's cross-examination, Crosby had led Baxter through the events at East Bankside on the day of David's accident. It became clear that Baxter, who said he prided himself on being 'one hundred per cent observant', had not seen anyone approach David as he sat on the quayside eating his lunch just before the accident; that neither Mr Dale nor Mr Pearson had gone anywhere near him just before they went into the main building and that he himself, at the time of the accident, was also in the building, standing at the entrance. As he volunteered that information, Julia had made a note on the pad in front of her. She well remembered that location: it was where the suspiciously new-looking hard hats had been stored during her recent visit to East Bankside.

Kavanagh, who had also taken an instant dislike to Baxter, took him through the events of the day yet again, and asked him to go further back. 'Perhaps,' he suggested, 'you can confirm exactly where everyone was immediately before the main power went off.'

'I was in the cab of the spreader.'

'The machine that lifted the refuse containers onto the barges?'

'Yes.'

'From where you could clearly see David, eating his lunch on the quayside?'

'Oh, yeah.' Evidently Baxter was bored.

'So,' Kavanagh continued, 'Mr Dale, the site administrator, arrived and the foreman Mr Pearson went to speak to him. Then they both went into the main building. Then the main power went off. Correct?'

'Yep. Then I come down from my cab.'

'And you went and stood just inside the entrance to the main building, near the main power switch?' Julia had asked Kavanagh to emphasize that point. Now, looking at the note she had passed him, he understood why.

'That's dead right,' said Baxter.

'From where you could see Pearson and Dale in the control booth on the opposite side of the interior of the building. Then,' he added, 'you lit a cigarette?'

'Yeah.' Baxter looked at Kavanagh as if he were stupid. He'd just *told* Crosby he'd lit a cigarette.

'Why was the power turned off?' asked Kavanagh.

'Dunno. Something got snarled up with one of the rams. Something like that. Happens all the time.'

'All the time?'

'Once in a while.'

'Which is it? Once in a while or all the time?'

Baxter tugged at his straining shirt collar. 'Er . . . once in a while.'

'So: you were inside the building and you're an observant chap. Couldn't you see what the problem was?'

'I was having a fag. Wasn't my business.' Baxter, confident again, spoke smugly.

'And you didn't ask Pearson and Dale why the power was off?'

Baxter looked genuinely horrified at the idea. 'I didn't want to get shouted at.'

'Oh? They were shouting?'

Too late, Baxter saw his mistake. 'Er . . . no. I . . . I couldn't hear.'

'But something,' Kavanagh persisted, 'stopped you approaching them. Your machine had cut out for no apparent reason, causing you to cease work. No one could have objected to you asking why.'

'I didn't want to interrupt them.'

'Because they would have shouted at you?'

'They weren't arguing.'

'I didn't say they were. But if you couldn't hear what they were talking about, how could you tell they weren't arguing?'

'Well . . . they weren't waving their arms about, were they?'

'You don't have to wave your arms to have an argument, do you?' Kavanagh pointed out.

'I do.'

Kavanagh could well believe that. 'What was David wearing when he was sitting on the quayside?' he said, hoping to wrong-foot Baxter.

'Can't remember.'

'Nothing memorable?'

'No.'

'Not one of those luminous safety vests?'

'No.'

'Or a brightly coloured hat?'

'No.'

Then Kavanagh made a show of looking annoyed at himself. 'Oh . . . what am I thinking? Of course he wasn't. He wasn't even in a hard-hat area, was he?'

'Nope. It starts right next to my machine.'

Kavanagh smiled. 'Sorry, Mr Baxter.'

Baxter was pleased with himself. Nice to get one over this snooty legal geezer.

'So,' said the geezer. 'No hard hat. You're sure about that?'

Baxter hesitated before replying. Suddenly he wasn't so sure. 'Yes,' he said. 'I'm sure.'

'But he had one when he was on the barge. It's in the Health and Safety inspector's report. Mr Baxter, when did David go and get that hat?'

Baxter stared Kavanagh straight in the eye. 'I don't know.'

'The shelf of hard hats is right next to the power switch. You were standing there having your cigarette.'

'I don't remember.'

'Or maybe,' Kavanagh suggested, 'you were distracted by the argument between Pearson and Dale?'

'There wasn't no argument.' Dale had been adamant about that one. 'If,' he had said to Baxter, 'you say we were arguing – far less what we were arguing about – then you're dead meat. Understand?' Baxter had understood.

Jim Dale was the next witness called. Julia had already decided he was a wide-boy and his obviously expensive suit, the prominent Rolex and the suspiciously yellow tan made her even more confident of her diagnosis. But where Baxter had been harmless, Dale, she suspected, was dangerous.

Crosby's examination made much of the impeccable safety record at East Bankside Recycling Centre. Where

Baxter had been proud of his keen powers of observation, Dale congratulated himself on his rigorous safety standards and training procedures.

'One last thing,' said Crosby, after he had established that there had not been a major accident either before or since David Lomax's, 'can we clear up this matter of the possible "dispute" between you and Mr Pearson. Do you have any memory of that?'

Dale made a convincing show of attempting to remember. The truth was, he had a clear memory of their argument. It would have been impossible to forget. 'Not really,' he said at length. 'But these things come up from time to time.' He shrugged and smiled. 'I am, after all, his boss.'

'Do you know why David Lomax was on the barge, Mr Dale?' asked Crosby.

Dale adopted a forlorn air. 'I can't imagine,' he lied. 'Just a tragic accident.'

'Tragic indeed,' said Kavanagh, as he sprang to his feet. 'But you would have done everything possible in advance to avoid such a tragedy?'

Dale agreed that he would. Again, he lauded the efficiency of his training programme. Kavanagh seemed impressed as he listened to Dale's catalogue of week-long training programmes and regular safety drills. 'So how on earth,' he asked in wonder, 'could this have happened? Bright boy, rigorous training programme?'

'Maybe he's not as clever as he seems.'

'Or perhaps your training programme is not quite as rigorous as you make out.'

'You can ask the Health and Safety—'

'It didn't work,' interrupted Kavanagh, 'with Mr

Baxter, did it? He was having a cigarette in a no-smoking area.'

A sharp intake of breath greeted that remark. Kavanagh let the silence hang heavy in the court while Dale tried to formulate an answer. He failed.

'What was your argument with Mr Pearson about?' said Kavanagh.

'I've already said, I can't remember if it was an argument. It was over a year ago. How can I be expected to remember?'

'But it wasn't a day like any other, was it? It was the day that your perfect safety record was very badly blemished.'

Then Dale let himself down by glancing in disgust over to David, impassive in his wheelchair. 'It was his own fault,' he snapped.

Kavanagh thought that was as good a moment as any to end his cross-examination. He hadn't expected to get far with either Baxter or Dale, just far enough to sow seeds of doubt in the judge's mind. It was Crosby's next and final witness on whom he pinned his hopes. Bob Pearson, he felt, was the wild card, not least because David had told him he was the only person at East Bankside who had shown any sympathy towards him, both before and after the accident.

With Pearson, Crosby employed the same tactics as Kavanagh had with David. He asked him to hold his statement in his hands and asked him if what it contained was the truth. Looking even more tired and drawn than the Lomax family, Pearson said that, yes, it was true. Then Crosby sat down.

Kavanagh got up. 'You liked David Lomax, didn't you, Mr Pearson?'

'Yes. He's a nice lad.'

'Intelligent and trustworthy?'

'Yes.'

'A boy of above average intelligence, trusted by you, the site foreman and safety officer, put through a "rigorous" training programme by Mr Dale, and yet he contrives to get himself trapped between two ten-tonne containers, in an area to which he was strictly forbidden access.'

Pearson didn't rely.

'It's a conundrum, isn't it?' prompted Kavanagh.

'Yes.'

'It's almost unbelievable that he would have placed himself in such obvious danger.'

Again no reply.

'Do you have any idea how that came to happen, Mr Pearson?'

Oh, yes, thought Pearson, I most certainly do. He cast his mind back to the awful events of that day. Despite the passing of a year, he still had a vivid picture of what happened. A hatch on a container on one of the barges had broken open and was on the point of spewing out its contents. David, eagle-eyed as ever, had spotted it just in time. Baxter, dopey as usual, had been on the point of lowering a container from the spreader; a container that, because of the open hatch, would not have been able to sit in place on the barge. Dale had sent David Lomax out to the barge to fix the container. 'No,' replied Pearson as he forced himself back to the courtroom and Kavanagh's question. 'I have no idea why he was there. Rush of blood, maybe?'

But Kavanagh had noted the hesitation. 'You don't seem completely happy with that answer, Mr Pearson.'

'Well, we all make mistakes . . .'

'Do we? When was the last one you made?'

'What?'

'You should be aware. You're the safety officer. What,' he repeated, 'was the last mistake you made at your place of work?'

Pearson looked miserable. 'I don't . . . well, it was just a figure of speech. I don't know why he was out there. I wouldn't wish that on anybody.' Then, like Dale before him, he glanced over to David. But the look he gave David was entirely different from Dale's. It was of infinite regret and deep sadness. 'I wish,' he said in a small voice, 'that it hadn't happened.'

So did Kavanagh. But he wanted to find out why it *had* happened. 'Why did you switch off the power, Mr Pearson?'

'I can't remember exactly. Funny noise or something from one of the rams.'

'But you're not sure?'

'No.'

'You were distracted?'

Of course I was distracted, Pearson wanted to shout. Dale was distracting me. He was shouting at me. 'No,' he said. 'I wasn't distracted.'

Kavanagh was far from convinced. 'You were in the middle of an argument with Mr Dale.'

'We were talking,' corrected Pearson.

'But you started talking outside the main building. You couldn't have heard this "funny noise" out there, could you?'

'I don't remember.'

Kavanagh looked down at his notes and sighed. 'You were talking with Mr Dale. You followed him into the building. You turned off the main power as you passed and then pursued Dale into the control booth. That's correct, isn't it?'

'Yes.'

'Mr Baxter didn't hear a "funny noise" from inside the building, did he?'

No. There was no funny noise. Dale invented the noise. 'I didn't ask him.'

'And did he ask you why the power had been turned off?'

'No.'

'Hmm. You remember some things very well. Baxter says he didn't notice anything wrong inside the building. He didn't hear any noises. Why was that?'

'He's not very observant.' That, at least, was an incontrovertible fact.

'No. He isn't, is he? He certainly didn't see David Lomax pick up a hard hat from the shelf.'

'He didn't need one ... Oh!' The 'oh' was hardly more than an intake of breath – but it said a great deal. 'I mean,' corrected Pearson, 'he didn't need one normally.'

But Kavanagh knew he was on to something. 'What do you mean? Why didn't he need one on this occasion?'

'Because he wasn't going anywhere.'

'But he *did* go somewhere. He went onto the barge. He was wearing the hat when he went onto the barge. A sensible young man, taking precautions. Where did he get the hat from, Mr Pearson?'

I gave it to him. There were no spare hats on the shelf back then. It was my hat he was wearing when he was crushed. I gave it to him because you needed one on the barge. And he didn't have one of his own. Dale had thought it a needless expense.

'Don't know,' he replied.

Kavanagh let him stew. Then, sure that he was on

the right track, he resumed his relentless questioning. 'You turned off the power because of a problem you can't recall and Baxter failed to notice. In what circumstances other than "funny noises" would you switch the power off?'

Pearson fidgeted nervously. 'Mechanical faults.'

'Anything else? You're the safety officer. Safety reasons, surely, would be other good reasons?'

'Possibly.'

'If you saw someone on the barge you'd switch off the power, wouldn't you?'

'Of course.'

'Would you switch it off if you knew someone was going to be on the barge?'

'Yes.'

'And you'd make sure that person had a safety hat, wouldn't you?'

'Yes.' ·

Kavanagh inclined his head towards the increasingly wary witness. 'You gave David Lomax a safety hat on this occasion, didn't you? That's why he didn't need one from the shelf?'

Pearson didn't seem to want to reply.

'You gave it to him because you knew he was going out there. The problem wasn't inside the building, was it, Mr Pearson? It was outside. I would suggest,' he concluded, as Pearson remained resolutely silent, 'that the power was turned off to enable David Lomax to go and fix that problem.'

And you would be absolutely right. 'No,' he replied. 'That's not true.'

'You sent David Lomax onto that barge—'

'No! I never sent him there.'

No, thought Kavanagh, I don't think you did. But

someone else did. 'All right,' he said. 'Let's look at what happened next.' He shuffled through his notes, and turned anew to the witness. 'About three minutes later you came out of the control booth and told Baxter to return to work. Without checking the spreader or the barge you turned the power back on. You were the one who had the rush of blood. You, Mr Pearson, are the one who is directly responsible for the way David Lomax is today.'

Pearson hung his head. 'I never knew he was on there.'

'But you failed to take any precautions before turning the power back on. Why?'

Because Dale was shouting at me and I was confused. 'I don't know. I mean I didn't mean to—'

'Perhaps you were preoccupied with something else?'

Pearson met Kavanagh's eye. He knows, he thought. He knows exactly what happened. 'I don't think I was preoccupied.'

'What was your argument with Mr Dale about?'

It was about safety. Of all the bloody, bitter ironies in the world, it was about safety. The Health people were coming that afternoon and Dale was in a flap. Especially about getting the barge loaded before they saw . . . 'We weren't arguing,' he snapped.

'But Baxter was too scared to approach you. Something was going on. Was Dale angry with you?'

'No.'

'Did he tell you to turn the power back on?'

'No.'

'So it was your decision to do that. You take full responsibility for the action that led to David's injury on the barge.'

'I told you!' shouted the distressed, exhausted man. 'I didn't think he'd be on there then.' Again, he was too late in realizing his mistake.

'Then,' repeated Kavanagh, emphasizing it, 'no one should have been on the barge "then".'

'No.'

Kavanagh lowered his tone. 'You thought he'd be off there – by "then"?'

Pearson didn't reply.

'He took longer than expected to fix the problem, Mr Pearson. Am I right?'

Pearson's shoulders drooped in defeat. He could no longer carry on the pretence. Slowly, he nodded.

'What was David doing on the barge?' asked Kavanagh gently. 'What was the problem?' Behind him, Julia craned her neck. Like the Lomax family, the judge and the entire prosecution team, she was dying to know. From the looks on the faces of the 'suits' from the Sanctuary Insurance Company on the opposite benches, they were also keen for enlightenment. Dale and his cronies, it was becoming apparent, had spun a fine little yarn.

At last Pearson looked up. 'One of the container doors wasn't closed,' he admitted.

'And what would be the cause of that?'

'Too much stuff packed in.'

'In the container?'

'Yes. He shouldn't have gone out there, but it's a simple job – I've done it myself.'

'But for some reason this simple job took David Lomax more than three minutes. Long enough for you to be able to forget he was out there. Why would that be? Mr Pearson? Why?'

'You'd have to ask him.'

268

Kavanagh was scathing. 'You know full well David can't tell us anything about the incident. He lost his memory as a result of it.'

Duly chastened, Pearson glanced over to David. Everyone in the court could tell he felt nothing but sympathy for the young man. 'He shouldn't have been out there,' he said, in a half-whisper.

'Mr Pearson,' urged Kavanagh, 'why did David's task take so long?'

Very upset now, Pearson tried to avoid Kavanagh's eye. 'I couldn't say . . . Maybe he started checking what was in the bloody thing . . .'

'The container?'

'Yeah.'

'What might he have seen?'

'All sorts of . . .' Then, biting his lip, Pearson trailed into silence. He was well aware of Jim Dale's presence in the room. And Dale was looking murderous.

'Why would it have detained him?' persisted Kavanagh.

'He'd have been looking at it, that's all!' Suddenly Pearson was shouting. 'He didn't know, you see,' he added, in a smaller voice. 'It was a secret.'

'What was?'

Pearson addressed himself to Dale. He was both accusatory and apologetic. 'I told you it wasn't right.'

'Mr Pearson.' Kavanagh, like everyone else, was desperate to know. 'What would David have been looking at?'

Pearson exhaled deeply. He knew the game was up. And all he felt was relief. He had never wanted to play it in the first place. 'We do a lot of business with hospitals. Health authorities. Their waste. We're supposed to treat their stuff and seal it. Not,' he added with a venomous look at Dale, 'just bung it in cheap black bags. They split open, for God's sake! That's probably how David got hepatitis into the bargain, poor sod. As if he needed anything else.'

'What exactly was in these bags?'

'I don't know.'

'What have you seen in similar bags?'

'X-ray plates. Chemicals.' Pearson screwed up his nose in disgust. 'Blood. Even bits of people! We were filling one large barge a day. Dumping it on an open site. Cost-cutting.' His voice grated. 'God only knows what happens down that end.'

Kavanagh was dumbfounded, like everyone else in the room. 'You mean,' he said, recovering himself, 'that you were dumping untreated hospital waste on an open site?'

Pearson nodded. 'I told Dale it was wrong. That's what we were arguing about. That's why I was distracted.' He spoke to the court at large. 'All this. This isn't about David. A few thousand quid compensation. This is about the company. Staying afloat.'

As he spoke, the representatives of Sanctuary Insurance looked at Dale. If the looks could have killed, Dale would have been dead. He was indeed deathly pale under the fake tan, and his mouth was set in a thin, furious line.

'Mr Pearson,' said Kavanagh, 'you are saying to this court that your company would rather lie about what happened to David than risk exposing its methods of dumping dangerous waste?'

Pearson couldn't speak.

'In your evidence, you too attempted to conceal this from the court.'

Pearson nodded, then found his voice. 'I had to. Dale said the accident was my fault because I turned the main power on. Said I could be prosecuted.'

Kavanagh looked up in surprise. 'And you were prepared to accept all the blame?'

'Dale knew he had me. My wife, you see, she's dying of cancer. I couldn't lose my job, couldn't go to prison. What would have happened to her?' Then he said to Dale, 'But it doesn't matter now. She got taken into hospital this morning. She won't be coming out again,' he added, almost inaudibly.

Another horrified but this time sympathetic silence reigned. Even Sam and Gina Lomax, confused by the barrage of information thrown at them, looked sad for him as they contemplated Pearson's awful dilemma.

'Mr Pearson,' continued Kavanagh, after a respectful pause, 'did you tell David Lomax to go on to the barge?'

'No.'

'Who did?'

Pearson looked at Dale.

'Was it Mr Dale?'

'Yes.'

'Thank you.' Kavanagh sat down.

Crosby had no more witnesses to call. Even if he had, there would have been little point. Judge Swarbrick, like everyone else in the court, had heard enough. His decision would not be difficult. Crosby stood up. 'That concludes the case for the defence, my lord.' And, he thought, what a feeble case it turned out to be. Still, it wasn't his fault. He'd encountered people like Dale before. He'd probably meet them again.

Swarbrick then addressed the court. 'I'll hear your concluding speeches tomorrow morning. I'll reserve judgement for two weeks.'

*

'I don't understand,' said Sam Lomax, as he rushed up to Kavanagh seconds after the court rose. 'Did we win?'

Kavanagh smiled. 'Technically, we have to wait two weeks, but I think you could book a holiday, yes.' As he was congratulated by a delighted Sam and Gina, he noticed Pearson out of the corner of his eye. Too ashamed to come too close to David or his family, he was hovering uncertainly in the background. Then David saw him. He wheeled his chair towards his ex-colleague and looked up at him. He saw tears in his eyes.

'I'm sorry about your wife,' he said.

That was the last thing Pearson had expected to hear. But then, after all, it was David speaking. He smiled in grateful acknowledgement. 'Thank you. So am I. But . . . David . . . I'm . . .'

'What?'

'I'm very sorry. About . . .'

David reached up with his good arm. 'Yes,' he said. 'So am I.'

CHAPTER TWENTY

'He's got it.'

'I beg your pardon?'

'Mr Aldermarten, sir.' Tom Buckley waved a large white envelope at Kavanagh. 'He's got silk.'

'Good God! Er, I mean . . . well . . .' Kavanagh was far too flummoxed to find the right words.

Tom supplied them for him. 'Perhaps congratulations are in order, sir?'

'Yes. Quite. Absolutely.' God, thought Kavanagh, I'm even beginning to *sound* like Jeremy. 'Yes,' he added with more conviction. Then he looked at the unopened envelope. 'Presumably Mr Aldermarten doesn't know?'

'No. He's not in yet.'

'Then I think we ought to arrange a little surprise for him, don't you think?'

Tom grinned. 'Yes. I think that would be fitting. I reckon he deserves a little party.' And heaven knows, he thought, so do I. Tom was heartily sick of Jeremy Aldermarten arriving each day in hope and then skulking off to his room with a face as long as two weeks. The lack of news from the Lord Chancellor's Office had started to make Jeremy's – and therefore Tom's – life a misery.

'All right, then,' said Kavanagh. 'Mr Foxcott in?'

'Yes.'

'Good. I'll have a word with him about the ... surprise.'

As he walked down the corridor, Kavanagh reflected that he'd had quite enough surprises, over the weekend, to last him for a month. Life had delivered a good few over past weeks. Some had been good, others terrible.

It had been a fortnight since the conclusion of the Lomax case, and the gratifying, although not entirely unexpected, aftermath of the prosecution's victory was that Judge Swarbrick had awarded the Lomax family the entire three-quarters of a million in damages that Kavanagh had asked for. The last that he had heard of Sam and Gina was that they had booked a fortnight's holiday in the Canaries – without their son. He had been glad to hear that. If ever a couple deserved a break, it was Sam and Gina. Kavanagh had been convinced that, had they lost the case, one or both would have had a heart-attack. Or perhaps a stroke.

A stroke. That had been the nasty surprise. Out of the blue, Kavanagh's elderly father had had a stroke at home in Nottingham and had been rushed to hospital. Thankfully, Alfred Kavanagh was making a rapid recovery and claimed that his hospitalization was a 'fuss over nothing'. The doctors, Kavanagh had been delighted to hear when he had rushed up to Nottingham, had said that it had been a fairly mild stroke. His ever capable mother Marjorie had told him that he mustn't worry about them. They would be fine. Their other son Grahame was living nearby, after all. They had never admitted that they would have preferred it to be the other way round. As Kavanagh well knew, it wasn't that they disliked Grahame. Cynthia, his wife, was the problem. She had never forgiven her husband for not being as successful as his brother. And, being socially ambitious, she had never been able to hide her jealousy of Lizzie. While Lizzie herself never mentioned that her father was a peer, Cynthia never stopped talking about it. 'Dear Lord Probyn,' she would say of the man she had met only twice in her life, '*such* a nice man.'

No, thought Kavanagh as he knocked on Peter Fox-cott's door. Cynthia was not going to be much of a comfort to his parents. There was no doubt that his father's brush with mortality had been a shock to them all. And even though Alfred was due to leave hospital within a week, Marjorie was going to have her work cut out looking after him. Something would have to be done.

'Come in! Ah, James. You've heard the news, I take it?'

'Indeed I have.' Kavanagh grinned. 'Jeremy Aldermarten QC. Quite a thought.'

'Indeed.'

Both men were silent but each knew what the other was thinking. 'Well,' said Kavanagh, 'it's not entirely surprising . . .'

'Isn't it?'

Kavanagh went on, 'It'll be good for River Court.'

'Mmm.' Then Peter became serious. 'S'pose so. But with Jeremy's elevation and Julia leaving, we're going to have to get someone else.'

Kavanagh sat down. 'Yes. You're right.'

'Helen Ames,' began Peter, with a wary look at his colleague, 'has been sniffing around these parts.'

'*Helen Ames?* I thought she'd left the Bar?'

'She had a baby, James. It's something, I believe, that you recover from.'

'Hmm.' There were few people that Kavanagh

actively disliked, but Helen Ames was one of them.

Peter knew what was coming. He held up a hand to stall Kavanagh's objection. 'Look, we can discuss all that later. For now, I suggest we organize a little celebration for Jeremy.'

Half an hour later, Jeremy Aldermarten arrived at River Court and walked, as he had every day for a week, straight into Tom Buckley's room. He looked, as he had every day for a week, apprehensive. The room, for once, was empty. And on Tom's desk there was a small yet prominently placed pile of post addressed to Jeremy. On the top was a tatty little brown envelope.

Jeremy's face fell. He snatched up the pile and, swearing under his breath, walked out and down the corridor towards his own room. His expectant expression had been replaced by one of bitter disappointment. Yet as soon as he opened his door, it changed yet again – to one of shock. The entire complement of River Court's staff stood in front of him. Everyone was grinning broadly and holding a glass of champagne. Jeremy nearly dropped his letters and his briefcase as Peter Foxcott, in the centre of the little group, raised his glass. 'I give you,' he announced, 'River Court's newest silk . . . Mr Aldermarten!'

Everyone raised their glasses. Jeremy, his mouth wide open, remained transfixed in the doorway. 'What . . . ?'

Then Kavanagh stepped forward with the large white envelope and a glass of champagne. Both were for Jeremy. 'You got it. And now,' he added with a smile, 'you cost twice as much and you'll probably never work again.'

276

Jeremy could hardly believe his ears. 'I got it? I *got* it.' He tore open the envelope. 'I bloody well got it!' Then he turned to Tom, standing grinning in the corner. 'You rat, Tom Buckley! You bloody rat!' Everyone laughed. They had all been in on the joke of the – empty – brown envelope. And they were all, despite their sure knowledge of Jeremy's impending increase in pomposity, delighted for him.

As Jeremy was swallowed up by the cheering, back-slapping throng, Tom made his way over to Julia Piper, who was standing next to Kavanagh. 'My only pay-out,' he said, handing her a wad of notes.

Julia hadn't a clue what he was talking about. She looked, uncomprehending, at the money. 'The bets on Mr Aldermarten,' explained Tom. 'You won.'

Kavanagh turned to Julia. 'You mean,' he said, 'that you bet on Jeremy getting it? He'll be touched by your faith, Julia. I must tell him.'

'Don't you dare, James. To be honest,' she added, *sotto voce* as Tom walked away, 'Tom blinded me with science. I thought I was backing him not to get it.'

Kavanagh fell about with mirth. 'Well, I suppose I should be glad you're not a gambler.'

'No, I'm not.' Julia pocketed the money. 'What does "six to four on" actually mean?'

Again Kavanagh was convulsed with laughter. 'I'm not going to tell you. Heaven knows how much you'll start winning if you actually know what you're doing.'

Julia was mock-affronted. 'That's the first patronizing thing you've ever said to me, Jim. You disappoint me.'

Kavanagh, serious now, regarded her over the rim of his glass. 'And you disappoint me.'

'I do?' Julia couldn't comprehend what she was hearing.

'By leaving us.'

'Oh.' She looked away. 'Please let's not go into that again. It's done now.' In two weeks' time she would be in Kenya. In six months' time she would be married. And after that . . . Well, marriage wasn't a death sentence, was it? And Kenya wouldn't be for ever. She could still come back to the Bar. Lots of other people did. And one woman was desperate to do so right now, if the rumours were true. Keen to divert the conversation from her impending departure, she said, 'I hear that Helen Ames has been around here a lot recently.'

'Oh, God, don't,' Kavanagh said. 'You know what I think of her.'

'No,' Julia replied. 'I don't, actually. Old foes?'

'You could say that. It was years ago and Helen—'

'Ah! There you are!' It was Jeremy, bounding up to them and dashing Julia's hopes of hearing what she hoped were salacious details about the redoubtable Ms Ames. 'Discussing . . . marriage, no doubt.' The last words, accompanied by a particularly unfriendly look, were addressed to Julia.

'No.' Kavanagh missed the look and, anyway, wouldn't have understood its significance. Jeremy's proposal to Julia – and the several refusals she had had to give him before he had finally clicked that perhaps she was serious, after all – had remained a secret between them. 'No, we were talking about work.'

Ah. Julia studied Kavanagh from under her lashes. So he's keeping the Helen Ames business pretty close to his chest.

Jeremy waved his letter from the Lord Chancellor.

'I'll take the day off tomorrow. I think I deserve it, don't you?' he said.

'Oh, absolutely,' replied Julia. 'And I'm sure you've got a lot of DIY to catch up on. Framing things and whatnot,' she added nastily. Well, I've already congratulated him twice, she told herself. And someone's going to have to take him down a peg or two.

But Jeremy had already ambled off to flourish the letter in yet more faces.

Kavanagh and Julia sipped their champagne in silence. Then, Julia asked, referring to Kavanagh's remark to Jeremy, 'what have you got on now, anyway?'

Kavanagh grimaced. 'The Wicks appeal. It's tomorrow.'

'Oh, my God. Better look smart, then. The paparazzi'll be all over the place.'

'I know.' Kavanagh pulled another face. 'But thank God they're armed with cameras and not guns. If I win, a lot of people will want to shoot me . . .'

Months ago, the trial of Sam and Caroline Wicks had made the headlines of every newspaper. The tabloids had had a field day. The combination of wealthy families torn apart by jealousy and greed had been irresistible, especially when a double murder – or, in tabloid parlance, a 'bloodbath' – was thrown in.

Kavanagh had had the unenviable task of defending Caroline Wicks. A pretty but awkward and, he suspected, slightly simple girl in her twenties, she had been accused with her brother of murdering their father and stepmother in cold blood at the family home, a sprawling farmhouse in Surrey. The bodies had been found by their younger half-brother Duncan.

The evidence against the Wicks siblings had been strong. Although neither lived at the farm, they had admitted to visiting that day, to talk, they claimed, about a business scheme in which Sam wanted to involve his father. In court, it had emerged that this was hardly unusual. Duncan had claimed that his father had given Sam endless amounts of money for his 'schemes', all of which had failed. He had known that, this time, his father was going to refuse. But he hadn't known, when he returned from working on the farm, that Sam and Caroline would have gone and his parents would be dead; shot through the head with one of the family's shotguns.

Bitter salvos had been fired in court by Duncan Pembridge and Sam Wicks. What made the scenario more interesting to the press was that the dead man, David Pembridge, was father to all three. The surname Wicks had been taken by Sam and Caroline after their parents' bitter divorce. Wicks, Kavanagh had explained to the court, had been their mother's maiden name. Their mother was dead, too, although, unlike their stepmother, from natural causes. Of course, the press had gone to town over Sam and Caroline's public adoption of their mother's name. It implied they loathed their father – even before the appearance of their 'wicked' stepmother and the brother they were obliged to recognize as a relative.

While the evidence against Sam and Caroline had been overwhelming, much of it had been circumstantial. Statements from Duncan and Mrs Tully, a neighbour, contradicted their claim to have left the farm at one o'clock, two hours before the murders had taken place. They said they had both seen Sam and Caroline driving away at three. Sam and Caroline, however, insisted that after they had left, burglars must have broken in and murdered their father and stepmother. A great deal of missing family silver lent credibility to their story. The fact that Sam's fingerprints were found on the shotgun did not. But then, as Sam had pointed out in court, Duncan's and his father's, as well as several unidentified prints, were also on it.

That Sam had been able to be so vociferous in court, all those months ago, was explained by his having chosen to conduct his own defence. An avenue open to every citizen, it was rarely taken and strongly discouraged by solicitors, especially when the defendant had no legal training. But everyone involved had reckoned without Sam. He was sharp, intelligent, had a good grasp of facts and a fanatical belief in his own abilities. While remanded in custody, he had zealously consumed every legal tome on which he had been able to lay his hands. It had been another aspect of the trial that had excited the media. And the fact that his sister Caroline's defence was conducted by James Kavanagh QC led to all sorts of stories about conflicts of interest and – this had tickled Kavanagh – an editorial on the subject of barristers being a waste of money.

As everyone at River Court knew, Kavanagh had found the whole episode trying, and partly because Caroline Wicks was so devoted to her brother that he had not been able to establish much of a rapport with her as a client. Her allegiance was to Sam and Sam alone. She had been incapable of grasping that, as far as the murders went, she and Sam were not 'in it together'.

But it had been Sam who had caused Kavanagh the most grief. His enthusiasm for his self-appointed task overflowed, in court, into arrogance and, on many occasions, near contempt. Not only had he fancied himself as a barrister, but he had decided he and Kavanagh were a 'team'. Kavanagh had thought otherwise and had tried to keep his distance. In the end, Sam had done his sister no favours. In spite of Kavanagh's valiant defence, both Sam and Caroline had been found guilty of murder and had been sentenced to life imprisonment. On pronouncing the sentence, the judge had made plain that he was glad to see the back of Sam Wicks. He had been a nuisance in court and had upset everyone. But that had been no excuse for the judge, throughout the trial, to convey to the jury the strong impression that he felt both Sam and Caroline Wicks were guilty.

And therein lay part of the reason for the forth-coming appeal: an appeal that Kavanagh was due to make in the Royal Courts of Justice the following day.

He did not, therefore, stay long at Jeremy Aldermarten's celebratory drinks party. Not that he would have wanted to anyway. Jeremy, he noted as he left the room, was becoming positively insufferable. He had also spilt champagne all over his letter from the Lord Chancellor.

CHAPTER TWENTY-ONE

In fact, Kavanagh was dreading the appeal. Such occasions, even for experienced QCs, were fraught and intimidating. Today, three judges, all of whom had studied in detail the transcripts of the trial and the papers submitted thereafter, would decide whether there was sufficient reason to overturn the verdict and release Sam and Caroline Wicks. For Kavanagh, there was an added stress: the conflict of personal belief versus professional propriety. He felt that the judge at the original trial had indeed been biased, and that the evidence against Sam and Caroline was inconclusive. But he disliked Sam Wicks: he suspected him capable of murder. Yet he couldn't afford to let that belief cloud his judgement.

And there was the problem of Caroline. While in prison, she had attempted suicide. Although she had been referred to a psychiatric unit, she was now back in jail. Her solicitor had voiced his fears to Kavanagh that she would try again before too long – and probably successfully. Then Sam's solicitor, Gerry Wainwright, had told him that Wicks had requested that Kavanagh lodge the appeal for both of them. Kavanagh had felt morally obliged to accept: it was the only way that Caroline had any chance.

Lizzie had been furious. 'But it's not your responsibility! You don't have to handle it.' That was true, she knew. He had done his duty at the trial. Another barrister could handle the appeal.

'I know,' Kavanagh had replied. 'But there isn't another barrister who knows what this appeal is about in the way I do. That's not vanity, Lizzie, it's fact. If you really want to know, there are a lot of things about this case I don't like – starting with that brother of hers. But it's my responsibility to see it through, and I'm bloody well going to do it. All right?' Lizzie had been so stunned by his impassioned outburst that she hadn't been able to reply.

Now, before the judges, he was pressing his case for the release of Sam and Caroline. 'May it please your lordships, I appear on behalf of the appellants Samuel and Caroline Wicks. My learned friend Mr Creggan,' he added with a nod to the man on his right, 'appears for the prosecution.' Creggan had been the prosecution counsel in the original trial, and was not best pleased about the appeal, mainly because his client Duncan Pembridge was apoplectic with rage. Sam and Caroline, he had screamed, would only be released over his dead body.

As Kavanagh addressed the judges, Duncan looked down at his half-brother and sister from the public gallery. His face was a mask of hatred. Sam, as usual, was a bundle of nervous energy and was looking at Kavanagh with hungry concentration. Caroline was almost catatonic. Hunched close to her brother, she stared at the floor, seemingly oblivious of what was happening.

Lord Justice Fenwick, the senior judge, leaned forward in his chair. He had an air of amused detachment that Kavanagh, never having met him before, found disarming. He didn't know if the judge was always like this, or if he found the appeal a bit of a joke.

It transpired to be the latter. 'Mr Kavanagh,' he said, 'we have all read the papers in this appeal. Since the grounds ultimately amount to stating that the learned judge's conduct of the trial was prejudicial, we thought it only right to inform you that we have not, for ourselves, found, on reading the transcript material, evidence to substantiate that complaint.'

Kavanagh hadn't expected quite such a lethal opening but his reply was equally eloquent – and equally icy. 'My lord, I am grateful to your lordships for that indication. One answer to your lordships' point would be that the full reality of a situation can never be wholly reflected in a simple transcript.' None of these three judges had been in court at Sam and Caroline's trial, and the transcript conveyed only the words, not the emotions of the general atmosphere. 'I hope to persuade you,' he continued, 'that your initial impression is wrong, and I am going to ask your lordships to look first at the learned judge's general attitude, to Mr Wicks in particular. We say that throughout the trial he gave the jury the impression that the defendants were guilty.'

'Mr Kavanagh,' Fenwick was still smiling, 'so far as we can ascertain, on numerous occasions the learned judge was not only tolerant towards Mr Wicks but went out of his way to help him.'

But Kavanagh was ready for that. 'May I then refer your lordships to page forty of the transcript, between sections E and G?' he retorted.

The bewigged judges flicked simultaneously through the papers and found the relevant passages. If Kavanagh had felt so inclined, he would have found their performance comical.

When he had read the pages in question, Fenwick said approvingly, 'Ah, yes, this is where the learned judge stopped the defendants chatting among themselves before they gave evidence.'

Kavanagh, though, had been there at the time. Sam and Caroline had indeed talked to each other at that point, but the judge's statement that they had been about to give evidence had been wholly erroneous, which Kavanagh then proceeded to correct. 'They were not about to give evidence,' he said. 'That is the heart of this matter. The judge's implication in front of the jury that they were colluding was wholly unjustified and manifestly prejudiced.'

Fenwick gave the point due consideration. Then, after a murmured consultation with his colleagues, he leaned forward again. 'But, Mr Kavanagh, the learned judge was very quick on another occasion to tell Mr Pembridge, and therefore the jury, that Mr Wicks was carrying out a "perfectly proper cross-examination". That does not sound like prejudice against Mr Wicks, does it?'

No, thought Kavanagh. It sounds like we're all nit-picking here. He was interested in the overall picture. 'My lord,' he replied, 'the grounds for this appeal are cumulative.' He asked the judges to refer in their transcripts to the point when Mrs Tully had given evidence against Sam and Caroline. The judge had congratulated her. That, said Kavanagh, was a clear endorsement of her evidence. Not so, said Fenwick, it was just a common courtesy. And so it went on: Kavanagh trying to paint the broader picture; Fenwick referring to details. In the public gallery Duncan Pembridge began to look confident. His murderous siblings would stay in prison. Sam, increasingly agitated in the dock, had difficulty in restraining himself from taking part in the proceedings. Several times, he looked as if he was going to rise to his feet and make an objection. The policeman by his side made it clear that such behaviour was out of the question.

The only person who displayed absolutely no interest was Caroline Wicks.

After half an hour of objection and counter-objection, Judge Fenwick's smile disappeared. He was fed up. 'Mr Kavanagh,' he said, 'I'm most reluctant to stop you, but – and I'm sure I speak for my learned brothers as well as for myself – there is no more that can be said on the point that will assist us.'

Kavanagh was having none of that. 'Then I must seek your lordships' indulgence because I want to say two more things.'

Fenwick sighed. 'On the same issue?'

'My lord, yes.' Sensing another objection in the air, he hurried on. 'First, the jury were not given a fair summary of the defence's case on Duncan Pembridge's motive for giving evidence against the appellants.' Behind Kavanagh, Sam Wicks silently concurred. The jury had heard little of Duncan's many grudges against him and Caroline. With its many omissions, the judge's summing-up speech had been a disgrace. 'The learned judge,' continued Kavanagh, with reference to that speech, 'made no mention of Duncan Pembridge's failure to tell the police or the jury about the spare key his mother kept hidden under a plant pot at the house. In the circumstances of this case, he *had* to do so.'

Sam nodded. Quite right. The spare key was missing when the bodies were found. Clear indication that the burglars had known where it was. Or the *burglar.*

In the gallery, Duncan Pembridge began to sweat.

'Second,' said Kavanagh, 'the learned judge's direction to the jury about Mrs Tully's identification of the accused was wholly inadequate.' At that, Sam nodded again. The Tully woman had always hated his father's first family. She'd been a friend of Duncan's mother. And she'd claimed to have been all but pushed off the road by Sam's car as it sped away from the scene of the murders. Stupid bitch, he thought. How on earth could she have positively identified anyone if she'd been struggling to keep control of her car?

That was Kavanagh's point. 'The judge failed to remind the jury that Mrs Tully was herself driving a car, that she was struggling to avoid an accident and that she was unable to tell the court with confidence who was driving.' Kavanagh looked at the judges with all the authority he could muster. 'My lords, these matters render the convictions of Samuel and Caroline Wicks wholly unsafe and wholly unsatisfactory.'

Then Creggan, the barrister who had acted for Duncan Pembridge, stood up to begin the reply for the prosecution. He had won the trial all those months ago. He had no intention of losing the appeal.

CHAPTER TWENTY-TWO

Julia Piper's leaving party was, at her own request, a modest affair in one of the wine bars most frequented by herself and her colleagues. She didn't want any fuss. She didn't want any speeches or presentations and she had been adamant that she didn't want any presents. Peter Foxcott had thought that was a piece of nonsense and, after a whip-round, had sent an enormously expensive present out to Nairobi ahead of its recipient. Julia had also declared that she didn't want anyone but her River Court colleagues to attend the party. Lizzie Kavanagh was the only exception. She wasn't a close enough friend to be invited to the other, more extravagant bash that Julia's bridesmaid-to-be was throwing for her, but Julia liked her and had decided she was, in any case, 'a barrister by default'. Lizzie would have been furious had she heard that.

The party took place two days after the conclusion of the Wicks appeal. Kavanagh had tried his best to dismiss the case from his mind, but with the press still churning out 'exclusives' and sensational scoops, he was having an uphill job. He was also behind with his paperwork.

On the evening of the party he was delayed by a lengthy and boring conference with his least favourite solicitor and clients who, he knew, hadn't a hope in hell of winning. He rushed back to River Court to find the place deserted. 'Shit!' he said under his breath, as he realized where everyone had gone. Well, he would just have to be late. He rushed into his room and scanned the papers on his desk. Most of them could wait till tomorrow, but he needed to scribble a few notes to Tom.

Ten minutes later he was on the point of leaving when the phone rang. He swore again. There was no one else in the building to answer it. With an irritated sigh, he lifted the receiver. 'Kavanagh,' he barked.

Silence.

'Hello?' Kavanagh felt suddenly vulnerable. In the dark, in the deserted building, a sudden chill ran down his spine.

And then the caller spoke. The voice was low, measured – and menacing. 'How do you manage to sleep, Mr Kavanagh?'

Warning sirens screamed in Kavanagh's head. 'Who is this?' he snapped.

'Doesn't the truth mean anything to you?'

'I don't think—'

'You make me sick!' shouted the caller. Then the line went dead.

For a full minute Kavanagh sat staring at the dead instrument. Not again, he thought. Not more threats. He had never forgotten the last time it had happened. *Your address is in the book, Mr Kavanagh.* And then Lizzie had been followed, threatened in broad daylight. *Tell your husband I was asking after the family.*

He reached for the phone again, but stopped with his hand in mid-air. The police wouldn't be able to help him. They probably thought that he deserved anything he got. They probably agreed with all the reporters at the Appeal Court verdict. 'How does it feel to be responsible for letting a killer go free?' some of them had shouted at him. Winning the appeal had given him little satisfaction.

He stood up, picked up his coat from the back of his chair and left the room. Then he walked, more hurriedly than usual, out of the building.

He was lost in thought as he made his way to the Fleet Street wine bar. So lost in thought that he was completely unaware of the shadowy figure following him through the darkness.

The party was in full swing when he arrived. Lizzie, thankfully, was already there. He made straight for her and enveloped her in a bear-hug. 'Goodness, Mr Kavanagh,' she laughed, 'I do hope this isn't how you normally behave in Fleet Street watering-holes.'

Kavanagh smiled in response. Lizzie didn't notice that the smile failed to reach his eyes. Later, he thought. He would tell her later. It would not be fair to ruin Julia's party. Julia herself, he noted with amused approval, was already fairly well oiled and – this he noted with disapproval – was laughing uproariously with Helen Ames. He would have to get used to Helen. He would have to try to change his mind about her being a money-grabbing champagne socialist. She had assured him that having a child had changed her: that people were now more important to her than money. And he would do well to believe her – especially as, a month from now, she would be his colleague at River Court.

Lizzie had resumed her conversation with Alex Wilson so Kavanagh, now with a drink in hand, made his way over to Helen and Julia. He didn't get that far. He was stopped halfway across the room by a familiar but frightened-looking girl. 'Mr Kavanagh?' she began. 'I, well . . .'

'Caroline!' Kavanagh's surprise reached everyone in the room. They all looked round at him – and at the stranger in their midst.

Caroline Wicks was looking far more scared than she had at her trial or at the appeal. She looked, thought Kavanagh, terrified and lost – just as she had after Judge Fenwick had given his verdict at the appeal. Where she should have been ecstatic, she had been worried. 'I don't know what to do, Mr Kavanagh. I'm so . . . so afraid.' It had been an extraordinary thing to say; a startling admission from someone who had just been saved from life imprisonment.

Now, looking at her, Kavanagh knew that his growing suspicions were about to be confirmed. He knew what Caroline was going to tell him. He knew, as Duncan Pembridge knew, that a killer was on the loose. Duncan's words on the phone came back to him. *Doesn't the truth mean anything to you? You make me sick!*

But, as he continued to stare at Caroline, he was thinking, most of all, about one of the basic truths of criminal law. About how one cannot be tried twice for the same crime. In the eyes of the law, Sam Wicks was innocent of murdering his father and stepmother. No matter what Caroline might say, nothing could alter that verdict.

Lizzie was the only person in the room, full of supposedly compassionate lawyers, who had the presence of mind to usher Caroline into a smaller, private room where she wouldn't be the centre of attention.

'I followed you from your office,' she said to Kavanagh. 'I had to tell you.' Then she looked up and uttered the words that should have been spoken months ago. Words that confirmed the most appalling miscarriage of justice. 'Sam did it.'

Kavanagh had known this was going to happen. Behind him, Lizzie's hand shot to her mouth to stifle a gasp. 'Why didn't you say this to the police?' asked Kavanagh.

Caroline twisted her handkerchief in her hands. 'Sam said if he went to prison there'd be nobody to look after me.'

'Oh, God.' This time Lizzie couldn't disguise her reaction. She looked at her husband. Both were thinking the same thing. In coming here, Caroline was risking her life.

Then Caroline said, 'Please help me. I've got no one else to turn to.'

Kavanagh shook his head slowly. 'I really can't.' The words sounded awful. But they were true. 'It's no longer anything to do with me.'

Caroline was horrified. 'But you can sort it all out! Tell the right people what happened.'

This time it was Lizzie who replied. 'Caroline,' she said gently, 'you have to go to the police with what you've told us.'

'They'll only lock me up again. I lied in court.' The words came out in a whisper. Then she fixed her terrified, pleading eyes on Kavanagh. 'You talk to them for me, you're one of them. You can tell them I didn't mean to hurt anyone. They'll listen to you.'

Kavanagh looked down at the wretched, pathetic creature in front of him. It was impossible not to feel sorry for her, yet neither was it possible for him to do anything to help. His involvement with Caroline had been purely professional. But the terrible irony of that involvement distressed him more than he cared to admit even to himself. It had been his job to serve Caroline's best interests. In the eyes of the law, he had done exactly that. In reality, he had released her from prison and into the clutches of a brother who had killed twice. And Caroline was the only person alive who had been at the scene of those crimes.

She saw Kavanagh's agonized indecision. 'Please help me,' she beseeched. 'Please help me to—'

'Help you to do what, Caroline?'

In sudden panic, Caroline whirled around. Lizzie and Kavanagh also turned to the newcomer. But Kavanagh, like Caroline, had already identified the voice. It was that of Sam Wicks. He was standing at the doorway, and, as he saw his sister freeze, a smile hovered round his mouth. A smile that contradicted the expression in his eyes. 'Mr Kavanagh,' he said as he approached Caroline, 'charges a lot of money for his time, love.' Then he put his hands firmly on her shoulders. 'You can't afford him.'

Caroline turned her anguished face towards him. 'I didn't say anything, Sam!'

'Hush, now. Be quite, Caro.' The words were soothing. The way they were spoken was not. Then Sam said to the Kavanaghs, 'Sorry for any embarrassment. Caroline, as you may have noticed, isn't feeling well. Come on, love.' He pulled her to her feet.

Caroline reached desperately towards Kavanagh. 'I don't want to go with him! I don't want to go!'

'You need to rest, Caro. You're upset.' Sam favoured the Kavanaghs with one last, triumphant look. Lizzie was frozen into shocked silence by the episode she had just witnessed. Kavanagh's face was a mask of tortured indecision. His compassion told him to interfere. Yet the lawyer within him held him back. Caroline, now limp with despair as she realized no one was going to stop Sam, allowed herself to be propelled through the door.

Sam glanced back over his shoulder as he left the room. 'Enjoy the party!' he said. As he dragged his sister out into the street he murmured soothing words to her. Yet in his mind he was cursing her. Stupid Caroline, said the inner voice. Stupid for telling tales. Stupid to go running to Kavanagh. And even more stupid leaving his address beside the open *A-Z* in the flat. It hadn't been difficult for him to find out where she had gone. She who had been expressly forbidden to leave the flat without him. She would have to be punished.

Kavanagh snapped out of his torpor. After the momentary, awful silence that followed Sam's departure, he reached a decision. 'Stay here,' he barked at Lizzie. 'I'm calling the police.'

'Jim?' Lizzie's face said it all. Hadn't he sworn that he couldn't do anything more for Caroline Wicks? Hadn't he done his professional duty by securing her release?

But he had also just seen a killer walk out of the room. 'You heard what she said, Lizzie. He's a murderer. I can't stand by and do nothing.'

'No.' Lizzie knew he was right. But her agreement was accompanied by an awful, unspoken weariness. Why did his work always have to interfere in their lives? Why should Julia's leaving be ruined by unfinished business? And why, oh why, did the business of being a barrister never end?

Kavanagh seemed to be reading her thoughts. 'I know. I know what I said. But look what I've done.'

'Caroline could be lying.'

'No. You saw her face when Sam came into the room. I've never seen such naked fear. And she's right to be terrified, Lizzie.'

'Supposing nothing's wrong when the police get there?

Kavanagh shrugged. 'I get prosecuted for wasting police time.' But as their eyes met they both knew that was unlikely. Something was going to be very wrong.

Then Lizzie forced her mind back to the party. 'What about Julia? This hardly makes for a rousing send-off.'

Kavanagh thought quickly. 'She doesn't have to know. I'll phone from the car. Can you go back to the party?'

'But what do I say?'

'Nothing. Just say Caroline was upset and that her brother came to collect her.'

'Well, I guess that *is* the truth.'

'Yes. One of the few truthful things that's been said in this whole ghastly catastrophe.'

Lizzie wasn't sure how she managed to get through the rest of the party. The words 'ghastly catastrophe' kept ringing in her ears as she half-heartedly made polite conversation to her husband's colleagues. No one expressed much concern about Caroline Wicks; those who had witnessed her arrival had already known from Kavanagh that she was slightly unstable.

Like his wife, Kavanagh had difficulty enjoying the party. His phone call requesting the police to go round to Sam Wicks's flat took two minutes and he was back at the party before anyone had even queried his absence. Yet he felt drained for the remainder of the evening. Not even several hefty glasses of wine could dull the pain he felt over the Wicks case. He had always known that neither he nor justice was infallible, yet this was the first time he had had that fact thrust so forcefully in his face. For the first time in his career, he felt a failure.

'Cheer up, Jim!' Startled, Kavanagh turned to find Peter Foxcott standing – none too steadily – by his side. 'No point in moping about it,' Peter continued as he draped a comradely arm round Kavanagh's shoulders.

'Er . . . moping about what?'

'Julia, of course!' Peter leaned closer. 'Between you and me, Jim,' he said in what he thought was a conspiratorial whisper, 'I reckon she'll be back. That fellow David'll only be in Nairobi for a year or two.'

Kavanagh was more than a little surprised. 'But you've taken on Helen Ames!'

Peter chuckled. 'Only for a year or two.'

'Oh.' A slow grin spread across Kavanagh's face. 'How very reassuring.'

'Anyway, she's not *that* bad.'

'She isn't?'

'No.' Peter wobbled, spilling his wine. 'Nothing's ever quite as bad as you think.'

Kavanagh smiled at his colleague's trite, unoriginal remark. But perhaps, he mused as Peter weaved off, there was an element of truth in it. Two years ago he had thought his marriage was over, a few months ago he had thought his daughter had taken leave of her senses. Barely a month ago he had assumed Matt would die in a motorbike crash. None of those things had happened. Lizzie was here to stay; Katie had ended her unsuitable affair; and Matt had completely lost his interest in motorbikes. Now he was mad about cars.

The smile vanished as the image of a car as a mangled wreck came to Kavanagh's mind. Cursing himself, he went off in search of Lizzie. She would put the smile back on his face.

But, as was often the case, it was Jeremy Aldermarten who fulfilled that role. Propping up the bar with Julia, his voice carried loud and clear to Kavanagh as he passed them. 'I suppose,' Jeremy mused, in all seriousness, 'the idea of marrying you was a pretty mad impulse. I expect you've saved me from a terrible fate.'

Julia's eyes nearly popped out of her head. 'Well,' she said, as she took a slug of wine, 'I wouldn't put it quite like that . . .'

EPILOGUE

Caroline Wicks was rescued. Sam told the police that it was attempted suicide. The police thought otherwise. Caroline, they pointed out, would have been unable to help herself to so many pills. Not with her hands tied behind her back.

Sam was tried and convicted for attempted murder. The judge recommended – strongly – that he serve the entire twenty-five years of his sentence.

The consultant in the hospital to which Caroline was admitted recommended that she sought psychiatric help. Her half-brother Duncan Pembridge paid for it. Caroline, he had decided, wasn't that bad.

All Pan Books are available at your local bookshop or newsagent, or can be ordered direct from the publisher. Indicate the number of copies required and fill in the form below.

Send to: Macmillan General Books C.S.
               Book Service By Post
               PO Box 29, Douglas I-O-M
               IM99 1BQ

or phone: 01624 675137, quoting title, author and credit card number.

or fax: 01624 670923, quoting title, author, and credit card number.

or Internet: http://www.bookpost.co.uk

Please enclose a remittance* to the value of the cover price plus 75 pence per book for post and packing. Overseas customers please allow £1.00 per copy for post and packing.

*Payment may be made in sterling by UK personal cheque, Eurocheque, postal order, sterling draft or international money order, made payable to Book Service By Post.

Alternatively by Access/Visa/MasterCard

Card No.   ☐☐☐☐☐☐☐☐☐☐☐☐☐☐☐☐

Expiry Date ☐☐☐☐☐☐☐☐☐☐☐☐☐☐☐☐

Signature _____

Applicable only in the UK and BFPO addresses.

While every effort is made to keep prices low, it is sometimes necessary to increase prices at short notice. Pan Books reserve the right to show on covers and charge new retail prices which may differ from those advertised in the text or elsewhere.

NAME AND ADDRESS IN BLOCK CAPITAL LETTERS PLEASE

Name _____

Address _____

_____

_____

_____

8/95

Please allow 28 days for delivery.
Please tick box if you do not wish to receive any additional information. ☐